POWER PLAY

CARA DEE

Power Play
Copyright © 2018 by Cara Dee
All rights reserved

This book is licensed for your personal enjoyment and may not be reproduced in any way without documented permission of the author, not including brief quotes with links and/or credit to the source. Thank you for respecting the hard work of this author. This is a work of fiction and all references to historical events, persons living or dead, and locations are used in a fictional manner. Any other names, characters, incidents, and places are derived from the author's imagination. The author acknowledges the trademark status and owners of any wordmarks mentioned in this work of fiction. Characters portrayed in sexual situations are 18 or older.

Edited by Silently Correcting Your Grammar, LLC.
Formatting by Eliza Rae Services.

CAMASSIA COVE

Camassia Cove is a town in northern Washington created to be the home of some exciting love stories. Each novel taking place here is a standalone—with the exception of sequels and series within the CC universe—and they vary in genre and pairing. What they all have in common is the town in which they live. Some are friends and family. Others are complete strangers. Some have vastly different backgrounds. Some grew up together. It's a small world, and many characters will cross over and pay a visit or two in several books—Cara's way of giving readers a glimpse into the future of their favorite characters. Oh, who is she kidding; they are characters she's unable of saying good-bye to. But, again, each novel stands on its own, and spoilers will be avoided as much as possible.

If you're interested in keeping up with secondary characters, the town, the timeline, and future novels, check out Camassia Cove's own website at www.camassiacove.com. There you will also see which characters have gotten their own books already, where they appear, which books are in the works, character profiles, and you'll be treated to a taste of the town.

*

Get social with Cara
www.caradeewrites.com
www.camassiacove.com
Facebook: @caradeewrites
Twitter: @caradeewrites
Instagram: @caradeewrites

Shh! This kinky game is about to start.

PART I
POWER

PROLOGUE

Madigan Monroe

At some point, I'd have to decide if I was writing a love letter or an apology.

I wasn't a fucking writer either way. Tearing the sheet off the notepad, I crumpled it into a ball and threw it in the trash can under my sketch board. My elbows hit the tabletop, my fingers disappeared into my hair, and I cursed in frustration.

Wasn't this whole situation proof of how different Abel and I were? He'd sent me a text message, and here I was, trying to reply via *letter*. But then, if we were so goddamn different, why had I felt some sort of connection to the kid since he was, well, literally a kid?

He probably didn't remember the first time we met. I sure did. Lately, it was going on a fucking loop in my brain.

"Thank you for flying out."

I kissed the top of Adeline's head and hugged her harder. "Of course, hon." Two young boys were sitting outside the hospital room I didn't wanna enter. I feared it was gonna break me.

Adeline wiped her cheeks discreetly and plastered a forced smile on her face. "Let me introduce you to his sons." She couldn't say his name. Then, I found myself struggling to do the same. "Jesse, Abel, this is Madigan, a friend of mine—and your dad's."

I couldn't fathom how she was holding up. She was about to become these kids' new mother, when she was only a few years out of her teens herself. Jesse, a preteen, and Abel, this shaggy-haired little boy of five or six.

A doctor left the hospital room, quietly letting Adeline know it was okay to go in. I couldn't bring myself to—not yet—and neither could Abel. He wanted to wait a little bit. So Adeline and I exchanged a look, and I nodded. I'd look after him while she and Jesse went in to see...fuck, Morgan.

I sat down in the vacated seat and shrugged out of my leather jacket.

Yesterday, everything had been fine. Now I'd learned I was mere months away from losing a friend to cancer.

"Adeline says Dad's gonna become an angel soon," Abel mumbled next to me. "I told him not to take the job."

Jesus Christ. I swallowed past the sudden burst of emotion and leaned forward, resting my elbows on my knees. Glancing back at him, I could only hope my words didn't make shit worse. "The good thing about angels is they never stop watching over you."

He pushed away some hair from his forehead and squinted at me. "He can do that here. 'Cept when I'm in the bathroom."

I chuckled and sniffled at the same time. "This will be

different. My nana is an angel too. I can't see her, but she's always there."

He looked around, as if trying to spot her.

"Doesn't matter if I'm at home, at work, or if I'm traveling. She watches over me," I told him.

Abel studied me. "Does she like you that much?"

I grinned. This kid was something else. "Apparently. She makes sure I never forget these." I dug out a small packet of Nutella from the pocket of my jeans. A mild obsession of mine, thanks to my grandmother. "Want one?"

He hesitated and tugged a little at his ear. "Um, yeah." He accepted the packet, and I tore off the foil cover. "You're not a stranger, are you? I'm not allowed to take candy from strangers."

"I promise. I used to work with your dad."

He bobbed his head and stuck a finger through the chocolate. "Adeline writes a list when she's gonna buy stuff at the store. Does your nana do that for you also?"

I shook my head. "She just makes me remember. She used to say—" I was cut off when the door opened, and Adeline poked her head out.

She was doing her best to keep it together. "He knows you're here and is personally offended you're stalling."

Great. Lay on the guilt. I blew out a breath and nodded once, then rose from my seat.

"Madigan already gave you sweets, huh?" Adeline was smiling at Abel.

He nodded and mouthed something to himself, and it took me a beat to realize he was trying to verbalize my name. "Madgan," he whispered. "Mad...i...gan." He looked up at me. "Can I call you Mad?"

"Sure thing." I ruffled his hair, which he definitely didn't like. He backed off with a little scowl and patted down his hair. Too cute.

There was only one thing left to do, and that was to face my friend. Morgan sat on the edge of his hospital bed, buttoning up his shirt. He'd aged ten years since the last time I saw him less than a year ago. He'd come over from Detroit to see me in LA after wrapping up some unfinished business there. He used to live in Reseda, for fuck's sake. His career had finally taken off. Had he even hit forty yet?

His eldest, Jesse, sat in a chair, lost in his Game Boy.

Morgan glanced up from his shirt and spotted me, and a tired smile graced his mouth.

I shook my head and moved over to him. "What the fuck did you do?" I cupped his face and pressed my forehead to his.

"Because this is my fault," he drawled.

I couldn't respond yet. Instead, I kissed his cheeks, his forehead, then his lips. "Can I order you to get well?"

"You bossing me around was fun once upon a time, playboy." He sighed and grabbed my hands in his. I squeezed back, and he kissed my knuckles. "I'm afraid I won't be able to obey this time around."

He might as well have taken a swing right at my heart. Sitting down next to him, I asked all the questions that'd gotten stuck in my throat when I was on the phone with Adeline. I learned about the weeks of tests that'd led up to now, and I listened to the painful truth about how aggressive the cancer was.

"They've given me three to six months," he finished.

I averted my eyes to get my shit together, and I cleared my throat. "What do you need from me? I gotta do something. Before I—" I stopped myself and pressed a fist to my mouth. "Just tell me what to do, Morgan."

He smiled sadly at the others. Jesse and his game, Adeline

and Abel. The latter two were sitting on the floor by the door, speaking quietly to each other.

"Jesse's gonna be angry," Morgan murmured. "I've asked Adeline to be there for him through that."

She was gonna try to do everything. It was the person she'd become.

"Can you check in on Abel from time to time?" he asked me. "He's...different."

I'd heard about that. Couple of months ago when I spoke to Adeline, the plan was for Abel to go through some tests. Morgan suspected ADHD or whatever.

"I'll be there." I hugged him to me. "Right now, I don't want you to speak like you're dead already."

He was undeterred, though. "Promise me, Madigan. Whenever Adeline needs you, please be there for him. For them."

"I swear." My voice broke at the end, and I blamed him. Seeing his eyes well up was gonna do me in. "Look at me. I'll be there, Morgan."

He nodded and swallowed hard, and I brushed my thumbs under his eyes. Then he turned toward Abel and drew in a deep breath.

"Come here, ace."

Abel got to his feet and was licking Nutella off his fingers on his way over.

Morgan picked him up and sat him across his lap. They were so alike, all three Novak guys. Abel was gonna grow up and have the same sharp features as his father. The hair would probably never smooth out. Morgan's hadn't. The dark waves shone with lighter, natural streaks and walked hand in hand with the kindest grins I'd ever known.

"What do you say we go out for dinner?" Morgan rubbed Abel's stomach. "Huh? Can you smile for me, son?"

Abel made a face instead, crossing his eyes and poking out his tongue.

I was the one who smiled, and it was great to hear my friend laugh.

I left my desk and walked over to the fridge. There was nothing like a beer at four in the morning. Then I returned to my seat and stared unseeingly at the notepad.

I had to tell Abel *something*. Via text message or not, he'd poured his heart into a few crushing words, and he deserved a response.

Morgan would fucking kill me if he knew. I sighed and leaned back, the chair squeaking as I looked up at the ceiling. *Have I failed you, Morgan?* Maybe I got too close. Abel wasn't a goofy six-year-old anymore. He was turning twenty in a few months, and somewhere along the road, I'd made him think he was in love with me.

Somewhere along the road, I'd crossed the same fucking lines. The shame crippled me sometimes. To even *think*...

"What the fuck am I doing?" I groaned.

I'd wasted two days on this. Two days. That was how long it'd been since I woke up to that text from him.

I think ive been in love with u since I was 12.

Even at twelve, he was my favorite person in the world. I remembered those days vividly. He'd been overwhelmed by his struggles with his bipolar disorder, yet he never failed to make people smile. I could be moping about another shitty ex-boyfriend, and there he was... Abel would fly into a room and sniff out who was down in the dumps.

"Don't drop me!" Adeline shrieked. "Oh my God, this won't work! Jesse!" She was wrong. This worked just fine. Jesse didn't even look winded as he ran down the basketball court with Adeline on his back. She was a tiny shit.

So was the boy piggybacking me.

"Faster, Mad!" Abel laughed.

I grinned, out of breath, and stole the ball from Jesse. Then I dribbled around him to make Abel laugh some more before I ran toward the end of the court. "You ready to throw it in the hoop, trouble?"

"Yeah, gimme." He secured his legs around my hips and stuck his hands out. "I'll show you how it's done."

I chuckled and flipped him the ball, and on the second try, he managed to score.

"Fuck, yeah! That's a good boy." I held up my fist for him, and he bumped it with a victorious shout.

"Mom, we won!" he yelled. "Mad and I won!"

Adeline huffed, and Jesse released her. "Okay, okay, let's eat, then."

It was a nice day in the park. The sky was perfectly blue, and people were out and about. It was in moments like these I wished Morgan could see how far his boys had come.

I threw a wistful smile at our surroundings, seeing families everywhere.

"What's wrong?" Abel demanded. He wriggled free until his feet hit the pavement, and then he came around me to grab my face. I let out a surprised chuckle and had no choice but to lean down.

"Nothing's wrong, sweetheart. I promise." I stared into his blue eyes. They seemed even bluer in the sun. "You've gotten some freckles this summer."

"Freckles happen," he replied frankly. Next, he grabbed my hand so we could join the others on the blanket in the grass.

"You swear nothing is wrong? Wanna hear me make farts with my armpit?"

"I swear, and abso-fucking-lutely."

I'd never been a parent to Abel. Was that why my thoughts had shifted so easily? Too goddamn easily.

Both he and Jesse had lucked out with Adeline and Lincoln adopting them. Which, in some ways, made this worse. Adeline and Lincoln were two of my closest friends; I was a blessed son of a bitch to call them family. And if they knew I'd been startled awake about a year ago by a dream in which their fucking son was riding my cock—

Nausea traveled up my throat, and I rammed a fist into the wall closest to my sketch board.

There was no *question* I'd failed Morgan.

And I wasn't gonna confess shit to Abel. It was so damn wrong. No, I had to let him down gently, say I didn't reciprocate, and pray I could still be "his Mad." I gripped the pen tightly and put it to the paper.

No. Fucking. Words. Came. Out.

I growled.

I sure as shit didn't shoulder the responsibility of a respectable parent. The right thing to do was to discuss this with him, hear him out, and promise I'd always be there as his friend. It was what Lincoln would do. He was the man who'd, over the years, earned the title of being Abel's dad.

It'd started the minute it was announced we were leaving Michigan for Washington.

I could recall the exact words Abel said to me the day he'd started calling Lincoln Dad. *"I mean...he's always there, he's nosy, he's fun, and he's cool. And I can trust him. Plus, he snuck me fifty bucks because I told him he's Dad now. And he got a little mushy, but that's a secret."*

Abel had been around fifteen, and he was right. He could trust Lincoln. Me, on the other hand? Given that I couldn't fucking trust myself, it'd be a bad idea to tell him he could trust me.

That was the whole thing with the boy I'd watched grow up before my eyes. Abel needed his people to have fixed roles. They needed titles. There was Mom, Dad, uncles, brother, sister, friends...and his Mad. Mad was a reliable teddy bear. Or, that was who I was supposed to be. But I hadn't been, not in over a year.

Not since the little troublemaker had morphed into a hard-working young man who played hockey for the Penguins and knocked heads with the best of 'em.

I couldn't do it. I wheeled back my chair and scrubbed at my face. Whether in an apologetic tone or one filled with forbidden hope, I couldn't write to him. It would be a final nail in the coffin no matter what, and I was too much of a coward.

Abel having his alleged feelings for me was entirely different. He was young and would grow out of it soon enough. I was supposed to know better.

In a way, this wasn't about me cowering away from rejecting him. I didn't wanna watch myself get rejected. Because soon enough, he would move on.

I had a feeling I wouldn't.

CHAPTER 1

A YEAR AND SOME CHANGE LATER

Abel Novak-Hayes

I was one miserable moron.
"I thought I'd find you up here."
Looking over my shoulder, I saw Dad stepping out and lighting up a smoke. I faced forward again, arms resting on the railing, and looked out over the ocean. Technically, we lived in the woods, high up on the mountainside, and a few trees were obstructing my view of the Chinook Islands. It was cold as fuck too. Our rooftop had always offered peace for me, though. Whether it was February or August, I came up here to clear my head when I was home.

It was dusk in February now, and I was pushing it without a jacket.

Dad joined me at the railing and blew out some smoke. "So what's bothering you?"

I side-eyed him. "Nothing."

"Oh." He nodded. "I meant without the layer of bullshit. What's actually bothering you?"

I scowled. Why were parents so fucking nosy? "What makes you think anything's wrong?"

"I don't know where to begin." He pushed down the sleeves of his Henley, hiding the ink that covered his arms. "Jesus, it's fucking frigid." He took another drag from his cigarette. "Let's start with your suspension."

I didn't care about that much. It was only two weeks, and we weren't going to the play-offs at this rate anyway. It'd been a different story when I played in Pittsburgh. Now I was with Vancouver, and...well, they weren't the best team. "We've talked about this. I lost my head. End of story."

"See, on TV it looked more like you were trying to sever *his* head," he pointed out. "The guy ended up in the hospital, Abel."

I'm aware.

I swallowed and peered down at the ground below. I estimated it was about a forty-foot drop to the driveway, maybe a little more. Since our house sat on a cliffside, there was no space for a yard, hence the setup on the roof. Once in my life, I'd contemplated jumping.

"He pushed my buttons," I muttered.

"He must've pushed them pretty fucking hard." He was studying me, and I kept my gaze forward or down. He had a way of dragging the truth out of me.

"What's next? You gonna ask me if I'm taking my meds?" I maintained a blank expression and pulled up my hood.

He shook his head. "I trust that you are."

Okay, good. 'Cause I was.

"You went straight to your medication..." He nodded

slowly, pensive. "That's some button. Is that it? Did he say something that made you cross-check him?"

"Oh, here we go." I was done with his digging—and the cold—so I turned around and headed over to the seating area. "No, Dad, everyone loves to hear that even zombies wouldn't go for their useless, bipolar brain." I fiddled with the heater until I felt the heat coming on. Then I slumped down in one of the four love seats that surrounded the low table and stared blankly toward the pool. "Look, I know I shouldn't have lost my temper—"

"Gimme a minute," he said. "Let me enjoy the memory of you slamming your stick across his neck for a moment."

My mouth twisted up slightly, and I was grateful he wasn't Mom right now. They had very different approaches, both awesome to me, but right now, I didn't need her fussing. I wanted his ability to relate. Dad wasn't as concerned about always being the good guy.

"Okay, I'm over it." He stubbed out his smoke and walked closer, taking a seat next to me. "What you did was wrong. We don't beat dumb fucks—we ignore them. You know that. What I'm more interested in is why he got to you. You're used to trash talk on the ice, son."

God*damn* him and his digging. In order to get out of this one, I had to give him something substantial, something big enough that he'd buy it. Because I couldn't sit through another lecture on self-worth and how I should see what an amazing dude I was.

I wasn't. My brain was damaged, and I had to live on a strict schedule to prevent anxiety attacks. A strict schedule I'd neglected a lot lately.

I chose to bring up the one thing that I was done trying to understand myself. "Can people go through breakup grief from losing friends?"

It had been a little over a year since I'd lost my friendship with Madigan, and it continued to tear me up every day.

Dad frowned a little, confused. "I thought things were good with Gray. He was here last weekend."

I nodded, brief glimpses of my twenty-first birthday dinner flashing through my thoughts. "It's not him," I said. "This is the second birthday in a row that Mad didn't show up." And it fucking hurt.

I was sorry for what I'd done. If I'd known confessing my feelings for him would push him away, I would've kept my mouth shut forever.

"Mom and I have been wondering about that," Dad murmured, scratching his jaw. "We figured you'd just drifted apart. I mean, your differences..."

Yeah, I was sick of hearing that. It was only one difference people got stuck on, the fact that I was twenty-one and Madigan was almost forty.

We used to live in Detroit, and Mad had quickly become my biggest supporter when I started playing hockey. And back then, everyone thought it was "cute" when I said I was gonna marry Mad one day. As it turned out, no one had taken me seriously because of my age. So what if I'd been fucking twelve? He'd been my best friend, the man I adored and looked up to, while my family viewed him as my uncle or some shit.

It pissed me off.

I *hated* when people used age as a weapon to ward something off. By that logic, Mom wouldn't be my mom. Seeing as she was only sixteen years older than me and had been in her early twenties when she'd adopted my big brother and me. Dad had a decade on her, but she was a year or two younger than Madigan. So...did that mean she couldn't be my mother?

Huh? No. Yet, it was impossible for people to comprehend Mad and me together as equals.

I wasn't twelve anymore, but I was sure as shit treated like it at times.

Goddammit, I pretended to like *coffee* for Madigan's sake. I even watched the news to look more mature, 'cause I had a feeling watching cartoons wasn't grown-up enough.

I guess it didn't matter. The one who found me and my feelings the most ridiculous was Madigan himself.

"Abel, if this has got you so upset, why don't you talk to him?" Dad asked.

And expose myself further? Make myself even more powerless and pathetic? No thanks. It hurt enough the first time, and I hadn't recovered from that blow yet. I wasn't gonna beg him to be my friend. I'd obviously been wrong. To him, since he was so close to my parents, I guess I was the nephew, after all. Just some kid.

"Maybe you're right," I lied. "Maybe we drifted apart." I added some bullshit about us always living far apart too. I played for the Canucks in Vancouver. Before then, I'd been on the East Coast since I was drafted at eighteen, so I couldn't fault my folks for thinking it'd been a natural "breakup." I wasn't home that often, although it hadn't stopped Mad and me from texting and calling several times a week before I'd told him I was in love with him.

I'd forced my body to move on. It was time to make my heart and mind follow.

My room was on the second floor of the house, and it was a quiet floor these days. Jesse, my big brother, lived in Los

Angeles. His room remained untouched. Casey, another family friend slash uncle type person who'd been with us forever, had bought a house in Downtown, the district south of us. His room here remained untouched too.

Leaving my door open, I let the lights in the hallway be enough as I crossed the room and looked out the window. Best feature of my room, no doubt. Floor-to-ceiling windows with a balcony that stretched along the outside of the house. Same view as we had on the roof, only now it was darker out. Dinner would be ready soon, so there was no use in firing up my computer or watching a movie. My phone was good for now, and I made it over to my bed and got comfortable.

I texted Gray first.

whatre u up to?

Then I reached for the remote on the nightstand and turned on the TV to find a playlist. My entertainment center took up most of the opposite wall, and I didn't like seeing it anymore. The photos meant more to me than the trophies, and there were no new photos. The one that hit me the hardest was a black-and-white one of Madigan squeezing me in a tight hug, wide grins on our faces, taken right after I got the call from the Penguins.

Rock music started playing on the surround sound system as Gray responded, and I turned down the volume a bit.

Dinner with Isla and Jack. They're leaving tomorrow. You?

I'd forgotten. Isla was his stepsister, and Jack was her boyfriend...and Gray's stepdad's college friend. I'd almost pissed myself laughing when I heard about Gray's stepdad finding his daughter with Jack... It was funny now too, months later.

Much like Aiden, said stepdad, Isla was an author, and she was going on some book tour this spring.

Waiting for dinner. Im bored.

I placed a hand under my head and watched as he typed a reply.

You've been in town a few days! How can you be bored already? Am I not giving you enough attention?

No, he fucking wasn't. He'd been here for my birthday, and we'd gone out afterward—me with my valid driver's license and him with his fake ID. He didn't turn twenty-one until November, though it had never really stopped us from going out.

Can I come over when u get home?

His roommates were rarely there, and I'd rather be at his place than here. Madigan was too big a part of this family, making his presence permanent and unavoidable. He was in pictures, memories, and many of Mom and Dad's anecdotes about their everyday life.

Best part of playing for the Canucks was I lived only an hour and a half away now. When I wasn't on the road with the team, I came down from Vancouver on Saturday morning and drove home again after dinner. Unless I crashed at Gray's and I headed home on Sunday.

I hadn't slept here since…shit, Thanksgiving, I guess. I managed to dodge it for Christmas.

Gray's text brightened my mood a little.

Mi casa es su casa, baby.

"Helloooo." My baby sister appeared in the doorway. The only person I shared this floor with.

"Hey." I patted the spot next to me on the bed, then grinned as she barreled toward me. She was still high on birthday celebrations—and wearing her princess crown from when she'd turned seven the other day. "Wanna snuggle?"

"Yeah, Daddy said you needed cuddles and huggles."

Gee, thanks, Dad.

"I guess he's right." I dropped my phone somewhere behind me before turning on my side. "When's dinner ready?"

"Mommy said soon."

Okay, then. I touched her wild curls, pushing them away from her cute face, then pressed her button nose with a soundless *boop*. She grinned crookedly.

Lyn had everyone wrapped around her finger, especially Dad. He was equally afraid of her because of how much she took after Mom, both in appearance and personality. Basically, he was fucked the day she started looking at boys differently.

"What's an urgent matter?" she asked.

My eyebrows went up a fraction. "Sort of like an emergency. Why?"

She shrugged and placed her hands under her cheek on the pillow. "Uncle Madigan is coming for dinner 'cause Daddy called with an urgent matter. And he cussed, but I'm not suppos'ta repeat cussing."

That made me sit right up. "Wait, what—he did what?"

She beamed. "Uncle Madigan is coming for dinner."

"*Why?*" I asked, frustrated as fuck all of a sudden.

Despite that Mad was clearly avoiding me these days, we were a tight-knit family, and it was impossible to escape one another completely. We sat through the random family dinner here and there, and it was always so fucking awkward and uncomfortable for me. Now, though, I'd gotten better at keeping to myself, and I hadn't seen him in months.

It was understandable for me to chicken out. Not so much for him. He wasn't the one who'd put his cards on the table.

"Because of an urgent matter," Lyn said frankly.

I huffed. And wondered what the fuck Dad was up to. He wasn't gonna turn into some meddler, I hoped. We already had Mom for that.

As my pulse spiked, I texted Gray again.

CHAPTER 2

Dinner was ready fifteen minutes later, and Lyn had barged downstairs when we heard laughter from Dad and Madigan. Now, as I stood in front of the mirror by my door, I heard my sister squeal, "Uncle Madigan!"

"Hey, gorgeous girl." Madigan's rich chuckle traveled up the stairs and made me queasy.

I ran a hand nervously through my hair, giving up before I'd started. My hair had a life of its own. In the end, I tugged up my hood and put my phone in one of the pockets in my sweats. I could not look hotter.

With an internal eye-roll, I left my room and headed downstairs.

When you lived with anxiety, you learned to recognize the signs of an attack coming on, and the pressure on my chest sure as fuck wasn't because I was thrilled to see Mad. Standing in the hallway with Lyn climbing on him as he chatted to Dad, he looked too handsome for words.

He and Dad were created from the same stock. While Dad was once the guitar player in one of the world's biggest rock bands, Mad was the tattoo artist to the stars. His older brother had been the drummer in the band; it was how they'd all met back in the day. Their shared history meant they had all these inside jokes that made me jealous. It wasn't unheard of that they ended up buying the same vintage tees with some old rock band on them, just 'cause they had the same taste. Levis and tees, beards or scruff, heavy on the ink, and always bitching about the music today's generation listened to.

Madigan spotted me as I reached the last step, and his grin became more forced. "Hey, Abel."

I jerked my chin, chewing on one of the hood's drawstrings. "Hey." I didn't stop, instead passing them to go right and get to the kitchen where Mom was pulling something from the oven. My fingers shook slightly, and I clenched and unclenched my fists. "Can I help?"

She jumped a little, startled to see me. "Oh. I'm sorry, sweetie." She chuckled breathily and put a pot roast on the stove. "No, I think everything's ready. Just grab what you wanna drink from the fridge."

"Okay." I went for the fridge and grabbed a bottle of water. My fingers were still trembling, and I clenched my jaw as I tried to get rid of the tremors. It was this fucking town, being home and being near that motherfucker, that caused this. I had my shit together in Vancouver. For the most part.

A hand clamped down on my shoulder, and I stiffened. It was Dad.

"Talk to him." He spoke for only me to hear. "Now that I know there's an issue, I can see it clear as day. It's tense and shit."

"Seriously," I hissed under my breath. "Are you bored? Why are you meddling?" One would think a hotshot music producer who ran a big studio in Seattle would be busier than this. I *knew* it was a bad idea when he'd handed over a lot of the responsibility to the guys working for him in the city. He was a whiny fucker without Mom and didn't like to travel without her, so these days, he recorded most stuff in his own studio in the basement.

For the record, only he would classify a two-hour commute "travel."

He scowled. "Mom meddles. I give a shit."

"Come on, boys," Mom said. "Let's eat."

I stared at Dad for a beat longer, a match I'd never win, before I averted my gaze and closed the fridge door. To make matters worse, I'd end up sitting next to Madigan. Mom and Lyn always sat next to each other when it was just us, and Dad sat at the head of the table.

I sat down across from my sister, leaving Mad and Mom on either side of Dad.

"I'm gonna watch you eat," Lyn whispered and bit into a roll.

"That's creepy," I whispered back.

"Nuh-uh." She shook her head. "It's fun. You eat more food than anyone in the world."

I snorted a quiet chuckle and filled my plate with rice, vegetables, and pot roast.

"Gravy, hon?" Mom offered.

"No, thank you." I went easy on fast carbs and fat.

"I forget you're on a diet." She made sure everyone else got gravy. "How many calories a day are you on now?"

I lifted a shoulder and dug into my food. "I'll probably go down a bit while I'm home." Opening my water, I took a big gulp from it. Right now, I needed about five thousand calories to maintain my weight. "This is awesome."

"I'm glad you like it." She blew me a kiss and took a sip of her wine. "So this is a pleasant surprise, Madigan. It's not often you show up for dinner anymore."

"It's because he doesn't like us," I said around a mouthful of vegetables. "He avoids the people he doesn't like." *Man*, it was satisfying to say that. Whoever said passive-aggressiveness wasn't a good way to deal with heartbreak?

"What the hell?" Madigan let out a chuckle, but his humor was skin-deep. His eyes showed confusion.

"I called you over 'cause you're never around anymore," Dad said flatly. "That's all there is to it. I know you still adore me."

Mom found him funny, as did Mad. I said nothing and continued shoveling food into my face.

For a while, the "grown-ups" talked about work and life. Madigan talked about the tattoo shop he owned with Jameson, his best friend. Mom talked about the facility she ran for men, women, and children escaping abuse. Dad talked about music and everything that was wrong in the industry these days.

Fun times.

In the meantime, I ate and did my best to focus solely on that. Not on Mad's voice, not on his movements, not on his laughter. Except, I failed, and my brain was flooded with memories of better times. Like when he'd visited me in Pittsburgh one weekend without telling me first. Just a surprise on a whim. We'd gone to dinner and a comedy show. Or the times he took me to games before we left Detroit. Or when he pressed his forehead to mine and talked me through my panic attacks.

"You've got this, sweetheart. Count with me, okay? One... two—that's perfect, in through your nose. I'm so proud of you."

The last mouthful of food was nearly impossible to swallow, and I stared unseeingly at my plate as the pressure on my chest grew.

Snap out of it, you useless idiot.

The sound of the doorbell wrenched me out of my state, and I hauled in a ragged breath.

"I'll get it!" Lyn shouted and bounced off her chair.

"Are we expecting anyone else?" Mom asked, confused.

Dad shook his head, wiped his mouth on a napkin, and followed Lyn to the hallway. "Hold up, baby girl."

Mom, for some reason, had to set another plate. Most people would dread salespeople. She assumed it was a dinner guest.

"Abel." Madigan's hand covered mine, and I blanched. That looked so fucking weird that I couldn't stop staring. "Is something wrong? You seem anxious."

He brushed his thumb over my skin. It left tingles and caused a drawn-out shiver, something that was pleasurable as fuck, but the contact was too strange to process.

"I'm fine." I withdrew my hand and held it in my lap.

"Adeline!" Dad hollered from the hallway. "Someone just called me gorgeous. I'm leaving you."

What the fuck? I looked at Mom, who snorted and asked who Dad was leaving her for, and then I frowned toward the hallway.

"No, the correct response is 'I promise to call you gorgeous more often,'" Dad muttered. When he appeared in the doorway, the relief that hit me almost bowled me over. It was Gray. Holy fuck, Gray was here. It felt like I could finally breathe. "Take a seat, kid," he told my buddy. "You can probably eat."

"Hi, honey." Mom smiled at Gray. "Are you sure you wanna be stuck with him?"

"Not even a little," he replied with wide eyes. "Remind me never to address him as gorgeous again." At Dad's scowl, Gray added, "I'm sorry, you're just a bit too high maintenance for me, Mr. H."

"I'm easy as fuck," Dad argued.

"Of course you are, you sexy beast." Mom was humoring him. "Easiest lay I ever had."

"All I heard was sexy beast." On the way back to his seat, Dad stole a smooch and decided to keep Mom.

"Daddy, you cuss *so* much." Lyn sauntered back to her seat too. "Uncle Casey has a swear jar at home. There are lots of dollars."

That was a discussion Mom was more than happy to get into, so I tuned out and focused on Gray. He sat down in the empty seat next to me, giving me a breather from the man on my other side.

"What're you doing here?" I asked quietly.

Gray squeezed my hand under the table. "You seemed like you needed me to run interference." Having no clue how he'd come to that conclusion, I only stared while he filled his plate. "You sent me a text," he said. "I put two and two together and figured a certain someone was coming for dinner." He set down the bowl of gravy and retrieved his phone.

All I'd texted him before leaving my room was...something about dinner. I didn't really remember.

"Here." He showed me the text, and my eyebrows went up.

Mdgan fr diner and I cant.

"Wow." I tugged at my ear, embarrassed.

"I assumed you weren't drunk," he said, pocketing his phone, "so that left anxiety."

"What are you two whispering about, boys?" Mom asked teasingly. "A date, maybe? I'd love to bring happy news when I have lunch with Chloe tomorrow."

I rolled my eyes. Our moms thought we were more than friends, and it wasn't hilarious anymore.

Dad narrowed his eyes and pointed his fork at us. "If you two are dating, no more sleepovers with the door closed."

"Jesus Christ." I scrubbed a hand over my face.

"Sorry to disappoint, Mrs. H, but we have the same taste in men," Gray said.

"What taste would that be?" It was Madigan, of all people, who asked.

There was no way I was getting into that with him.

Gray had no such qualms. "Older, bossier, definitely not a hockey player."

"*Hey.*" I smirked and grabbed my water bottle. "You're just jealous I beat your score."

Gray played hockey too. At hobby level. He wanted to be a coach and work with kids or something, which was a waste if you asked me. He was fast as hell on the ice; only one person faster ever played for our old high school's team. Me.

"Older?" Dad scowled, then faced me. "Son, you're not coming home with some old sugar daddy. In fact, give Gray a go. He called me gorgeous."

"Jesus Christ," I repeated. "Dinner was great, Mom. Thanks. We're gonna go to my room."

"I'm eating, man," Gray protested. I gave him a look and felt my jaw tensing. "On second thought, I'm still full from my dinner with the family."

Thought so.

We dumped our dishes in the sink and started leaving the kitchen.

"Abel, can I watch a movie with you?" Lyn asked.

"Tomorrow, okay?" I glanced back at her.

"She makes a great chaperone," Dad noted.

"They don't need a chaperone." Mom glared at him. "They're adults. Leave them be."

Thanks, Mom.

Lyn snickered and grabbed her glass of milk. "Abel has penises on his computer."

"Oh my God, don't go through my shit!" I widened my eyes, mortification flooding me. My sister's comment started mayhem in the kitchen between my parents; there was a lecture from Mom on privacy, bitching from Dad, and I couldn't face Madigan to see his reaction. Instead, I pushed a laughing Gray out into the hallway and toward the stairs.

"Do you wanna watch penises together?" he asked over his shoulder.

"Just kill me." I took a calming breath and let it out slowly. Next, I heard Madigan's voice. "Abel, wait up."

No, seriously, just kill me.

I paused on the stairs and exchanged a look with Gray. I didn't know what to do here. My anxiety was getting worse, but I'd never been able to resist that motherfucker.

"I'll be in your room," Gray said quietly.

Okay, then. My friend was deserting me. Steeling myself to be alone with Madigan, I waited on the stairs and stuck my hands down into my pockets.

Mad cleared his throat, coming to a stop on the step below mine. He was still taller than me.

"You're angry with me."

I raised a brow and made eye contact briefly. "What gave you that idea?"

He stared at me, his jaw ticking with tension under his trimmed beard, and I averted my gaze. Lowered it, to be accurate. To his inked forearms. It was where he wore his family and his memories, and my first jersey number was there in an Old English font.

"If I've hurt you, I'm very sorry," he murmured. "The last thing I ever wanted was for you to get hurt."

Fuck you.

I cracked half a grin and nodded. "Great. Are we done here? I have a hot guy in my room, and everyone seems to think I gotta find someone my age."

His eyes flashed with something sharp. "I thought you were just friends."

"Yeah, well." I scratched my nose and looked up the stairs. "I gotta move on, right?" It was the closest I could get to broaching the topic that had ruined everything. "It was good seeing you again, but you can go play with Mom and Dad now. They're your age." Turning away from him, I felt my heart start to pound painfully, and I took two steps at a time to escape.

"*Abel.*"

I managed to resist this time.

Gray and I spent the rest of the night playing video games and raiding the mini fridge under my desk, and then he slept over. My parents had always been good at helping me relax, as had Madigan, but lately, I'd come to rely more on my friend.

When I struggled with depression, my episodes of rage and being hyper, and my panic and anxiety, it hurt me more to see my folks hurt. Seeing me that way was painful to them, so it made things worse for me. It was a fucked-up situation, but I couldn't help it. It tore at me when Mom got upset and when Dad yelled at my doctors, 'cause I didn't think they hated anything more than being helpless. As a result, it'd made me retreat a little.

I was doing shitloads better these days. Each episode was milder in comparison to what I went through as a kid, with the exception of my panic and anxiety attacks that came and went as they wanted. Even so, keeping a lid on it in front of my parents was the best alternative for me, 'cause Gray's methods of helping me were perfect right now. He went all in for distractions and random stuff. With him, there was no talk of what my therapist recommended or any textbook coping mechanisms. It was video games, movies, hitting the gym, and often just spending a quiet moment together in bed.

Dad's and Madigan's approaches were similar, but it was different with Gray. I wasn't trying to make him proud of me, nor was I in love with him. We were equals and handled each other's bullshit as buddies.

Gray made me feel normal, like I didn't have bipolar, like I was just another dude.

Although, right this second, he was annoying me. Squinting sleepily in the dark, I read the alarm clock and saw it was four in the morning, and he was texting someone.

"Quit waking me up with your pining," I grumbled.

"Sorry. Craig sent me this." He turned around and showed me the too-bright screen.

Meet with me.

"It's weird when you call him that." I yawned and pulled the covers higher. "And he should divorce his wife before he chases your tail."

Gray was in my position; only he was hooked on my old hockey coach from high school. Our coach, I should say. As it turned out, Coach Fuller had a thing for Gray too, but he was supposedly straight and definitely married. To a woman.

Gray deserved better. He was one of the best people I knew.

"What should I write back?" he asked.

"*Nothing*. Haven't we learned from my mistake?" I could attest that no good decisions were born at four in the morning. At that hour, we caved. We gave up all control and handed the power over to someone who shouldn't have it. Four a.m. was for broken hearts and fools.

"Dammit," he whispered. A moment later, the room went dark again, and he put his phone away. "When I told your dad we have the same taste in men, I forgot to mention we're into unavailable fuckers."

I smiled tiredly as he shifted closer and pressed his body to mine. He was all toned muscle and warm comfort, easy to get lost in. He nuzzled my neck and stroked my back.

"Need a distraction?" I guessed.

He nodded jerkily. "Yeah."

Cupping his jaw, I angled his head better and covered his mouth with mine.

CHAPTER 3

"We should go out soon." I threw my gym bag into my truck, then got in behind the wheel. "Find a hot Top to rail us or something."

Gray adjusted his beanie and fiddled with the stereo. "You can say I'm bad in bed."

I laughed, turning away from the curb. "Yeah, you suck."

He sure as fuck didn't, and he knew it. We were mostly bottoms, me more so than him, and it'd been a while since we got laid by someone other than each other.

"Wanna get lunch?" Ten-thirty wasn't too early, was it? We'd been at the gym for two hours, and I was starving. Plus, we were already in the Valley. The southernmost district of Camassia had a lot more to offer. Called Little Seattle by the town residents, it was where the weekend crowd migrated for a decent selection of clubs, bars, and restaurants. It was where the community college was, as well as the town's only mall. Cobblestone streets were lined with brownstones and old factories turned trendy lofts.

Gray lived here.

So did Madigan.

"Let's go to Coho." He referred to a steakhouse, and I approved. They had awesome burgers. "I get a discount now. Last week, they wouldn't even let me pay."

My forehead creased. "Why?"

"Isla's boyfriend's brother runs the joint."

Oh. Cool. "Well, lunch is on me," I said. "I feel like I need to buy you flowers or something after last night."

He'd been so nice to come to my aid, and then, at four fucking a.m., I was taking all my frustrations out on his ass.

Gray sighed contentedly and leaned back. "Dude, last night was so good. I needed that."

If the tables were turned, I'd be agreeing with him. Being the one who inflicted that pain, though… It made me highly uncomfortable.

"Did you decide on another tattoo yet?" he asked. "Are you gonna do it here or in Vancouver?"

"Here," I replied. "I gotta pick a day Jameson is working and Mad isn't in the shop." And yes, I'd decided on a design and where to put it.

"Or maybe you quit avoiding him," Gray pointed out. "Last night after you tore up my ass, you kindly explained that I'd never move on from Craig if I didn't erase his number—"

"Why do you have to make me feel worse?" I reached over and punched his arm.

He snickered. "And you're right. As long as he's married, I should ignore him. But it's the opposite with you and Madigan. You should show you're over him by acting natural around him."

I chewed on my lip, mulling it over, and turned onto the street where Coho Bar & Grill was. "I can't lie well, though. He'll take one look at me and I'll get fidgety."

Around friends and family, and definitely around my

team, there was hardly a trace of my insecure side. Or submissive side, I guessed I should add. I knew better these days, and I was on the subbie side of the spectrum. Around assertive and dominant men like Madigan, I grew flustered and unsure. It was like pulling the rug from underneath me.

"We'll work on it. If you can fake a love for coffee in front of him, you can make him think you're over him too." He patted me on the shoulder, then pointed at an empty spot. "You can park there."

We continued talking about my strategy for Madigan over the best burgers I'd had in a long time. The steakhouse was cool, both casual and romantic-like. Rock music played on the speakers, candles floated in bowls of water on the tables, and pots of herbs hung from the ceiling along with string lights.

Gray and I sat at the bar where two guys and a woman worked. The dude who was a carbon copy of Isla's boyfriend had his back to us as he worked the grill, and the other two handled orders and waiting tables. I'd been introduced to Alessia, a short, curvy chick who had the nicest smile and snuck us sweet potato fries on the sly.

"Your family knows the right way to expand," I mumbled around a mouthful of my chicken burger. "Best thing we got was when…uh." I came up empty. My brother was single, I had no idea who Madigan was seeing, and Casey chose to hook up with Dad's cousin. "I guess Uncle Ellis's marketing skills…? But he was already in the family."

Gray chuckled. "You're avoiding the subject."

I took a bite of my chicken burger and shrugged. "I miss having Mad as a friend, but I don't see how faking it is gonna work. Besides, won't seeing him more often make it worse? It already hurts being in the same room as him for five minutes."

Gray was about to reply when Alessia came back with a bowl of eggplant chips. Once she learned we didn't eat regular fries, it seemed she was set on making us try everything else on the menu.

"Adam just put these on the menu last week," she said, sprinkling some sea salt on top. "I can't recommend them enough." Adam was the grill master behind the bar with his back to us, and he'd heard Alessia, judging by the little smirk he wore when he tilted his head. "So you two are cute together. Have you been together long?"

I smiled and tried a couple chips.

"Funny, I was gonna ask the same about you and Adam," Gray said.

That made her blush for some reason. "Oh, we're not—"

"Are you bothering the customers, love?" Adam came over and locked his arms around her chest, effectively pinning her arms to her sides.

Watching her reactions to him was like looking in the mirror. Adam and Gray eased into a conversation about Isla and Jack, and all I could see was Alessia's expression and her reaction to Adam's close proximity. The flush on her cheeks, the discomfort in her posture, the insecurity flickering as she wrung her hands and averted her gaze. Jesus Christ, it might as well have been me when I was around Mad, with the exception that I tried to pull off standoffishness.

"So, um." Alessia cleared her throat softly, her voice quiet. "You're a hockey player like Gray, right?"

I nodded. "I play in Vancouver."

"That's cool." She smiled a little. "Why don't you play for the Seahawks?"

I hid my amusement by wiping my mouth. She was kind of adorable.

Adam, who'd heard her, shook with silent laughter. "She doesn't watch much hockey."

"It's all right." Right this moment, I wanted her to be comfortable. "The teams can get confusing."

"What?" Alessia glanced up at Adam quickly.

He grinned down at her. "The Seahawks play football."

"Oh. Sorry." Her embarrassment was palpable to me, something I'd always struggled with. It made me anxious to sense other people's emotions that easily. It could get exhausting really fast.

"We'll let you get back to your lunch," Adam said. "Nice talking to you, kids."

Then it was just Gray and me again, and I'd lost my appetite. Being in love fucking sucked. Seeing other's unrequited love sucked too. It all fucking sucked.

"Do you wanna head over to the tattoo shop after this?" Gray asked. "Can't hurt to get it over with, right?"

"No, I wanna go home." I put my napkin on the plate and got out my wallet. "I'm tired."

Hiding was easier.

Yet, the following day, I found myself parked outside Camassia Ink. It was lunchtime, a good hour of the day to stave off panic. White-knuckling the wheel, I leaned forward and took deep breaths to calm myself down.

Gray's words had gone on repeat all night, and I'd woken up several times with my heart pounding. If given the choice, I knew what I would go with. Be in love with Mad and still have him in my life...or end up not having him around at all...

I missed him so fucking much. Of course I'd go with the former.

I missed his voice and guidance, I missed the gentle giant buried underneath the roughness and hard edges, and I missed laughing my ass off at his crude sense of humor.

I missed when he took me to games in Detroit.

"One day, when you get drafted, you're gonna walk up to a Canadian player and offer him a cup of tea."

I scrunched my nose. "Why?"

He smirked, eyes on the road and hands on the wheel. We were on our way to a game, and I was pumped. The Wings were playing the Habs.

"Everyone knows Canadians are basically Brits in flannel and mullets," Madigan went on. *"They drink tea like their lives depend on it. But for the longest time, they haven't been able to because the Wings have all the cups."*

Back then, the joke had flown right past me. I hadn't made the connection between teacups and Stanley Cup trophies, so my first question had been, "You think the NHL will want me when I grow up?"

"Abso-fucking-lutely," he'd said.

Screwing my eyes shut, I tried to shake the memories and focus more on my breathing. It was getting out of hand, this whole situation. I'd managed to keep a lid on my anxiety around Madigan before. Dinner the day before yesterday wasn't a new thing. Rare or not, I did see him on occasion.

"Fuck," I ground out. Were my lungs getting smaller? I broke out in a cold sweat and started hyperventilating. *Breathe, breathe, breathe.* I sucked in a dry breath that made me cough, and then my eyes were stinging and welling up.

You motherfucking loser. No wonder he doesn't want to have anything to do with you. You can't even breathe on your own.

"Useless, s-stupid." The self-hatred flared up and burned hotly, and I fisted my hair. The rage, panic, and pressure closed in on me, and I didn't know what was worse. That I was past the point of no return, or that I was aware enough to see the hole I was crawling inside. I'd gotten myself into this fucking mess because I was as dumb as a box of rocks.

The door was suddenly wrenched open, and the shock caused me to flinch away. I couldn't open my eyes, not even when I was hauled out of the car. Instead, I covered my face and as much of my head as possible.

"S-s-stop," I managed to choke out.

"Like hell I will." Shit, it was Madigan. "Don't fight me, sweetheart."

I wasn't aware of doing *anything*, much less fighting. Next, I vaguely registered the scents of disinfectants and strong arms around me. We were going somewhere; there was noise—music—voices, stumbling, heat, sweat, burning lungs... I was swimming in all of it.

He was speaking, but I couldn't hear the words. Just his low voice and lips pressed to my temple. At the same time, he was guiding me somewhere. Up a set of stairs—to his apartment, I guessed.

"I can't—" *do anything.* The rage won out, and I welcomed it. I could breathe when I was furious. There was control and rhythm in anger. The second we reached the landing, I shoved him away from me as hard as I could, then slammed my fist into the nearest wall. "Useless piece of shit!" I shouted hoarsely. Every ounce of the fury was directed at myself. "Just throw yourself off a fucking cliff, you motherfucking retard!"

"Quit it, Abel!"

I was pushed up against a wall and restrained, only fueling my self-hatred. "No, let go of me!" Using my shoulder,

I got him in the chest and managed to get free. It wasn't merely my hands shaking; it was like my entire being was becoming unglued. Soon, I was fighting both Madigan and the chest pain. "Fucking worthless," I groaned through a sob. "Don't touch me, don't touch me, *don't touch me!*" The last part came out in a scream, and it unleashed my hysteria. I gulped, black spots filled my vision, everything wobbled, and I couldn't find an escape. Oh God, just kill me. I wanted to die, I had to get away, where did the stairs go, I yanked at my hair—

"That's enough!" Madigan's growl shook me, and then his arm was planted across my chest. My back hit the wall again, and he was quick to cage me in and restrain my wrists.

I was damaged, pathetic, and now weak, too. Could I do anything right? Another sob ripped its way out of me, and I struggled to get my hands free so I could hide my face. The shame and despair crippled me as I realized this was the biggest attack I'd had in years. The thought of going through new trials and new meds made me wanna die.

"Listen to my voice, sweetheart. You've got this. I believe in you."

I whimpered and clutched his T-shirt, unsure of whether to cling to him or push him away. "Why can't I b-be normal?"

"Fuck normal," he gritted. "We're not gonna go over this again, Abel. You know better."

I didn't. He used to say I was perfect the way I was, that I was perfect for *him*. But that was before he thought there was a risk I would misinterpret his intentions. He was too late for that, and he'd fucking lied to me. If I were so goddamn perfect, he wouldn't avoid me.

"You don't want me around anymore." As soon as I said that, the levees broke, as if they hadn't already shattered, and I fell apart. He let me cover my face with my hands, though he didn't back off. I needed him to. I needed him to leave me alone. Except every time I told him to go, he refused.

"I've given you enough space." He cupped the back of my head and hugged me to him. "Hug me back, you little shit."

Even as the grief grew stronger and I kept crying like some loser, I obeyed and wrapped my arms around his middle.

"You don't know how much I miss you, Abel."

I didn't believe him. "Don't—don't l-lie to me."

Deep breaths. I drew in a long, shaky breath. My nose was stuffy, so I exhaled through my mouth. Another breath, and another. One day, this pain had to be over.

A fresh round of tears rolled down my cheeks, but they were lessening. Every breath came easier than the last, and it was impossible to be unmoved by his comfort. He held me tightly and worked like glue, putting me back together.

"I've never lied to you." He pressed a kiss to my forehead, and I hated him for it. "I did a shitty thing that I'll regret for the rest of my life, but I would never lie to you."

"What did you do?" I croaked and wiped at my cheeks.

He shook his head and loosened his hold. "Nap time first. I'll explain later."

"Nap time? I'm not a fucking child." I sniffled and looked away, though he wouldn't accept that. He cupped my cheek and brushed away a stray tear, and I was forced to look him in the eye.

To my annoyance, his eyes flashed with amusement. "Humor me. I know you're exhausted."

"You're still an asshole."

"Born that way." He took my hand and produced a key from his jeans, then opened the door to his place.

I wobbled inside with barely any physical strength left and looked around the sparsely decorated studio for the first time in over a year. A kitchenette, sleeping alcove, corner for his sketching and stenciling, and another corner with two cushy chairs and a small entertainment center completed his studio. The man lived modestly, despite the wealth he came from, despite the big money actual celebrities paid to fly him out to wherever they were.

My bleary gaze got stuck on a few sketches he'd pinned to the wall behind his sketch board. He'd drawn Lyn and me together from a photo I knew we had at home. There was one sketch of a hockey stick, and the details were so vivid. At the end of the stick, a Penguins logo was peeling off to reveal half the orca that represented the Canucks. Lastly, there was a sketch of all the jersey numbers I'd worn.

Growing up, I had seen him with a sketchbook more times than I could count. I knew exactly how he'd sit, chew on his pen, eye his work critically, and rest one foot on his knee. When he got restless, he would bounce his foot or drum the pen against the edge of the sketchbook.

"I need another hug." In the middle of the floor, he drew me to his body again, and I couldn't even hate him anymore. This was what he did to me. My nose wasn't as stuffy now, so I was invaded by the rich, masculine scent of his body wash and cologne.

He rendered me powerless.

Oddly, I'd never disliked it when it was him pushing that feeling on me. It was comforting and safe. *He* was safe. Or, he used to be. A safe place to land, 'cause he'd take care of things.

It probably wasn't okay I felt that way. I had to take care of myself.

"I hate you," I lied.

He tightened his hold on me. "I'm sorry I've hurt you. So fucking sorry."

"Whatever," I muttered. Pushing halfheartedly at his ribs, I broke the hug and stared at my feet. My eyes felt heavy. The best part of the end of a panic attack was the numbness that set in. "I'm sorry I..." The words got stuck in my throat. "I'm sorry I told you how I f-felt."

"Don't apologize for that, sweetheart," he whispered. "I was the one who... Fuck."

Yeah, he was the one who'd ignored it. Not that my approach had been very smooth—or classy, for that matter. I blamed it on the four-a.m. thoughts. The defeat that seeped in before dawn. I'd been all the way across the country, lonely as fuck, and I'd sent that goddamn text message. The words still haunted me.

I think ive been in love with u since I was 12.

With one text message, I'd handed over my heart on a platter, and he had walked right by it.

"I should go home," I mumbled. I was done feeling antsy and exposed, and I—

"Not so fast." He gripped my arm, only to wince and let go. Then he pressed a hand to his shoulder and rotated the muscle. "You throw a good punch."

I frowned and looked down at my hand. My fingers twitched. There was hardly any pain, even now that the dust had settled and the adrenaline was gone. And I'd slammed my fist into a *wall*...hadn't I?

"I caught it." He answered my unspoken question and grabbed my hand again. "You think I'm gonna let you break your hand before the play-offs?" Without waiting for my response, he ushered me over to his bed and tugged at the hem of my hoodie. "Take it off."

I suppressed a shudder at that one. For as slow as my brain was to catch up on other shit, it was surprisingly quick on anything that could be sexual.

I looked away but had to ask. "What're you doing?"

There was no way I'd take my clothes off and get into bed with him.

"Can you let me fuss and be selfish for one fucking minute?" There was no heat in his voice, and I'd rather deal with anger. Anger was easier to push away from. "I want you to nap, and then we'll deal with dinner."

Had he lost his mind? What was it with him and nap time?

I took a step back and pulled the hoodie over my head. "On one condition. We talk before I sleep—"

"What the fuck is this?" He quickly stepped closer and held the hem of my tee that was riding up. "Who did your ink?"

I peered down at the piece on the left side of my rib cage. "You jealous?" I smirked tiredly.

"A little." He frowned and traced a finger along the number forty-four. Same jersey number he'd tattooed on his arm, only mine was bigger and in a simpler, bolder font. "I feel like you cheated on me." He drew a low snicker from me, and he continued to the next tattoo. A hockey stick that was broken in half and had barbed wire circling it.

"I came here to talk to Jameson about adding to it," I admitted.

That made Madigan scowl, and he let his hand fall. "You don't want me to do it?"

More than anything.

"Are you gonna rat me out to Mom and Dad?" I asked.

He cocked a brow. "Lincoln and Ade don't know?"

I shook my head.

"You're trouble," he sighed and moved to the bed where he sat down. "You're an adult, though. It's your business."

Nice to know he viewed me as an adult. "So, you do know my age. Interesting. Do you remember my birthday too?"

He laughed through his nose and leaned back on his hands. "I deserve that. I genuinely tried to make it last weekend, but I was outta town."

Dad had told me. Mad had been in LA to tattoo some old musician.

"And the year before that? When I turned twenty?" I shuffled closer and sat down on the foot of the bed after kicking off my shoes. My body felt twice as heavy as before, but the emotional numbness was nice.

"It was too soon," he murmured. "I feel awful for how I behaved that Christmas."

When he'd turned up with a date just two weeks after I'd sent him that message? Yeah, that sucked. Not only had he never responded or even acknowledged what I'd said, but he'd brought someone home for dinner on Christmas Eve. I'd freaked out so badly that I'd returned to the East Coast early. And I hadn't gone back home until two months later for my birthday.

"That was a punch in the gut." I nodded. "Worst way to get rejected."

With a heavy sigh, Mad fell back against the mattress and scrubbed his hands over his face. "We weren't together—him and me, I mean. He was dating a buddy of mine from Seattle and was gonna be alone for the holidays. I knew what it'd look like if I invited him to Ade and Lincoln's house, so I went with it. I was a coward. There's no other word for it."

Jesus Christ. "Going through all that was easier than just taking me aside and letting me down gently by saying you didn't feel the same? You're a fucking dick, Mad."

He stared at the ceiling and clasped his hands over his stomach. "It's not that simple, Abel. It's not about what I f— You know what, it doesn't matter. I should've done what you said. I should've talked to you, and I chickened out."

I didn't know what to say or how I felt about this. Part of me hoped closure would help. The other part of me thought he was a year too late. The damage had been done, and I'd crashed embarrassingly hard.

I would've liked to believe I'd handle the situation better if I hadn't lost my friend. It was one thing to be rejected as a… um, love interest? It was a whole other situation to be abandoned by the man whose word I'd always trusted. When he told me I was good enough, I believed him. Or, I used to.

"Do you remember Morgan, Abel?"

I scratched my arm and nodded a little. "Some, yeah." I'd been six when my biological dad died. A handful of memories were crystal clear, and I treasured them. Morgan had called me Ace as a kid, and I had the ace of spades inked next to my jersey number now.

For the most part, I wasn't sure if they were memories or if they were stories told by Mom, Dad, or my brother. Jesse had been older, so he remembered Morgan better.

Morgan Novak. He was once the assistant of Dad's band's manager, so they'd all traveled together. Back then, Madigan had been part of the roadie crew since his big brother was the drummer. Mom…uh. Well, my folks were weirdly tight-lipped about the way they'd met, so we just assumed she'd been Dad's groupie.

"Before Morgan passed away," Madigan murmured, "he made me promise to visit and check in with you guys in Detroit whenever I could. Easiest promise I ever made to one of the best men I've ever known."

I frowned and fidgeted with the drawstrings of my sweats. "You talk about him like you loved him." That was weird.

Madigan chuckled tiredly. "You have no idea."

I looked to him sharply at that. *No fucking way.*

He met my gaze with a lot less urgency. "I loved him as a

friend, Abel. But I won't lie to you. We do share history from the band's last tour."

"Uh..." I grimaced automatically, though I wasn't sure I got it. "You're not telling me you hooked up with my father, are you?"

He didn't reply. He merely stared at me.

"Oh God," I mumbled and looked away. Holy fuck, that was bizarre. "Are you serious?"

"I am. Sweetheart, I have eighteen years of living on you, and I wasn't always a monk."

As if he was a monk now.

"Does that mean my father was bi?" I asked, trying to do the math. I knew my biological mother had abandoned us, but they'd been married at some point.

"Yup." Madigan dragged himself up to sit. "To be honest, the end of the nineties is kind of a blur for me. I was on the road for a whole summer with Lincoln and his band, and they didn't exactly go to bed after each show."

I side-eyed him. "Sex, drugs, and rock 'n' roll, right?"

"And then some." He ran a hand through his dark hair. "Morgan had a thing for Ade, too."

"Stop it." I palmed my face, half grossed out. "That's my mom you're talking about, idiot."

He found it funny. "See this? This is just it, Abel. Your parents are two of my best friends, and we share a lot of history. You're not gonna like some of it, and you should have a boyfriend you can talk to about everything."

My hands fell to my lap, and I stared at him blankly. If this was his idea of letting me down gently, it wasn't funny. Or gentle.

"Okay, fine," I said. "You, Mom, Dad, Morgan—you basically all fucked, got high, and drank together. Am I correct?"

"Fuck no, I'm gay." He put a hand on his chest. "I've never

been with a woman, and Lincoln's fucking obsessed with your mother." Great. That didn't rule out the rest, but whatever. "You see where I'm going with this, though? We're very different, Abel. We're into different things—"

"I get it." I took a breath to kill my brewing anger. This was Madigan trying to tell me we weren't compatible without saying he wasn't into me. I got it, and I didn't need to hear another word. On the flipside, this was my one shot at taking back some of the control I'd surrendered. Regardless of how much it hurt to know my feelings weren't reciprocated, this conversation had eased most of the tension.

Tension was one of the enemies of someone with anxiety.

I wanted my friend back, and one lie might take care of it.

"I don't feel that way anymore, okay?" I averted my eyes and cleared my throat. In order to sound more believable, I sat a little straighter and forced myself to make eye contact. "You don't have anything to worry about, I promise."

It was hard to read his expression, and I couldn't sense what he was feeling. While something tightened around his eyes, his faint smile seemed legit, and he even covered my hand with his.

"I had a feeling it would pass quickly." Fuck him. Fuck him so fucking hard. He shifted toward me and held my hand in both of his. "You think you can forgive me at some point so I can have you back in my life?"

I had no choice but to forgive him, 'cause I missed him more than I could describe. Before that, I had a question. "Why did you have a feeling it would pass quickly?"

He shook his head in amusement and gave my hand a squeeze. "Because you're a gorgeous young man who can light up a whole fucking room, and I'm a bossy old fuck who wants everyone to get off my porch."

Okay, as far as rejections went, he wasn't half bad at it.

I withdrew my hand and punched him in the shoulder I'd already punched once. Hard.

"For fuck's sake, Abel," he growled, rubbing his shoulder. "The next one will cost you."

"You could've told me this a year ago, asshole!" I yelled. "Do you realize how much this has hurt? Thanks to you, I gotta get back to therapy!"

Shit. I really did. The realization hit as the words left me, and it was the truth. My self-doubt had gotten worse and worse, the anxiety rising until I eventually exploded. First on the ice when I'd cross-checked some Finnish dude who called my bipolar brain useless. And then now. And it wasn't the extent of it. I'd been berating myself, calling myself useless and worthless left and right lately. Because of *him*.

"Abel—"

"This isn't okay." I ran both hands through my hair and tugged at the ends. "I've relied so much on you that when you split, I lost all my confidence."

My self-esteem couldn't make or break according to Madigan's actions. It needed to be mine and mine only. I had to reevaluate everything and find my backbone. First of all, I had to stop thinking about him before I thought of me. For claiming I was so bad at lying, I'd erected enough fronts in attempts to get him to like me, and now I didn't know where it left me. Confused as hell, that was for sure.

"Let me help." Mad shifted closer, and this time, I could sense the pain rolling off of him. He was churning with guilt. I saw it in his eyes. "I wasn't kidding about earning your forgiveness, kiddo."

I ignored the *kiddo* comment and chewed on my lip. "How? I don't even know if I need to have my meds adjusted."

"At least I'm good at this," he murmured. "How are you

with your routines and structure? You have a habit of forgetting stuff when you get anxious."

True...

Madigan patted my leg and stood up. "Give me a minute. I'll get a notebook, and we'll draw up a new schedule for you."

Wonderful, he was gonna act like my uncle slash caregiver again.

CHAPTER 4

I was already regretting this.

Over the next hour, Madigan sat by his sketch board and pretty much interrogated me on the tasks I'd neglected—tasks that made up my everyday structure. Without said structure, I floundered, grew uneasy, and lost track of time. If I wanted my mind at ease, my surroundings needed to be organized.

"When should you get up in the morning?" he asked.

Restless and bored, I wandered over to his entertainment center. "Five on a game day, eight on an off day, and seven if there's regular practice." I didn't want to put too much focus on this topic; it was a little embarrassing. Instead, I studied the photos on display in between stacks of books and movies.

"And when have you been getting up lately?" he asked next.

I sighed. "I don't know, with enough time to get to practice or whatever I'm supposed to do."

"Abel." There was some mild scolding in his voice. "You

need your two hours before you leave home. Stress upsets your stomach, and you'll end up crunching Imodium—"

"Yeah, fine, whatever." I ignored my ears heating up and eyed a photo of him and Jameson. It was taken outside the tattoo shop on the day they partnered up. Arms around each other's shoulders, cocky smirks, Ray-Bans, and smokes behind their ears. They were kind of two peas in a pod. "I thought I was supposed to nap."

"You will, after this." He tapped his pen against the notebook, pensive. "Are you eating regularly?"

"If by regularly, you mean all the time, then yes." My diet was the one thing I remained strict on, mainly 'cause I got the direct results in the morning if I strayed from what my nutritionist recommended.

That didn't mean I didn't cheat, but only when I was off work. If I had practice or a game, there was added stress.

"How many meals a day?" he wondered.

I lifted a shoulder and scratched my nose. "Including snacks? Six or seven." Eating was a big part of a hockey player's life, something that'd taken me a while to get used to. I burned through calories in no time, and if I missed a meal or didn't get enough, I lost weight fast. "I'm kinda hungry now."

He chuckled. "Help yourself. I keep your cereals in the cupboard."

I headed over to his kitchenette, curious about that. Wouldn't they have gone stale? Opening the left cupboard, I spotted two boxes. My favorite Oreo O's and the evil necessity of some fancy brand of a high-fiber oat mix.

"You hate Oreos," I stated. The box was brand-new and didn't expire for months.

"Funny how that works. I hate not having them in my cupboard even more."

I frowned at him over my shoulder, and he was still jotting

down notes. In no mood for healthy options, I filled a bowl with Oreo O's and opened the fridge to get the milk. Hell, he even kept almond milk around for me.

"Do you still run in the morning?" he asked.

"I'm *supposed* to..." I guess I'd been slacking with that too. Shoveling milk and delicious little Oreo bits into my mouth, I got curious about what else had or hadn't changed. Besides, he was boring, and I was nosy. I ignored the middle cupboard, knowing it was where he kept his plates and glasses, and opened the last one. "Jesus!" I jumped back as a big stack of those little Nutella to-go packets tumbled out and fell down into the sink.

I was instantly flooded with memories of Madigan's obsession with those things.

"My grandmother used to say 'something sweet every day keeps the sad face away, but for the diabetes, you need to do more than pray.'" He snuck me a small packet and draped an arm around my shoulders. "I won't tell anyone if you don't." With a kiss to the side of my head, he brightened my mood and helped me forget my latest tantrum.

During my outburst, milk had trickled out of the corner of my mouth, and I wiped it away before putting the packets back into the cupboard. I knew, I just fucking knew, if I patted him down now, I'd find one of these in his jeans.

I kept my back to him so he couldn't see my smile. "No diabetes yet, I hope?"

There was a pause before he responded, and I heard the smirk in his voice. "I've been praying really hard lately. So far, so good."

I grinned to myself, having missed this.

By the time I turned around, I'd composed my face, and I went back to shoveling milk and cereal into my mouth.

He eyed my choice. "Your first and last bowl of sugar today. I'll get you something better after you've slept."

"I can rest at home, you know." At the moment, I wasn't very tired. "It's Friday. I'm sure you have plans."

He hummed, nodding slowly as he wrote in his notebook. "I was gonna get a pizza with Jamie and catch up on paperwork. Exciting plans." Something gave him a pause, and he furrowed his brow. "Do you have plans?"

"Not this weekend," I said with my mouth full. "Going to Seattle next Wednesday before I go home."

I'd woken up to a text from Gray, where he agreed with what I'd said the other day when I told him we needed to go out. So he'd scored tickets to Afterfuck, something I was admittedly less excited about now that I was working shit out with Mad.

"With Gray?" he guessed.

I nodded. "Have you been to Twelfth & K?"

I assumed he had. And, belatedly, I hoped this wasn't a touchy subject. Twelfth & K was a fetish club in Seattle, and they hosted Afterfuck once a month, an after party of sorts for gay men. You had to have attended at least two regular events and go through a vetting process in order to get tickets.

Gray wasn't kinky, but he was a man with a functioning dick, and I'd dragged him along a few times. We'd head down on Wednesday, have our fun, and spend the night in my parents' condo before driving back up on Thursday. Then I had practice on Friday in Vancouver and a game on Saturday.

Madigan gave me a flat stare, his attention no longer on the scribbling. "How do you know about that club?"

"Well," I said slowly, deciding to pay him back by quoting him from earlier, "I have a lot of history, and you're not gonna like some of it."

He narrowed his eyes. "You won't like it there. It's a BDSM club."

"Okay." I finished my cereal, then put the bowl in the sink and wiped my mouth. The bed suddenly looked inviting again, and I aimed for it. "I guess you know best since you're so fucking old, and there's no way I already knew it was a kinky place."

Seriously, adults sometimes. I mean...I was an adult too.

Three years ago, Madigan accidentally shared a post on Facebook that sent me down a rabbit hole of research. Or, at least, I guessed it'd been an accident, 'cause shortly after, the article had disappeared from his timeline. It'd been about BDSM, and I could admit today I'd gone to my first event solely to be perfect for him. If he was into something, I wanted to like the same thing.

In the end, I'd found my place. It had fuck-all to do with him anymore. Since then, I'd heard bits and pieces that hinted of his...hobbies or whatever. I already knew he was a bossy motherfucker. It made total sense if he was a Dom as well. No need for confirmation, nor did it matter, 'cause it didn't change what I was into.

However, fuck him for assuming what I wanted in life.

"You're right. You're right." At Mad's words, I whipped my head around to face him. I was right? I mean, I knew I was right, but...I was right? "It's just a shock," he admitted. "It's difficult to think of you enjoying a place like that."

"Well, I do." And Gray was right. I needed to go out. Otherwise, I'd end up trying to convince Madigan I could be good for him, and I wasn't gonna go there. He would shoot me down. Again.

I sat down on the bed and yawned. "I think I wanna rest now."

The numbness was fading, and it'd be nice to fall asleep before my brain started overanalyzing everything again.

Madigan snapped out of whatever he was thinking about, and he walked over as I hogged most of his bed and got under the covers. The bed smelled of him, and it was hard not to bury my face in the pillow and inhale.

"Have I told you you're trouble lately?" He smirked ruefully and dipped down to tuck me in. I really was a kid to him, wasn't I? At the same time, it was nice. This was Madigan. Underneath the inked bad boy was a fussing caregiver.

I nodded and grinned. "You said it earlier."

"Worth mentioning twice." He touched my cheek. "Get some sleep. I'll finish your schedule, and then we'll have dinner when you wake up."

Yes, Sir.

It was a little disturbing how quickly Mad and his studio became a safe place again. What happened to making him earn back my trust? Yet, when I woke up, my mind was at ease, and there was no pressure. No pressure to be strong, no pressure to be confident, no pressure to be tough. Shit, I hadn't felt this way since I was a kid—before he made me nervous and my dick hard.

I could let go of all adult notions and not give a fuck. 'Cause in the end, it didn't matter around him. Unless I was getting a tattoo, he wouldn't see me as anything other than the twelve-year-old he once took to games.

It would probably do me good to let go of all the pretenses, too. I'd loved him the most before I knew I loved him, which was a confusing thought. It'd been easier back then. Fewer worries.

A ding caught my attention, and I lifted my head off the pillow and squinted. It'd gotten dark while I slept. There was another ding, and now it was annoying.

"Mad—" My sleepy voice was cut off as I spotted a note on the nightstand.

Just getting us dinner. Be back soon.

My stomach snarled in approval, and I hoped he didn't go for some healthy option for me. I wanted to veg out and enjoy the evening—*ding!*

"Motherfucker." I sat up, my feet hitting the floor, and I glanced around the room. On the coffee table, I saw Madigan's iPad. It kept flashing, so I dragged myself over and picked it up. A notification from Jameson popped up. I only saw the preview, but it sure as shit had my attention.

So this buddy of mine is into kink…

I glanced over my shoulder to check the entryway. Madigan really shouldn't have his iPad and iPhone synced. Whatever he was texting on his phone with Jameson was popping up here too.

I took a casual swipe with my finger, and look at that, there was no password. That was stupid of Mad. Chewing on my lip, I clicked on the texts to see their conversation.

How would Abel know about a fetish club in Seattle? Humor me.

Oh man, it was Madigan who'd started this convo. Since it was about me, I felt I had the right to snoop.

One day he discovered porn and his dick showed the way.

I snickered at Jameson's response. He wasn't entirely wrong. I *had* seen kinky porn—and gotten off to it—before I learned Madigan was into BDSM.

The next two texts were from Mad, and I wasn't surprised one bit to see what he'd written.

He said he's into that shit. It ain't right.

He's a kid.

There. I'd gotten my confirmation and final rejection. While I spent the rest of my life getting over him, I wasn't gonna pretend around him anymore. Never again was I gonna pretend to be interested in the news when I really wanted to watch cartoons or *The Avengers*. I'd had my last cup of gross coffee near him because fuck that. I was done trying to be mature for him.

Didn't he just turn 21?

"Yes, Jameson, I did." I sat down on the bed and scrolled down.

Doesn't matter. This is Abel we're talking about. I've known the boy since he was six.

I rolled my eyes. This was the story of my life.

Sounds legit. Can we change the subject? I gotta tell you something, and you'll never believe it.

My interest died at Jameson's request, except then I remembered the preview I'd seen. So I kept scrolling. Madigan had agreed to Jameson's topic change and called him an unhelpful dick, and then I saw Jameson's text.

So this buddy of mine is into kink. He gets off on hot guys calling him Daddy. Now he's judging the fuck out of a guy for being into similar shit, but between you and me, I think it's because Daddy wants Abel bad.

I blinked.

I read it over and over again.

My gaze traveled farther, to Mad's reply.

Eat shot.
*shit!

And Jameson's "Hahahaha."

Then I looked up again. "I think it's because Daddy wants Abel bad," I whispered to myself. *Daddy?* Seriously? I'd heard of Daddy kink, but... I shook my head quickly and furrowed my brow. There was no way Madigan wanted me. Was there?

I didn't find this discussion funny at all. My stomach tightened, and the pressure was back over my chest. I couldn't go through this again. Shaking my head once more, I scrambled off the bed and returned the iPad to the coffee table, and then I got back under the covers.

I stared up at the ceiling, restless and anxious and nervous and increasingly angry. I shouldn't have snooped. Hoping that Madigan would see me differently had already crushed me once. I blinked a couple times as my vision suddenly got blurry, and I pushed down my emotions.

Jameson was wrong. End of discussion.

Madigan was finally my friend again. I couldn't lose him twice.

An internal wall was slammed up, and I decided right then and there to focus solely on our friendship. No pretending, no bullshit. I was gonna be me, completely. That meant I was sometimes the angry hothead who cursed outrageously when my team lost. Sometimes I was immature as hell, and I always hated coffee. Other times, I felt weak and needed comfort. I'd lose the tough-guy attitude for those moments.

It would be like when I was little again. If he didn't want me when I acted older, he wouldn't want me when I acted—when I *didn't* act.

My mind calmed down at my decision.

I would find my way again, with Madigan around, and I would look elsewhere for love.

"It's final," I said to myself.

When Madigan returned a while later, I sat up in bed and rubbed my eyes. I hadn't fallen back asleep, but I'd dozed a little.

He flicked on the light by his sketch board. "You're awake."

"Hi." I yawned and dug out my phone. I'd slept on it. A delicious scent filled the room, and I perked up. "What did you get?"

He smiled and unloaded a bag on the coffee table. "Eggplant lasagna and salad."

I made a face. "You picked healthy food on a Friday."

"Wasn't I supposed to?" he chuckled and opened the containers. "Don't worry. It's just the pasta that's been replaced. You still get all the cheese, and I may have bought dessert, too."

Okay, I could forgive him for the eggplant.

As he pulled drinks from the fridge, I moved over to the chairs and picked the one closest to the window. Admittedly, the food did look delicious. The cheesy lasagna was surrounded by a salad with a mountain of spinach, fresh Parmesan, tomatoes, onion, and slices of avocado. Folding my legs, I put the container in my lap and reached for the TV remote.

Mad set Diet Coke, beer, and water on the table. "The local news is starting—"

"The news sucks." I opened a can of Diet Coke and took a big gulp while I headed straight for Netflix. "Can we watch *Luke Cage*?"

"I don't know what that is, but pick whatever you want."

Step one, complete. I was sticking to honesty. I could see Madigan watching me in my periphery, but I kept my eyes fixed on the flat screen and chose the first episode. Then I explained *Luke Cage*, *Jessica Jones*, *Daredevil*, and the other superheroes in the Marvel universe, making sure to mention the order he should watch them. *Jessica Jones* came before *Luke Cage*, but I'd recently seen that season at home.

I was met with silence from Madigan, so I had no choice but to face him. I couldn't read his expression. Was he amused or sad—no, wait. Both amused and wistful, and I figured it out because I had a clue as to why.

"Do you remember how passionate you used to be about Harry Potter?" he asked, and that was exactly why. He'd found my ramblings about Harry Potter funny and cute, whereas I'd found them a necessity. Because people kept jumping into the series all wrong.

"Gray watched the second movie first," I muttered and forked up a chunk of lasagna. "He did it to be a dick."

Madigan laughed quietly. "You'd get so furious."

Yeah, well.

I liked this. This was better. I had no expectations, and there was no one to impress. Maybe Madigan liked it too. He seemed to be in a better mood now with the heavy shit behind us.

CHAPTER 5

"Jesus Christ, Abel! I'm done. I'm dead." Gray shut off the machine and stepped away from the treadmill. Bent over, hands on his thighs. "I'm tasting blood."

"You're...supposed to," I panted. "Ten more."

"Go fuck yourself." He collapsed on the floor next to my machine and poured water into his mouth. "Maybe you like the taste of blood in the NHL, but not in this town. Not. In. This. Town. *Ugh*. I hate doing sprints."

I chuckled, out of breath, and sped up for another round.

"You better give me a blow job after this," he groaned. "Or is that out now that you're cozy with your Mad again?"

I'd snort if I had the air for it. The only words I could wheeze out were, "Only I call him that."

It wasn't until I slowed down to catch my breath that I could speak better. And no, nothing was *out*. Mad and I were only friends.

"I don't know, man..." Gray stood up with a grunt and leaned on my machine. "What if Jameson is right and Daddy Madigan wants little Abel?"

"Stop it." I stole his water bottle and chugged what was left. "Fuck." Another sprint began, and I gritted my teeth, tasting the familiar copper in my mouth. Spots filled my vision, my lungs expanded, and I ran for all I was worth.

"The Daddy thing is kinda hot," he noted.

"Yeah." I, for one, was gonna look that shit up in Seattle next week. I'd googled a little bit last night when I came home from Madigan's, and the fetish fit him to a T. A Daddy Dom tended to focus more on nurturing, and the whole thing called to me.

"You're in a better mood." Gray extended his towel to me, and I used it to wipe sweat off my face. "I like it."

Heaving a last breath, I quit the sprint program and slowed down to a jog. "So do I." Another story of my life. Without structure, my moods were all over the fucking place, though I suspected today's change was more than that. "Okay, I'm done. Let's stretch and hit the showers."

"You can tell me more about this Jameson on the way," he said. "I remember you saying he swings both ways."

I stepped off the treadmill and grabbed my own towel and water bottle. "You've met him, haven't you?"

"Briefly. He's hot. Is he single, though?"

"I think so." At the back of the gym, we grabbed a couple yoga mats and sat down. "After we eat, we could head over to the shop. My tattoo idea kinda got lost yesterday."

"Sounds good." He scooted a bit closer to me, and with our feet touching each other, we linked our hands and took turns pulling back. "You're bendier than I am."

"It'd be weird if I weren't." I'd started out as a goalie and still liked the position. When we played hockey for shits and giggles, I often volunteered to cover the goal, and we had to be flexible. "Pull back farther." I gripped his hands tighter as he eased me forward, and I groaned at the burn along the backs of my legs. "Does this mean you're gonna try dating again?"

He shook his head. "I'm not ready. I just wanna get laid."

Made sense. We were in the same spot.

"I doubt he'll turn you down." I smirked, eyeing Gray's thigh muscles working. Where I was fast and limber, he was cut and carried a bit more bulk than me. He had weight to throw around, and he was a few inches taller.

"If you're trying to get into my pants, it's working."

I grinned.

"Don't tell your dad, but I'm gonna call that man gorgeous." Gray stopped staring at Jameson through the shop window and pushed the door open.

I ran a hand through my damp hair and followed him. "You call a lot of men gorgeous."

"Don't tell him that either."

We waited while Jameson finished talking to a client by the register. I could spot Madigan working on a dude's back piece farther into the studio, half that area sealed off with a curtain. The other two chairs were empty, so maybe it was a slow day.

The red-painted walls were filled with photos from their portfolios. A political podcast filling the air made things less fun, but the sound of a tattoo gun always worked for me.

"And come back in if you have any questions or concerns," Jameson said.

The woman nodded and shouldered her bag. "Thank you so much."

Jameson's gaze landed on me first, and he smiled lazily

and rested his forearms on the counter. "Hey, kid. You feelin' better?"

Right, because last time anyone in here saw me, I was in the middle of a panic attack. Just great.

I nodded and walked closer. "Yeah. How're you?"

"Better now that I'm not alone with the grumpiest fucker on the planet." He must've meant Madigan, though I had no idea why. Jameson cast a curious glance Gray's way, so I took the hint and introduced them.

"Gray, Jameson Grady—Jameson, Gray Nolan."

"Good to meet you." Jameson nodded.

"You too, gorgeous."

I shot Gray a dirty look. How fucking obvious could he be? Then again, that was the goal.

Jameson's eyes flashed with interest. "Well, aren't you a flirt."

"And aren't you a Grady." Gray mirrored Jameson by resting his arms on the counter and leaning forward a bit. "Any relation to Jack and Adam?"

I frowned, having not considered that before, even though I knew their last names.

Jameson's brow lifted. "They're my older brothers."

"Is your gene pool made of liquid sex?" Gray asked.

"Okay, you two have fun," I said abruptly. "I'll wait upstairs." I wasn't sure they heard me. Knowing my way, I went behind the scenes and cleared my throat subtly to get Madigan's attention. I knew I was breaking the rules by disturbing him while he worked.

He finished the line he was filling in, then looked my way with a frown. Only, when he saw it was me, his frown was replaced by a small smile.

What I noticed were the dark shadows under his eyes. He hadn't slept.

"I'm here to discuss my tattoo," I said. "How many hours until you're done?"

He glanced at the clock on the wall. "We're wrapping up in twenty."

"Okay, cool. I'll wait upstairs. Gray and Jameson are flirting. Sorry for bothering you. Bye." The words tumbled out of me in a rush before I headed for the back room where a door led to the stairs.

It was the first time in over a year I used the spare key he'd given me years ago.

I let myself into his studio apartment and kicked off my sneakers. Then I grabbed a soda from the fridge and got comfortable on his bed with the remote. He'd cranked up the heat at some point, so I removed my hoodie and socks.

While I waited for Netflix to load, I sent Gray a message.

Im upstairs if u decide to stop humping Jamesons leg.

I sipped my Diet Coke and read his response.

We're going out tonight. You can't say no.

Uh, I was definitely saying no.

If Jameson is going, u dont need me as wingman. Have fun!

I'd already made Seattle plans for next week. That was enough. I'd get laid then. Spring chicken like me? I'd have a good selection of Tops to choose from.

Dude, his place is across the river way up in Westslope, and my roommates are having a party. I need you.

I grinned. He didn't need me. He just needed the key to Dad's yacht. Unbeknownst to Dad, we used it sometimes for occasions such as this one.

I can give u the key to the boat.

In return, Gray told me he loved me.

I was in the middle of a *Luke Cage* episode when Mad walked in, wiping his hands on a rag. I didn't know why he bothered. He always had ink on his skin and under his nails.

"You weren't kidding when you said Jamie and your friend were flirting."

"How bad is it now?" I chuckled.

"They'd be horizontal if they had a bed nearby." He took a seat on the edge of the bed and stole my soda to take a swig. Then he peered back at me. "You having a good day? I expected to be verbally beheaded when I woke you up this morning."

I smiled and sprawled out, placing a hand under my head. "It was good. I gotta get my ass back in gear." To be honest, I hadn't expected Mad to text me with my wake-up call, but I appreciated it. "What about you? You look like you haven't slept."

He shrugged a little and took another swig from the Diet Coke. "I brought it on myself. After how I treated you, the guilt isn't gonna go away overnight."

Oh.

I chewed on the inside of my cheek. "I don't want you to lose sleep over that. We're fixing things, right?"

He nodded. "It'll get better over time." He glanced down at my tee. "So you wanted to talk ink."

"Oh, yeah." I sat up and lifted my T-shirt, revealing my rib cage. "I want two words added next to the '44' here, and I want a set of handcuffs to connect them. The words, I mean."

He stared at my ink and rubbed his jaw and mouth, then lifted a brow. "Why handcuffs?"

Okay, I didn't want him to ask me that. My ears felt hot, and I tugged on the right one as I tried to phrase myself. "I thought we weren't going to talk about this." I lowered my gaze automatically, as well as my tee. "You don't want to hear about it, I think."

If I remembered correctly, and I did, he'd said it "ain't right."

"Are you seriously into BDSM?" He dipped his chin to make eye contact, and I felt compelled to hold it.

"Yeah." Where was a drawstring to chew on when I needed one? Instead, I twisted a piece of hair between my fingers. "I'm not a pro or anything, but I've been to a few events. Mostly in Seattle and Vancouver."

There was concern rolling off of him, though the main emotions I saw in his expression were confusion and…whatever you felt when you were trying to solve a math problem.

"By yourself?" He tilted his head slightly.

I realized he was doing his adult thing, his *Dom* thing. A side of him I'd seen countless times before but never thought much of. This was it, though. He took a gentler approach when he could sense I was uncomfortable.

"A couple times." I put my feet together and drew them closer to my body, needing to hold something. Otherwise, I'd fidget. I rocked slowly. "Mostly, Gray's gone with me."

"I see. Is he into BDSM too?"

I shook my head. "He's just horny and prefers to bottom."

His mouth twitched. "A horny bottom. I guess Jamie's dry spell is over."

I shrugged. No doubt, Gray would bend over for Jameson. Where his dry spell was concerned, I didn't know anything.

Madigan sighed and scrubbed his hands over his face. It was the first time I'd seen a tattoo on the side of his middle finger, and I reached out and grabbed his hand without a second thought. My brows knitted together.

Protect him.

It was the weirdest gut punch. "Who's he?" It was me, it

was me, it was me, it had to be me. I couldn't accept another answer. For some reason, I *needed* the answer to be me.

"You know it's you, trouble."

I nodded once, hugely relieved. The day he introduced me to the guy he'd spend the rest of his life with, I was going to die a little bit. But until then, in one way or another, I had to be his number one. I was his Abel.

"I'm gonna be jealous when you get a sub who you'll introduce to the family." I chuckled shakily. "I'm used to being your favorite."

I didn't care if I sounded childish and vulnerable. This wasn't about that kind of love. It was us, what we had, what we'd shared since I was little.

"Sometimes you kill me, Abel." He rubbed at his eyes, then smirked and shook his head at me. "You're irreplaceable."

"Okay, good." I bit my thumbnail, my heart pounding. This conversation was maybe getting too heavy, and I was still too in love with him to separate fantasy from reality long term. "So are you. But anyway, my tattoo. Do you think—"

"Hey." He hooked a finger under my chin and nudged it up. "We'll get there. I have some concerns I wanna talk about first."

"Um, all right." Feeling restless and fidgety, I slipped my hands underneath me and sat on them.

"First of all, I can't lie and say I'm cool with you going to kink events," he told me. "I'll get it through my skull somehow that you can do whatever you want, but I worry, all right? I know how some of these parties can get outta hand, and knowing you're there alone without guidance and company doesn't sit well with me."

Yup, he was totally a Dom.

"Second of all," he went on, "you mentioned me having a sub, so I'm gonna assume you know I'm in the lifestyle."

"You haven't been really secretive about it," I said.

"No, I guess I haven't." He appeared unsure of how he felt about that. "Can I ask how you discovered kink?"

Technically... "Porn." Though it hadn't been enough for me to want to research it until I'd seen Madigan sharing that Facebook post on BDSM.

Mad snorted and ran a hand through his hair. "Figures. Okay, we'll leave this subject for now, but I might bring it up again before you go to Seattle." If he insisted... "Now, let's talk tattoos. What were the words you wanted connected by the handcuffs?"

"Powerful and powerless," I answered.

"Of course you do." He blew out a breath. "I'm gonna get my sketchpad before I interrogate you. Christ."

I pinched my lips together, amused. Typical bossy type. He couldn't stand not having all the answers.

I'm gonna get so fucking laid.

Good for you, Gray.

I moved some shit around, so we can start tomorrow if you want.

The next text was from Mad. Fuck yes. There were some serious perks to being his favorite.

MH shoot confirmed for Tuesday, will call you when we have all the details.

I grimaced at the last text and left my room. "Mom!" I called, jogging down the stairs.

"She's at Chloe's." Dad's voice came from the kitchen, so I

went there. He was fanning out takeout menus on the kitchen island as I entered. "She's having a girls' night, so I've decided to have a guys' night. What's up? Did you sleep?"

It was never a good thing for Gray's mom and mine to join forces, but anyway.

"A little." I patted down my bed head. "Okay, you should be able to help me out here. I got a call earlier from the team's publicist, and they're gonna book me in for interviews and stuff. They're all stressing about it."

He nodded, studying a pizza menu. "Damage control after your suspension. Go on."

"Right, and so far, they've booked four interviews and bumped someone to get me on the cover of the next *Men's Health*."

"That's big, buddy."

"And I hate it," I finished. "My question is, what can I do to make this as small as possible? I don't wanna come off as an entitled asshole, but these things freak me out."

Hockey wasn't like football. Sure, we had sponsors and endorsement deals, but there was no comparison. I loved that hockey publicity was a lot more low-key.

Dad gave me his full attention and folded his arms over his chest, pensive. "You're valuable enough to the team that you can limit your travel, no doubt. If there's one thing you can use your celebrity for, it's privacy and personal comfort."

He would know. He was on the cover on some music magazine last fall, and they'd literally flown up from LA to do the photo shoot in Dad's basement studio. On the cover, he was sitting in his chair at the mixing console.

"I guess we could do it in Seattle?" I questioned. "I don't know. They scheduled one of the interviews in LA, but we'll already be in town to play the Kings."

"When's the shoot?" he asked.

"Tuesday." I made another face. I didn't wanna drive up to Vancouver for one little thing. If I could move it to Seattle, Gray and I could just stay there an extra night.

"I don't see why you can't have them come here," he said.

My forehead creased. "Where would you have a photo shoot in Camassia?" They required an actual studio.

Dad smirked faintly. "You realize Ellis runs an ad agency, right?" He spoke of his cousin and Casey's fiancé, and no, I hadn't thought of that. "I'm sure he can set it up for you. He'll be here in..." He checked his watch. "An hour. Just forward his information to the publicist, and they'll handle it."

"That's it?" I wondered. "I mean, it's okay to do that?"

He chuckled. "Son, you average almost half a goal per game. Trust, you can do that."

I smirked and blushed at the same time. "Have you been checking my stats again?"

"Fuck yeah. The reason we have kids is to brag about them to parents who raise fuckups. I'm nothing if not a motivational father." He was nuts. I was nothing to brag about, but that didn't mean I wasn't feeling ten feet tall right now. "I'm in the mood for pizza. Can you eat that?"

"Yes." I nodded. I wanted to celebrate with bad carbs and cheese for one night. "Who else is coming? I assume Casey."

He inclined his head. "Yeah, we've got sitters and everything. Casey, Ellis, Chloe's man, and Madigan."

"Oh. Cool." I sat down on the stool and snatched up the menu, stoked to see more of Mad today. Now that he was back in my life, I wanted to see him constantly to make up for lost time. "Can you text Mom and tell her not to plan Gray's and my imaginary wedding?"

"I'm flattered you think so highly of me, but I can't move mountains." He paused. "Did you work shit out with Madigan?"

"Yeah, it's all good now. I want the mozzarella and spinach pizza."

"You're horrible at making unhealthy decisions." He frowned. "What's next, a light beer?"

I grinned. "I kinda like rum and Diet Coke. Or vodka and Sprite Zero."

"Jesus Christ," he muttered. "All right, if you're joining guys' night, go shower and put on something other than sweatpants for once. I have snacks to open and music to pick out."

I knew how that was gonna go. When Dad had people over, he played fucking *records*. The old, huge ones. Mad had a big record collection too, and I didn't get it. They were so much work.

"Check me out, I clean up all right," I mumbled to myself. I was the clueless dude who texted Mom for fashion advice, and while I'd rejected her suggestion of a dress shirt, I did go with her choice of a pair of dark gray slacks that made my butt look great. She didn't say that last part.

I adjusted my junk and put on a bit of cologne, then pulled on a long-sleeved black tee. Hell of a lot comfier than button-downs.

After putting on socks, I pocketed my phone and left my room. Music was playing in the living room, and I knew Casey, Uncle Ellis, and Aiden, Gray's stepdad, were already here.

The doorbell rang as I descended the stairs. "Dad, pizza or Mad is here!"

He answered among chuckles from the living room. "I hope it's pizza."

And it was. Six pizza boxes were stacked on top of one

another, and I remembered I always kept a few bills inside my phone case.

Dad didn't like that, nudging past me in the doorway. "Your NHL blood money isn't welcome here."

I snorted and headed for the kitchen instead, and I was getting a soda from the fridge when the others joined me. They already had beers in their hands, so I closed the fridge.

"Hey, Abel. How are you?" Uncle Ellis smiled. Unlike Dad, Ellis was a polite, more formal guy.

"He's not wearing sweats," Casey said. "He's doing great." He smirked at my eye-roll and stepped closer to hug me. "We saw your last game. It was quite the...yeah."

I opened my soda and cocked a brow at him. "You finally figured out what channel hockey's on, huh?"

"Hey," he defended, "I'm known to watch some sportsing events." Rarely hockey. I knew he liked football on occasion.

I grinned and shook my head, then nodded hello to Aiden as the doorbell rang again.

Gray's stepdad was a quirky nomad-looking man, hot in a weird way. I didn't know if he was rugged or clean-cut. He was one of the few men who fucking rocked the man bun, but underneath his cargo pants and Henleys was a humble, kind dude.

"Did Mrs. Nolan kick you out?" I asked him.

He chuckled, his brows lifting a bit. "I didn't pick up on her hints, actually. Then I got a call from my daughter, who not so subtly told me to get the hell out. Thankfully, Lincoln called ten minutes later."

I laughed.

"Okay, let's eat!" Dad placed the six pies on the kitchen island as Madigan entered the kitchen, and I sent him a smile. My stomach flip-flopped around him, especially when I was the recipient of his warm grins.

We took our seats around the island, and I made sure to end up next to Mad. On the other side of me, I had Casey, with Dad, Aiden, and Uncle Ellis sitting across from us. Noticing Madigan hadn't gotten anything to drink, I left my seat and grabbed a beer from the fridge.

"Here." I chewed on my lip and took my seat again. "I didn't get the worst pizza." I lowered my voice as the others got sucked into a conversation about their kids. "I wanted a pepperoni, but I got one with spinach and tomatoes." And a shit-ton of mozzarella.

His eyes got heated with approval, and he gave my leg a squeeze. "That's a good boy. You're doing great with your schedule."

I sucked in some air and turned away, glaring at my lap. He couldn't fucking call me that. I couldn't let this slide—no goddamn way.

"You can't say that to me, idiot," I hissed under my breath and opened my pizza box. "It means something else to me." It meant something more.

That kind of talk smacked me squarely in the chest with yearning and pathetic need. I wanted to be someone's good boy—actually, I wanted to be *his* good boy, but apparently, beggars couldn't be choosers.

"I'm sorry, Abel. I didn't realize..." He trailed off, frowning in concern. "It hits you that hard?"

"I guess." I felt the need to apologize but knew he wouldn't tolerate that. Instead, I picked up a slice of pizza and shoved half of it into my mouth.

He'd often called me a good boy when I was younger. In retrospect, I should've seen the signs of my orientation. I always sought out the strongest minds, and praise from those people could turn me into mush. It was my superhero power.

I could sniff out a mentally strong man from miles away. I sort of made a habit of surrounding myself with those.

"I'll be more careful in the future." He paused and side-eyed me while he opened his beer. "One thing, though. That's the last time you call me idiot. If I hear another insult like that coming out of your mouth, I'll deal with you how I see fit."

I swallowed what was in my mouth, the pizza sliding down like a chunk of lead. He was serious, and it was seriously hot. *I'll deal with you how I see fit.* I licked my lips nervously.

"What about asshole?" Yeah, I went there.

I was my own worst enemy. For as much as I depended on order and a structured life, fire was irresistible and indisputably my favorite toy to play with. On the ice, it turned me into a hotheaded player, my sharp digs carrying as much speed as my next slap shot. In the bedroom, my attitude was my last defense, one I wanted to see tumbling down. I played with fire to get burned. It was how I submitted to dominant men. I just hadn't found a good match yet. Few Tops enjoyed that challenge.

Other than a small tic in Madigan's jaw, he was motionless and staring at me with enough intensity that I half regretted my bratting. Half.

"Choose your next words wisely, Abel."

Okay, more than half. He chipped away a bit of my defenses, and I broke the gaze to regroup. My heart thumped hard in my chest. The challenge was right there in front of me. The fire sure as shit didn't need any toying with, yet... Fuck. No, I shouldn't. He could probably banter this way and be fine, but for me, the lines would blur.

"I'll give you this one," I muttered.

CHAPTER 6

After dinner, the coffee table in the living room quickly filled up with top-shelf alcohol and snacks, the number of bottles enough to give Dad's rock-star past a solid nod. He still knew how to party. *However*... They were all fucking talk. In between sips of whiskey, crude jokes, a few shots, and the mandatory topic of "music today," they mostly discussed their children. They'd clearly not done that enough while we ate.

When Dad said he didn't get to see Theo—Casey and Ellis's newborn son—often enough, I took a shot of vodka in hopes that the booze would liven shit up for me. Then Casey got into a discussion with Aiden about makeup for little girls. Casey's daughter, Haley, was a couple years younger than my sister, and he looked to Aiden for advice since Isla was in her mid-twenties.

"I mean, how do you handle a situation like that?" Casey poured himself another drink, looking completely at a loss. "Ellis and I have decided that nail polish is all right, but unless it's Halloween, we don't want her face painted."

I'd laugh if the topic didn't bore me. Grabbing the bowl of

peanuts, I got comfortable in my chair and flung my legs over the armrest. Madigan was occupying the chair on the other side of the table, and he looked fucking fine manspreading. Not that I was looking at his crotch or anything.

"In the grand scheme of things, it doesn't matter." Aiden raised his glass. "Save your energy for when your little girl comes home with a man almost twice her age." He took a swig of his whiskey. "Damn—he might even be your old college buddy."

"That won't happen here," Dad said. "My baby girl's never gonna date, and we're working on fixing up Abel with Gray."

I rolled my eyes and reached for my drink.

"A bit delusional, don't you think, Lincoln?" Ellis chuckled.

"What is it with you guys and issues with age differences?" I asked. "Mom married your old ass, Dad. You should be grateful some of us are drawn to whiny curmudgeons."

"I love you, Abel," Casey laughed. "Lincoln, he got you."

"He said *us*," Aiden noted.

I winked at him. "That includes Gray. One day, he's gonna come home with an older guy too."

"We don't want those we love and want to keep safe to be exposed or taken advantage of." It was Madigan who spoke, and I narrowed my eyes at him. "Younger minds are often more impressionable."

"See? Madigan gets it, and he doesn't even want kids," Dad said.

"Sometimes, that's what we impressionable minds want." I never once broke eye contact with Mad. "I can't find what I want among my peers 'cause I want a guy who has more experience. While some look to a lot of places for support or guidance, I wanna look to him."

In my periphery, I saw Casey watching us like a tennis match. Dad was muttering under his breath about not being an old ass.

"That requires a lot of trust," Madigan murmured.

I trust you.

The realization that I trusted Mad implicitly, regardless of shit we'd gone through, wasn't a shock, but it was heavy nonetheless. I swallowed and looked away, quick to distract myself by finishing my drink.

"You're right, it does." It was all I could say.

"You're a smart young man, Abel," Aiden told me.

"Only time I remember he doesn't come from my swimmers," Dad said with a dip of his chin. "He's a hell of a lot smarter than me."

"Stop it," I groaned. Okay, so it wasn't always I handled praise very well. Besides, he was selling himself short. I'd learned a lot from him.

"You know what?" He ignored what I said and moved forward. "Whoever you bring home, whether he's old as fuck or jailbait, I'll be on your side."

I shook my head and smirked. Shit didn't work that way.

"I have a feeling that comes with conditions," Madigan muttered into his glass.

"I'm loving this." Casey was enjoying the show or whatever. "We need more mixers. Abel, give me a hand."

"Sure." I threw a handful of peanuts into my mouth and got up from my seat. Following him to the kitchen, I checked my phone and snorted at Gray's messages.

I don't fuck and tell, but this dude's monster cock...felt great in my throat.

For five minutes, he made me forget Craig.

Okay, he wants to go again. Have mercy on my ass! (But really don't.)

I texted him back, wishing his ass a speedy recovery, and almost walked right into Casey.

"Sorry." I pocketed my phone again.

Rather than getting mixers, he sat down by the island and patted the stool next to him. "Let's talk for a minute."

"That's never a good sign." I wrinkled my nose and approached slowly. "What's up?"

"You're a lot quicker on the ice," he said. "It's nothing bad. I think I know what's going on, so I wanted to say something about Madigan."

Fuck. Putting a blank expression on my face was harder than it should be. "What, um, what about him?" I was literally on the edge of my seat for this, ready to bolt if I had to.

There was a hint of humor in his eyes, as if he could read my mind and found the tension funny.

"You've known Madigan far longer than I have, but there's one thing I've witnessed that you haven't. Actually, there are two." He paused, thinking, and smiled at something. "I get to see what he's like when you're not around. But more than that, I got to see how he's changed as you've grown up."

I shifted in my seat, uneasy but intrigued.

"I realize you're hearing this from our family's most hopeless romantic," he went on, "but I hope whatever you're doing, you'll keep doing it. Just...cut him some slack and be patient. He's seeing two of you—the little kid you once were, and the man you're becoming."

I shook my head, feeling the need to interrupt. "I don't know what you think is happening here. Between Mad and me? Absolutely nothing."

"For now, maybe," he replied pensively. "You can't say you're not into each other, though."

"I can definitely say that," I argued. "Not for me, but for him. I—" Shit, was I really gonna tell the truth to Casey? Fuck it. He wasn't like the other grown-ups in the family. He was more of a friend. "About a year ago, before the holidays, I told him I...you know. I love him, okay? But he doesn't feel the same."

Casey smiled. "And you believe him? Abel, you're his whole fucking world. You were his priority when you were fourteen, and you're his priority now. Things have just changed. The man doesn't even date anymore. He's got himself trapped in a boxing ring where he's fighting himself, basically." He leaned in a little. "Note that this is the second time in two minutes I've mentioned sports."

It was also the second time I'd heard someone say Madigan could be into me. First Jameson and now Casey.

"Has he told you he promised your biological father he'd look after you?" he asked.

"Yeah." I tugged absently on my ear, processing what Casey'd said. All while doing everything I could not to get my hopes up.

"Add the fact that two of his closest friends are your parents," he said. "They were the ones who included Madigan in the family because his own family's shit."

I knew that much. The Monroe family wasn't just another deadbeat clan. They looked great on paper. Two Hollywood producers, two successful sons. Except, when parents neglected the kids and married their work, the family kinda lost its meaning. Madigan's older brother was, to this day, a frequent visitor in rehab, and Mad hadn't seen his folks in over ten years.

"I'm scared shitless of getting my hopes up," I admitted. It put a rock in my stomach just to say it. "We only recently became friends again."

"I noticed you seemed closer at dinner," he murmured. "Listen to me on this one, though. I go out with Madigan sometimes, and he's not trying anymore. I believe he's found what he wants, but he won't allow himself to go there."

It all made sense in theory. Even so, I wasn't sure... Looking over my shoulder and into the living room, I could glimpse Mad. He was talking to Aiden and Dad. Then Dad stood up, declaring it was time to change records, and Madigan chuckled and leaned back in his chair. As if he could sense me watching, he tilted his head and met my gaze, at which I quickly turned back to Casey.

Jesus Christ, it was terrifying how fast he could make my heart race.

"Think about what I've said," Casey told me and squeezed my shoulder. "I'm here if you wanna talk."

I nodded. "Okay. Thank you."

"Say it."

I jolted awake, disoriented and out of breath. "What the hell was that," I panted. I blinked and registered the dark shadows; I was in my room, and it was in the middle of the night. Then the images from the dream flooded me, and I collapsed on the mattress again.

"Please." I groaned and pushed against him. "I'll obey, I swear. I'll be good. Please!"

He pinned me harder to the mattress and slowly worked his cock inside me. "I wanna hear it, Abel." He spoke through gritted teeth as he stretched me to take all of him. Next, his whisper near my ear shook me. "Say it."

Please, Daddy.

"Fuck." I swallowed dryly and rolled over to bury my face

in my pillow. *Daddy, fuck me. Daddy, take me. Daddy...* Slipping a hand underneath myself, I gripped my cock and pushed it into my fist over and over. I was already wet, the pre-come seeping out of the slit.

"*Say it, baby boy.*"

"Daddy," I gasped.

Holy shit. I screwed my eyes shut and came all over the sheets, the force both embarrassing me and filling me with a frenzied need. I flushed all over and squirmed in the mess I'd made, and all I could think of was how I could get more.

I'd kneeled for dominant men before. I'd followed through on commands, begged, and called someone Sir. This was different. This was explosive and mortifying and intense and...*fuck.* I had to read more about this sort of kink. Right now, all I wanted was to crawl under Madigan's skin and stay there forever. I wanted to put my head in his lap, suck his cock, and have a lazy morning with Oreo O's and cartoons. I wanted his hands on my body and his puppet master fingers in my brain.

I wanted him to challenge me, and I wanted him to narrow his eyes and warn me when I taunted him. I wanted him to shut me up so hard that I forgot everything but him. I knew he had the mental strength to own me completely.

There was something else that I couldn't put my finger on. Hopefully, doing my homework would give me more answers. For now, I was done for. Lifting my head, I squinted at the clock.

Four in the fucking morning.

I was about to hand over everything to him—*again*—and I was powerless to stop myself.

I used the box of tissues on the nightstand to clean myself up, and then I grabbed my phone and opened our text convo. He'd told me not to throw insults at him, right?

"I'll deal with you how I see fit."
"Deal with this, your domly highness," I mumbled.
Dick. Idiot. Asshole. Bastard.
I pressed send before I could chicken out.

"Too fucking soon, dude." I glared down at my lap, more correctly, my dick, and shook my head. The research continued, and I told myself I'd wait at least half an hour before I could jerk off again.

I had two notebooks open where I jotted down thoughts and other stuff, and go figure, the internet had a lot to offer. Other than going to the bathroom and showering, I hadn't left my room this morning. The mini fridge under my desk provided me with soda and chocolate bars.

It was possible I had failed miserably with the routine Mad had drawn up for me, but he was already irritated with me. I might as well go for broke. His morning text had said it all.

I would've waited with the insults until after I'd put my tattoo machine on your skin, but that's just me. We'll discuss this later. Now, get up and head to the gym.

"Abel, everyone's here for brunch!" Mom hollered up the stairs.

"I'm not hungry!" I shouted back. I took a sip of my soda and moved the cursor to the next website. I'd found what I hadn't been able to pinpoint last night. Or before dawn. It had nothing to do with a Daddy Dom; I already knew I was drawn to every part of Madigan. No, it was the traits and preferences of those who identified as Littles. The mother ship was calling me home.

More than that, it was the dynamic. The nurturing and the letting go of adult stuff. I could be as boyish and immature as I wanted, and it was okay. There would be someone I could count on to enforce rules, someone I could trust to guide me, someone who would take care of me. In return, I'd obey and give up my control. I'd worship and devote myself to him.

Like all other fetishes, there were countless varieties and versions. Some were sadistic, some were littler than little. I read one girl's blog, and she identified as a toddler and only had nonsexual DD/lg arrangements. That wouldn't be me. I wasn't sure I saw age anywhere in this, but sex would be one of the components.

I just wanted to quit putting up this front. I had to pretend enough in my professional life. Teammates and media thought I was badass and bordering on too mature for my age. They saw the awareness I tried to raise for bipolar disorder and that I volunteered as a hockey coach for kids at the summer camp a teammate hosted. In reality, I was always looking for an escape, a safe place to breathe out and be myself.

As someone who had bipolar, it meant that sometimes I was manic. Sometimes I was volatile and angry. Sometimes I was hypersexual, sometimes asexual. Most of the time, I zigzagged in between mild states of indifference, exuberance, emotional exhaustion, and caution. I was energetic and curious by nature, which amped up my anxiety if I didn't go along with the structure set up for me. I was forgetful at times too.

And those thoughts were depressing.

I could be difficult.

I did my best in my everyday life not to be over the top,

and that was even worse. It was why I sought out escapes. Then again, who the fuck would want me if I let it all go?

"Abel!" It was my sister hollering this time. "Are you looking at penises again?"

"For fuck's sake," I sighed. I ignored her, glad the door to my room was locked. I was also glad Madigan wasn't here.

Sunday brunch was a thing in our family, and the usual suspects showed up. Uncle Ellis, Casey, the kids, and Madigan. Today, he was opting out because I had to be at the tattoo shop in an hour.

He's always been able to handle every side of you.

I bit at a cuticle and stared at the computer screen. Damn Casey and Jameson for making me hope again. It wasn't fair.

A little before noon, I knocked on the door to Camassia Ink. It was closed to the public, so it would be only Mad and me.

I was a little jumpy, probably because I'd had four Coca-Colas and two Snickers. Not my best decision.

Madigan appeared from the back room and unlocked the door to let me in.

"Hey, shit stirrer."

"Hi." I smiled nervously and passed him, shrugging off my jacket. I dropped it on one of the three chairs by the window. "Do you have any food? I'm so hungry."

He frowned. "You didn't eat after the gym?"

Oh, right. I cleared my throat and scratched my neck. "I was busy, so I didn't go. And I forgot to eat."

"Really." He folded his tatted arms over his chest and stared at me with an impassive look on his face. "In what universe is it a good idea to get inked on an empty stomach?"

"This one?" I took a chance.

He shook his head and pointed toward the back of the studio. "Get upstairs. Now."

Upstairs I went. He followed me, and the silence made me wanna fidget. Maybe it was time to do some damage control. When push came to shove, my defiance was playful and meant as a joke. It was the sparring I got a kick out of.

"You're not angry about the text I sent, are you?"

"No, I'm not angry, Abel." He waited until I stepped aside so he could open the door.

Perhaps he wasn't angry, but he was *something*. I didn't know what yet.

Once inside the apartment, he told me to sit down while he made me something to eat, and I went for the bed. It was comfier than the chairs. As I removed my hoodie and shoes, I studied him, my nervousness growing. He was too unreadable for my liking.

It put me on edge.

"It helps if you remind yourself how cute I am," I offered.

At that, Madigan side-eyed me over his shoulder, and I gave him my best grin to sway him. *Please let it work.* All I needed to know was that I hadn't genuinely disappointed him. That would be crushing.

Abandoning what he was doing, he walked over to the bed and squatted down in front of me. I didn't know how to react to that. He grabbed my right hand in both of his and pressed a firm kiss to my knuckles.

"Cute," he repeated. He nodded slowly, then rose to place his hands on the sides of my head and press another kiss to my forehead. *Keep going.* "We can agree on that. You're unbelievably cute." That was it. He let out a low chuckle and returned to the kitchenette. "You're also trouble, and we gotta discuss boundaries before my inner control freak takes over."

I touched my forehead. "Is that vanilla for your domliness dominating me?"

"Yes, Abel." He didn't appear to like it when I spoke plainly. "We should keep things appropriate, yeah?"

Uh, was that a question? Because I was the last one who'd give him the answer he was looking for.

"What do I know?" I shrugged and got comfortable under the covers, stacking his pillows against the headboard. "I'm just a slut boy who obeys."

He looked to me sharply, jaw cut and tense under his trimmed beard. "You're a fucking brat, that's what you are."

I puckered my lips at him, then yanked off my tee.

His mouth was drawn in a tight line, and he gave me a brief once-over before he returned to the food preparation. I didn't know what he was doing. There was lettuce and tomatoes and bread, maybe turkey or chicken, but also milk and cereal.

"Why are you undressing in my bed?"

"I wanna get comfy." I frowned down at myself. I hadn't even given it a thought, and now I was embarrassed. Shit, I'd really stripped. Only my sweats to go. "Sorry, I wasn't thinking."

His shoulders shifted with his inaudible sigh. "It's okay, sweetheart. It's just testing my restraint."

I wanted to talk about that. Given my morning research, I had a proposal because I needed to know. "What if you did get bossy with me?" I swallowed my nerves and rested my hands in my lap under the covers. "I mean, the cat's out of the bag. You know I'm a subbie now, and I'm looking for help. I wanna learn—see if I'm into this other thing I read about." I figured that was the restraint he mentioned. He wanted to give me orders rather than ask, thus helping me stick to my schedule. At this point, his hands were tied. He had drawn up this neat, everyday routine for me to follow, but I wouldn't. Not without a firm hand. "I'm not one of those who's in it only for the sex," I said. "D/s is amazing for me on a bigger level. It's something I want in my life. What I'm saying is, it's not like you gotta get intimate with me. You can still teach me stuff."

Madigan lowered the knife he'd been using.

I kept watching his back and the glimpses I got of his face, and it made me anxious to wait for his response. Was my idea too much? I just wanted to learn. I'd read a great deal about the psychology behind dominance and submission, and the only thing I could gather was how much this would benefit me. I couldn't imagine anything putting me at ease more than daily structure, established trust, and surrendering control to someone who knew what he was doing.

Mad was that person. For now, since he didn't want forever.

"What's this other thing you've read about?" he asked in a low voice.

Your primary kink.

I twisted a piece of hair behind my ear, nervous about his reaction. "Um, Littles. Daddy Doms and Littles."

He placed his hands on the counter and hung his head.

It was too much. I shouldn't have said anything. It was an intimate thing for him, and being some weird mentor to me would ruin it. I knew it. Fuck. Why did I open my stupid mouth? Why did I think this was a good idea? Just because he was perfect for me didn't mean I was perfect for him.

"If I don't help you, who will?" he asked, clearing his throat.

"Ignore what I said," I said quickly. "It was unfair of me to put this on you. I don't want you t-to be uncomfortable, an-and—"

"Abel."

I sucked in a breath and clenched my fists under the covers.

Madigan walked over to me, this time sitting down on the edge of the bed, and his hand landed on my leg.

"I trust you," I mumbled.

"That's what terrifies me." Leaning closer, he cupped my jaw and made me look him in the eye. "My priority is you, though. I'll help you." He gave me another forehead kiss that made my face redden and my heart hammer. "You can talk to me about anything, and I won't have to worry about getting more grays because you're out there getting advice from someone who doesn't know you as well as I do."

The relief was overwhelming—too overwhelming. There was no stopping my wide grin, and there was no stopping me from throwing my arms around him and giving him the tightest hug ever.

"Thank you, thank you." My head was already spinning. What should I ask first? Like, how did I find out if I was a Little? Could I be myself now? Even if that meant showing every dip and peak of the roller coaster that was my life?

CHAPTER 7

Maybe Madigan was a sadist. He decided the best place to discuss this arrangement was at his workstation in the shop with a needle piercing my skin. He'd given me half an hour of watching TV after I'd eaten an awesome turkey sub and tolerated some milk and oat mix cereal. Then I'd been sent down here and into his chair.

"No, keep your arm up," he said.

Returning my hand under my head, I peered down as he carefully removed the stencil. I'd given him free rein to design my tattoo, and I wasn't disappointed. The shadow of the word "Powerful" would blend with the shadow of my first jersey number, the letters bold and jagged. He'd make the texture metallic, unlike the second word. In an old typewriter font, "Powerless" would be inked near the bottom of the first word.

He'd skipped the handcuffs, opting for shackles.

"You should consider making a career of this," I said.

He was too focused to laugh, but his eyes crinkled in the corners.

"So are we gonna talk—"

"Quiet, boy."

Shit. I swallowed against the flutter in my stomach, and he wheeled his chair back to do whatever he did at his station. He was sexy as sin in his element. And he'd just used his Dom voice on me. *That* was gonna take a while to get used to.

I should've worn my damn jockstrap. Madigan getting dominant with me was bound to give me a hard-on in no time.

"What makes you think you might be a Little?" He wheeled closer again, tattoo gun ready.

"I don't know." I waited to speak again until the buzzing filled my ears and the needle made contact with my rib cage. Sucking in a breath, I zeroed in on the fiery pain and embraced it. It was the same every time I got inked, though this session might prove even more intense. "When I read this guy's online journal, I could relate a lot." Tipping my head back a bit, I watched the ceiling instead. I'd lose focus if I stared at him and the ink. "Since my mood can shift so fast and I'm easily influenced by my surroundings, I want a place where I don't have to be someone I'm not. It's exhausting as fuck—"

"You can quit the tough guy act right now, sweetheart."

I exhaled, tracing the paint strokes on the ceiling with my eyes. "It's tiring, Mad," I said quietly.

He brushed his thumb over my stomach, causing my abs to clench. "Tell me what you want in your safe space."

Besides you?

"I hate coffee," I blurted out.

He chuckled, confused, and wiped gently at the inked area. "You drink coffee plenty."

No. I forced it down for Sunday brunch when he and I happened to be at the house. Sometimes, I ordered it when I was meeting up with teammates.

"It's the most adult drink," I said. "It makes people look

grown-up—like they have their shit together. That's why I've lied about following the news too. Grown-ups watch the news, and I don't understand it. It's depressing."

The needle moved closer to a more sensitive area, and I released a breath through clenched teeth.

"I like mindless TV," I went on. "It shuts off my brain."

"It's an escape," he murmured. "Go on."

"And what's so good about being an adult anyway?" I closed my eyes and breathed through the pain. "You always have to know what you're doing, there are responsibilities, and too many expectations." I didn't mind some of it. Every summer when I had more off time, I liked to help out; I got to coach kids and follow in Mom's footsteps and do charity work. I worked hard and needed to feel useful. And I explained this to Madigan so he wouldn't get the wrong idea. "But at the end of the day..."

"I understand." He wiped at my skin again and cleared his throat. "At the end of the day, Daddy takes over, and you can let it all go."

"Jesus," I breathed.

There was a smirk in his voice. "Did I just make it real for you?"

"Um, yeah. I've never—I mean, it's n-new," I stammered. "The Daddy thing."

Madigan didn't reply, and my automatic reaction was to say something. Until I realized I didn't have to. He was gonna help me. I could leave this to him.

A couple hours later, I stood dazedly in front of a full-length mirror and inspected my new ink with a tired grin on my face. Madigan had excused himself to go outside for a cigarette as soon as he was ready, so I could just stand here and stare at my reflection without giving a crap. I really liked what I saw. Tilting my head, I took in every inch of his marks and decided right then and there that he would do all my ink from now on.

He'd managed to make the design look like rusty metal, and the shackles were a subtle yet badass addition to the two words.

Madigan reentered the shop, and he didn't look as relaxed and carefree as I felt. Despite the intense soreness, getting inked was hypnotic for me after a while.

"I thought I heard Mom say you quit smoking," I mentioned.

"I did." He went to the cleaning station and washed his hands with soap I'd seen in hospitals. "I cave sometimes when —" He shook his head and dried his hands, then grabbed a new pair of gloves. "Anyway. Let's get your ink wrapped. You happy with the work?"

"It's fucking amazing, Mad." I padded back to the chair and lay down. "You haven't asked about the symbolism of the tattoo."

He placed a roll of medical tape on my stomach. "I can venture a guess." He had a small bottle of something, and he sprayed whatever it was onto the ink. Next, he opened a packet with a sterile pad that he carefully applied to my tattoo.

I supported myself on my elbows and peered down curiously. "No plastic wrap?"

He met me with a scowl. "Fuck no. What kind of idiots have you worked with before?" *Um.* "Don't answer that," he muttered and got back to wrapping. "Whoever thought it was a good idea to seal an open wound in plastic should be brought back to life and shot dead again."

"Touchy," I noted.

"Just a bit." After applying the gauze, he grabbed the tape. "When you were little, the main trigger to your depressions were the tantrums and panic attacks you couldn't control. You said they made you feel powerless."

I watched him while he concentrated on what he was doing.

"It's a constant battle for you to regain some of that control." He slid his thumb over the tape he'd applied along the edge of the gauze strips. "Then there's kink. In kink, power isn't a matter of life and death. It's an exchange. You give it freely in order to be who you want to be. And being who you want to be can be pretty fucking powerful. The words go hand in hand. Or in shackles."

I didn't have to say anything. No one would ever know me as well as Madigan did. It was as thrilling and comforting as it was painful. Because I knew I'd never get over him.

Madigan helped me out of the chair, and I listened with one ear as he gave his scripted speech on tattoo care. I wasn't planning on leaving his place anytime soon, so I'd have him show me in a few hours how to do the lotion thing.

When I mentioned paying for the ink, he told me to shut my dirty mouth.

My automatic response sat on the tip of my tongue. *And what if I don't?* And it sparked my next question.

"You called me a brat," I said. "I know most of the Doms I've played with disapproved when I taunted them, so if you want me not to do that—"

"How many are we talking, Abel?" His forehead creased, and his mouth twisted up.

I flushed and tugged at my earlobe. "Not many. Like five or six? Just at play parties, except for one. We met up a few times—back on the East Coast."

"Got it." He nodded once and looked away, running a

hand through his hair. "Well, you have nothing to worry about." He gestured toward the back, and I took the hint to return upstairs. "Mouthy little subbie boys are my weakness."

Okay…so what was wrong with me? We had a lot in common, and it seemed like we'd be a good match. Following him back to his place, I mulled things over and chewed on the inside of my cheek. Was it only because he'd promised Morgan he'd take care of me? Or was it 'cause he'd seen me as a kid? This was wearing on me.

I'd basically claimed the bed as mine at this point, so I went straight there. I was still barefoot from before, and I was itching to get under the covers.

"Are you gonna punish me or something for the text I sent last night?" I asked. "Keep in mind that I'm cute."

He laughed through his nose and got us a couple drinks from the fridge, as well as something from a cupboard. I couldn't see what it was. "We're going to discuss the ins and outs of this little mentorship before we go there, but you're damn right. It may or may not involve you telling Lincoln and Adeline that half your rib cage is inked."

I grimaced. Dad wouldn't be an issue, but Mom…? She liked to think I was sweet and innocent, which was why I kept postponing it. Couldn't she just find out when she saw the cover of *Men's Health* in approximately two months? I'd be outside of the danger zone then.

"I'd prefer a spanking," I pointed out. "I like those."

"I'd prefer if you didn't like your punishment," he replied. "Kinda defeats the purpose."

I scrunched my nose. Next, he handed me an actual juice box, and it was probably weird that I found that hot. Was this a Daddy/little thing? I read the label, unsure. It was some organic cranberry-apple juice. Healthy stuff, in other words. Or better than soda anyway.

Madigan joined me in bed, only he sat on top of the covers.

"Something sweet." He handed me a to-go packet of Nutella.

"Thank you." That made me grin, and I tore into the packet and dragged a finger through the chocolate. Technically, this was a nut butter, meaning my nutritionist could shove it. Butters made from nuts were on the list of "OK" items. Technically.

"You couldn't wait for the spoon?" Mad was watching me with amusement. I hadn't even noticed the two spoons in his hand.

"Redundant." I spoke around my finger. "Do you think our nutritionist will let me use Nutella as butter from now on? If you think about it, it's hazelnut."

"If I think about it, there's also cocoa and a truckload of sugar," he responded. "Probably best this stays between you and me."

"I can keep a secret." I swiped another finger through the goodness and stuck it in my mouth. "Do you have plans today?"

He shook his head, leaving the spoon in his mouth, and retrieved his phone. "There's a pub meet for our local kink community if you want to go, though. It's just a munch."

Goddamn. I'd wanted to attend events here at home since I was eighteen, but I'd always been afraid I'd run into Madigan. The community was on the small side.

"We can do that?" I really fucking wanted to go.

"Of course. It'll be a good place for you to talk to others who identify as Littles." He scratched his jaw, squinting a bit. "Not that there are very many."

I didn't like where that thought took me. "Any exes of

yours I'll run into?" Maybe we shouldn't go. I wasn't sure I could handle meeting someone he'd been Daddy to.

Mad found that amusing for some reason. "Highly unlikely. As far as I know, you're the first male Little in our community."

Oh. I guess that was a relief. "Okay. Any exes I'll run into at the club in Seattle on Wednesday?"

"No, Abel," he chuckled.

"Have you killed them?"

"You figured it out." He snorted and took the two Nutella containers to put them on the nightstand. "It can't be that it's been a while since I dated or met someone."

Who could forget Casey mentioning that? Didn't mean I believed it.

"How long?" I asked.

"A while."

"How long of a while?"

"Abel." He gave me a look of warning. "Little over a year, all right?"

Little over a year. It was a little over a year since I texted him at four in the morning saying I was in love with him.

"No one's called you, um, you know, Daddy since then?"

"I didn't say that." He frowned. "Being someone's Daddy Dom—being *called* Daddy—means a great deal to me. It's nothing I get into with a casual play partner or one-night stand."

That made sense, though I wondered where that left me. Madigan loved me in his own special way, and we had a lot of history. I wasn't casual. Then, I wasn't his little boy or submissive either.

Perhaps it was a good idea I didn't call him that anyway. Given how attached I was to him already, adding significant titles would make it easier for me to forget we weren't a real thing.

"You met my last Little," he said. "Corey."

I *hated* Corey. I...didn't remember him. Wait, Corey? That was at least four years ago. I vaguely recalled meeting him once or twice for dinner at home. He hadn't seemed *little*, though. Not in personality or anything else. Wasn't he the paralegal or whatever? I scratched my head.

"You dated a paralegal, right?"

He nodded. "That was him."

Huh. He'd gotten a job in San Diego, if I wasn't mistaken. Or San Antonio. San something. He'd been a lot older than I was now, too. Early thirties, I guessed.

Fuck it. I didn't wanna talk about Corey. "We should talk about us instead," I insisted. "I like it when you make rules and stuff, like with my daily schedule and making sure I follow it. And I like being at your place 'cause it's relaxing."

"Rules and stuff." He smiled faintly and inclined his head. "There sure as hell will be rules and stuff. Whether or not you follow them is up to you."

"What happens if I don't?"

"Well..." He puffed out a breath, deflating his cheeks, thinking. "There's punishment, of course. Depending on the infraction. If you willfully disobey me and don't treat me with respect, you'll remember the punishment far longer."

I winced at the thought. Being playful was one thing, but I didn't wanna outright defy him and make him disappointed in me. And on that note, regret slammed into me regarding this morning. I'd ignored what he'd texted. No gym time, no breakfast.

"I was a dick this morning when I didn't go to the gym," I said. "First the text, then not doing what you told me."

Madigan cleared his throat and set his soda can on the

nightstand. Then he lay down on his side and pushed himself up on his elbow. "Only I get to tell you what you are from now on. Make that a rule. You're not allowed to berate yourself and resort to name-calling."

I mirrored his position, wanting to hear more. This was it. He was setting up rules for me. "But I call myself stuff all the time."

"And I don't like that," he murmured. "I'll help you create a new habit, one where you cut yourself some slack. You've always been hard on yourself." He paused. "Is that position good for the wrap?"

"It's not straining." I brushed a hand over my rib cage under the covers. "It doesn't even itch. What did you do to it?"

He chuckled. "Stay on topic. As for the text you sent me, I took it for what it was. I smiled when I received it."

"You did?"

"Mm." He folded a pillow in half and used that instead of his elbow. "It's a hell-raiser's way of asking for more."

I ducked my head and did my best to hide my grin. A strange sense of shyness fell over me, and it was as if he was slowly stripping me of my exterior.

Madigan went on, explaining the difference between punishment and funishment. Both could sting severely, but funishment was lighter and carried humor behind it. And no matter what, he went on, forgiveness meant just that. When it was over, it was over. He also told me that I was, under no circumstances, allowed to walk on eggshells around him for fear I'd disappoint him. Disappointment was part of life, and everyone messed up. Additionally, there was a big difference between being disappointed in something I'd done, and being disappointed in me.

I listened, I really did, but I stared too. His eyes crinkled at the corners as he told me he had no interest in mindless obedience. He wanted to be kept on his toes, and that made me happy. He didn't want me to follow blindly—*oh, that's hot*. My gaze fell to where he dragged his teeth briefly against his bottom lip near the corner of his mouth. He did that sometimes when he was mulling over what to say. Then his eyes had my attention again. He had a pair of captivating ones. Mostly gray and blue, with flecks of pale green near the center.

"Are you listening, Abel?"

"Yessir," I responded automatically, watching his lips twist. I licked mine out of reflex. "You want me to maintain a food and workout journal online that you can look at. I'll do it."

Lines appeared at his mouth and eyes when he laughed. It made me grin.

"You're too fucking adorable," he sighed.

"Thank you." I bunched up a pillow like he'd done and scooted closer. "Keep talking. I'm listening, I promise."

Was his beard soft or coarse? I felt it every time he kissed me on the forehead, but it wasn't enough. My fingers needed to determine that.

"I think I'm done talking for now." He looked content and maybe a little tired. "Do you have any questions?"

Yes, mainly one. "What's in it for you? You haven't listed anything you want me to do for you, and that won't fly with a submissive."

He hummed, watching me, and I couldn't fucking take it anymore. I reached out and walked two fingers over his jaw. Interesting. It was both soft and coarse. Mostly coarse, yet silky in a way.

"You know, I never would've guessed you were a sub," he murmured. "But a Little...? I should've seen it sooner. I think I did on some level..." He trailed off and wrapped his fingers around my wrist, bringing my fingertips to his mouth for a chaste kiss. "A Middle, more correctly. I don't see you acting like a kindergartner."

I grimaced. "No. What's a Middle?" My fingers weren't done, so I returned them to his jaw. They strolled up toward his temple where his hair shifted in brown and silver.

"A cheeky hell-raiser like you. Think...preteen more so than kid, personality-wise."

That seemed to fit the bill. "I liked drinking from a juice box, though. And I like cartoons."

"And that's okay." He closed his eyes as my fingers wandered into his hair. "That's nice." I felt the shortish strands along the side of his head before I eased into the longer wisps at the top.

"You didn't answer earlier," I said quietly. "What you get out of it."

"I get this," he murmured sleepily. "Right now, I couldn't ask for more. I get to have you back in my life, and I get to look after you."

I swallowed against the flutters and scratched his scalp gently. "You really missed me?"

For a split second, he looked haunted, even with his eyes closed. Then he took a deep breath and let it out slowly, and the contentment washed over him again. His forehead smoothed out, and he nodded once.

"More than you'll ever know."

My bottom lip trembled at a sudden onslaught of emotion, and I gave up on his hair. With a few grunts, huffs, and pulls, I managed to yank the covers free from under him—okay, maybe he helped me a little—and then I threw caution to the wind and moved into his embrace. Thankfully, he wrapped his arms around me and held me tightly.

I inhaled deeply and waited for my eyes to stop stinging. I barely acknowledged the dull ache of my new ink.

Don't leave me again.

"I'm so sorry for hurting you, Abel," he whispered against the top of my head.

I couldn't speak. My throat had closed up. All I could do was nod jerkily and press myself harder to his body. He was warm and all comfort and protection.

This was my home.

CHAPTER 8

I didn't know when I'd fallen asleep, only that I woke up when Madigan hiked my leg over his hip. I blinked against the cobwebs of sleep and rubbed my eyes. *Why can't I see...?* Ugh. I squinted toward the window behind me, the twist of my body reminding me I'd gotten inked today.

It'd turned dark out—*oh my God.* I swallowed a gasp as one groping motherfucker slipped a hand under my sweats and cupped my ass. Shit, shit, shit. Good time to notice I was embarrassingly hard.

Panic rose quickly.

Placing a hand carefully on his shoulder, I tried to ease away far enough for my dick not to be pressed against his hip. He could *not* wake up and find me this way. It was mortifying. And he was surprisingly strong in his sleep. Goddammit. Okay, what did I do? Maybe if I woke him up and moved out of the way while he gained his bearings...

"Mad," I croaked.

My eyes fluttered closed when he hummed and pressed

his lips to my neck. *Wake up, asshole!* I wasn't sure what was worse, warring against him or myself. 'Cause fuck if I didn't ache to press myself closer to him.

"Madigan, wake up."

He shifted slightly, but closer, not away from me. Fuck. With his face buried in the crook of my neck, he inhaled deeply and let his lips linger on my skin. I bit my lip and sent a panicked look at the ceiling. I'd shared a bed with him before, and he'd never had boundary issues then. What the fuck—*and there goes his hand*. He squeezed my buttock and pulled me toward him.

"I'm gonna kill you," I groaned.

My heart threatened to pound its way out of my rib cage, and it got worse when his breathing pattern changed. He was waking up, I was sure of it. It was like watching two trains speeding toward one another, knowing the crash was imminent. I kept my hand on his shoulder, fingers trembling, ready to use his body to shove myself off the bed. Ready to bolt, ready to escape.

His breathing sped up, the warm puffs of air hitting my neck. He was awake and rigid—unfortunately, not where I wanted him rigid.

"Are you awake now?" I whispered shakily.

He was gonna know I wanted him, even though a breeze could get me hard. What if he said I was too much? That maybe mentoring me wasn't a good idea? He could blame his groping on being asleep.

"Yeah. I can't believe I—fuck." Then he was gone, rolling away and off the bed. "I'm sorry, Abel." He left a chill in his wake and disappeared into the bathroom in the entryway.

I blew out a breath and looked up at nothing. He'd apologized, so that meant I was in the clear, right? I hadn't ruined everything. He was still my friend. As long as I had that, I could deal.

A small burst of jealousy flared up inside me as I wondered if he'd dreamed of someone, but I pushed that aside. I'd lost count of the times Gray and I had half taken advantage of each other in our sleep just because we were wrapped around one another.

Or maybe he wants you...

"Fucking Casey." I slapped my hands over my face and cursed both him and Jameson.

Well, at least I'd lost my boner.

The next time I woke up, it was almost light out, and I was disoriented. My stomach growled and tightened with hunger, and I lifted my head from the pillow and squinted at the clock on the bedside table. Shit, I hadn't eaten in forever. Did we... No, we didn't eat dinner last night. And at that thought, I was hit with the memory of how we'd woken up last time.

I turned my head quickly, relieved to see Madigan hadn't fled to Canada. He was asleep, still dressed in jeans from yesterday, and if he slept any closer to the edge of his side of the bed, he'd fall off.

As I yawned, I lowered my gaze and spotted a pillow between us. Lord, he'd actually put it there? And when had he returned from the bathroom last night? It'd been a while before I'd fallen back asleep.

"Mad."

He made a sleepy sound and stretched out on his back, then threw a heavy arm over his eyes. It made his muscles flex, and I eye-fucked him in his half-naked glory. Too bad he felt the need to sleep in his jeans.

"Madigan, wake up." I shook him carefully, his arm cold to the touch. Maybe because he was stupid and hadn't bothered with a blanket. "It's morning."

"Mm." He grunted, half asleep. "What time is it?"

I peered over my shoulder and read the clock on the nightstand. "Five-thirty." But we'd gone to bed so early.

"No rush, then," he whispered groggily.

"I'm hungry. Can I have Oreo O's?"

I studied him with some apprehension while he let out a yawn and scrubbed tiredly at his face. Maybe he didn't remember last night—yet—or maybe it was like the time I confessed my feelings for him, and he was just going to ignore it.

"Sure." Rather than...well, staying put, he dragged himself out of bed.

"I can do it myself, you know." I sat up and continued to observe him.

He opened the fridge, seeming adamant about keeping his back to me, and shook his head. "Let me take care of you."

I swallowed hard and stared at my lap. The ache was physical; it literally hurt to want him so much. And then he said sweet stuff like that...? I wished I could be someone else, someone he couldn't resist.

"I'm just, um..." I didn't know why I felt the need to announce I was going to go to the bathroom, so I shut my mouth and headed for the entryway.

Count your blessings. Nothing's going to change again. He's your friend, and he's even agreed to help you with the kinky stuff.

After relieving myself, I took out a new toothbrush from under the sink and brushed my teeth. Also, while I gave myself a pep talk, I had time to remove the wrap from my ink.

I inspected it in the mirror, smiling and not caring that toothpaste foamed at the corner of my mouth. My new ink was fucking gorgeous.

Madigan knocked lightly on the door. "Sweetheart, where's your medication?"

I squinted in thought. I always kept a Ziploc baggie for nights I spent away from home... *My wallet*. "Um, probably in my jacket that's still downstairs in the shop."

"Okay, I'll be right back."

In the meantime, I carefully cleaned the ink with the lotion or ointment-type spray he'd put on the sink. Tomorrow when I did my photo shoot with *Men's Health*, this was gonna look so good. The skin wouldn't be so irritated, yet it'd be before there was any scabbing. After throwing away the gauze wrap, I washed my hands again and left the bathroom.

Madigan returned a couple seconds later.

"Oh, lemme see." He handed me my pills and placed a hand along my side, his thumb teasing the area below my tattoo. "Perfect."

"There won't be any scabbing by tomorrow, right?" I asked to make sure.

His forehead creased, and his smile was rueful. "From now on, only I get to put ink on your body." *Yes, Daddy*. How would it feel to actually be able to respond that way? "My work doesn't leave scabs unless it's a cover-up or a sensitive area."

"Oh." I looked down at my torso. "Does the rest not look okay?"

"No, it does." He went down on one knee and pressed a kiss to the spot above my belly button. My eyes widened, and I gulped past the shock of what he'd done. Was this okay? I mean, for all I cared, he could kiss me anywhere, but it was new. Different from forehead kisses. Maybe it was part of his Daddy Dom stuff? I would *love* it if we could hug more and even cuddle. "It looks good."

I chuckled shakily, trying not to get hard. Give me a break, he was on his knees before me. "You can come with me tomorrow and see me flex it in front of a camera." It was a joke—mostly.

That had his attention, and he rose from the floor. "What camera?"

I filled him in on the photo shoot and how Dad and Uncle Ellis had made it so I could have it here in town.

"Dad is teaching me to make more demands," I joked.

"Good. The less travel, the better." He nodded and gestured for me to have a seat.

I watched him while he made me breakfast, and I knew I had to kill the unease regarding last night. Otherwise, I would obsess over it and create more problems.

My face heated up as I tried to phrase things, and I tugged at my ear, finding it impossible to get comfortable in the chair. *Um, about last night when we grinded against each other...* I winced.

"Are we okay?" I blurted out in the end. "I mean, about w-what happened—"

"We don't have to discuss that." His voice wasn't harsh or anything. Hell, it bordered on cautious, yet, at the same time, it brooked no argument. He didn't wanna talk about it. "I feel horrible. I like having you here very much, and I don't want you to feel uncomfortable around me." Uh, *I* wasn't the one uncomfortable with what happened. "I promise it won't happen again."

I clenched my jaw but said nothing. He was making it sound like he'd taken advantage of me, which was ridiculous.

Right now, though, I chose to be selfish. "It's not like I was complaining. But anyway, everything is good? You're still gonna help me with the kink stuff?"

It wasn't until then that he faced me as he walked over with my food. Although, saying he made eye contact would be a stretch. "I'll be by your side for as long as you want me to." He set a tray on my lap, and I eyed the cereal, another juice box, and small sandwich. "Eat your breakfast."

Yes, Daddy.

The more I responded to him internally, the more I itched to say it out loud. I wanted to try it.

Opening the Ziploc, I poured two pills into my hand and chased them down with some cran-apple juice. Then I turned on the TV and found cartoons on Netflix.

Madigan didn't eat, claiming he wasn't hungry this early. Instead, he sat down in the chair next to me with a cup of coffee and a magazine about tattoos. My attention was split between watching him and watching the TV.

"Will you be doing much traveling this year?" I asked.

He flipped a page in his magazine and took a sip of his gross coffee. "Not really. I have a few clients in LA and New York, then the convention in Orlando."

I knew about Orlando. He went every year; they invited him because he drew a crowd, and he always tattooed someone famous. The chances of me going to the play-offs were slim, so maybe I could go with him...? It wasn't until April.

"Do you know who you're working with this year?" I wiped a trickle of milk off my chin.

"Lincoln, actually." He seemed to relax with the new topic. "Last year was a bust. I got stuck with some teen pop star, and I lost my shit. So I told them I'd bring the talent next time."

I hummed in acknowledgment and crunched on a few

cookie bits. Dad liked to believe the world had forgotten his musician days and that he was only known in the inner circles of production and stuff like that now. He was wrong. He had heaps of fans who were, like, his age and who'd been around when he was huge. They were often the people who attended the annual tattoo convention in Orlando, or so I suspected, so it made sense for Mad to go with my dad.

"I wanna go." I jutted out my lower lip.

"Who says you can't?" He smiled and reached over to pinch my lip.

It made me grin. We were good. Last night hadn't ruined anything.

"Calm yourself." Madigan hugged me from behind as we walked downstairs.

"I'm restless." Understatement. As comfortable as I was at his place, he lived in a fucking studio, and there was only so much I could do before I started climbing the walls. "You need a bigger apartment. You're too rich and too old for this bachelor shoebox."

He chuckled and released me. "I like my shoebox."

I pushed open the door leading to the back of the tattoo shop, and I was greeted by music. Jameson and their apprentice, Justin, were here.

"Hello." I nodded to Justin, whom I'd only met briefly before, as he got ready to give a girl a piercing in her belly button. He nodded back, a smirk playing on his lips. Jameson was by the counter, and I stopped there. "Hi. Is my friend alive?"

I was surprised I hadn't heard from Gray yet. Not since the "oh my God, his monster cock" blah, blah texts.

Jameson looked up from the laptop he had stashed behind the counter and glanced at me, then Mad, then back at me. "He's fine. Very fine, actually. What about you two?" There was a lot of smirking going on.

Madigan sidled up next to me. "All good."

I flicked my gaze between them, feeling like I was missing something.

Jameson laughed and scratched his nose. "Uh-huh. Sooner or later, you'll—"

"Whatever. When's my first client?" Madigan abruptly peered over the desk and flipped open their planner. "Figures. God forbid I get some time off."

I shrugged on my jacket. I was gonna go home and pack my gym clothes, then go work out. I had ants in my pants, as Mad called it, and needed to burn off some excess energy. Gray had classes today, so I'd have to wait to bother him.

To be honest, I knew today was gonna end on a bad note. My parents were working, Mad was gonna work too, Gray was in school, my grandfather was probably out fishing as usual, and I didn't feel like calling any other of my buddies in town. When I was bored, I did weird shit.

You might wanna warn Madigan about that.

He'd try to stop me, though. Then I'd go even more stir-crazy.

No, I could handle it. I was a big boy.

I spent three hours at the gym, and it worked to an extent.

Then I kidnapped my sister.

I told her teacher my mom must've forgotten to tell them Lyn had a dentist appointment and that I was taking her. It worked like a charm, and then I was buckling Lyn into the back seat.

"I don't wanna go to the dentist," she whined.

"We're not." I got in behind the wheel and checked the rearview. "We're gonna go shopping."

"Yay!" She clapped.

See, it was never a good thing for a guy my age to have more money than he could spend, and shopping was a good way to pass time. First, we went out for a late lunch, and then I brought her to one of the two toy stores in town. I picked the mall in the Valley 'cause it was where we could do the most damage. Lyn lost her shit over princess LEGOs and a pink guitar.

"Like Daddy plays!" She placed the guitar in the cart after batting her lashes at me, and I checked my phone while she continued on her quick visit to Spoilville. Mom was gonna be so pissed.

I fired off a text to Gray.

wanna hang out after class?

I texted Madigan next.

Seriously. are u gonna live above the shop forever?

Lastly, to level out the crazy, I sent a message to my old therapist. It would do me good to talk to her occasionally about everything. Regardless of how much Madigan was going to take care of, he wasn't my keeper or my shrink.

Check me out, making mature decisions.

"Can we buy Theo a present, Abel?" Lyn stalked over with a big box of action figures.

"He's a baby," I said. "The only thing he plays with are the fingers we stick in his face." Additionally, Uncle Casey and Uncle Ellis were even stricter than Mom about material shit. Maybe not Ellis so much, but definitely Casey. He'd get pissy. "You know what we can do? We can get Mom and Dad something."

The way I saw it, I could butter them up before I told them I had tattoos.

Couldn't hurt.

"Okay, what do we get?" Lyn put on her serious face and looked around her.

"Maybe nothing in here," I chuckled.

We went to pay, and I received my response from Madigan as I handed over my credit card.

Maybe not.

I replied.

Ur a Daddy Dom. U could have a playroom!

Tilting my head, I thought about it some more—the moving part. A place of my own. Why didn't *I* move? I shared a condo with two teammates in Vancouver; that was it. I'd actually never had a place of my own, and I was twenty-one years old.

Lyn and I brought all the bags back to the car, and by "Lyn and I," I meant she carried a new stuffed animal while I grabbed the rest.

"Can I get a new dress, Abel?" she asked sweetly.

I closed the trunk and considered my options. Shopping for clothes was the only thing that stood between me and finding a Realtor. So I gave her a nod. I could go for some new sweats and hoodies, too.

I did something bad.

In my defense, it was Mad's fault. Accidentally on

purpose walking past a Realtor's office once we were done with all the shopping, I'd seen the listings in the window, and one was to a loft right across the street from the tattoo shop.

"You can't tell Mom and Dad about this." I eyed Lyn in the rearview.

"Tell them what?"

"That's my girl."

"No, I mean it. Tell them what?"

I laughed under my breath and turned left to follow the real estate agent.

Five minutes later, I parked outside a sandwich shop that was across from Camassia Ink, and I hoped Mad—or Jameson—wouldn't see us. Madigan was going to be busy all day, but you never knew.

I grabbed Lyn's hand on the sidewalk and told her to put on her hat. Light snow had begun to fall, and it was cold as fuck.

"Thanks again for agreeing to show me the place today," I told the agent.

"No problem at all." She smiled brilliantly and produced a key from her purse. "Shall we go up? Unlike many of the buildings in this neighborhood, there's a new elevator installed, and—"

"Abel!"

"Aw, fuck." I grimaced and reluctantly turned toward the tattoo shop. Dammit all. Madigan was crossing the street, and he didn't look too happy. Which…um, well, why didn't he look happy? He couldn't possibly know I was about to look at a condo.

"Hi, Uncle Madigan!" Lyn waved madly.

"Hey, princess." He spared her a quick smile before reaching the sidewalk and facing me. He wasn't wearing a jacket. "When you let your little sister skip school because you're bored, the polite thing to do is keep the sound on. Your mother's been calling you for an hour."

My stomach fluttered with nerves, and I pulled out my phone. Shit. How had I missed this? "I didn't know it was on silent. I must've hit the button by accident."

Other than a dozen missed calls from Mom, there was a text from Dad.

Don't spend too much money this time, and answer the phone when Mom calls.

He knew me too fucking well. It was possible it wasn't the first time I'd cured boredom with Lyn and shopping.

"All right, I'm sorry." I picked up Lyn and positioned her on my hip. "We're heading home soon, just…doing some shopping."

By some miracle—or perhaps he was simply too busy with a client—Madigan didn't acknowledge the real estate agent standing less than ten feet away. It helped that my sister babbled rapidly about the toys I'd bought her.

"Uncle Madigan probably has a client waiting," I told her to cut off her cute rambling. "You can tell him about the toys next time he comes over to dinner."

"Your brother's right." Madigan stepped closer and pressed a loud smooch on Lyn's forehead. It made her giggle. "How does the day after tomorrow sound, huh?"

While she nodded furiously, it raised a question for me. The day after tomorrow was Wednesday, and I had plans with Gray then. Was that still on? I mean, would Madigan have rules about me going to kink events? Would he insist on tagging along? Would he forbid me? Did he even care? Crap. I got fidgety just thinking about it.

Madigan returned to work, and I glanced over at the

Realtor in her fancy red sport coat, eyes glittering at the possibility of making a sale today.

I was fucking doomed.

CHAPTER 9

When the doorbell rang downstairs, I left my room in a sprint.

"I got it!" I hollered. Down the stairs, almost stumbling, heart rate picking up. Then I ripped open the door and yanked Gray inside. "You're late, idiot. Let's grab food in the kitchen, and then—"

"*Hey*. Slow down." He removed his jacket and beanie.

I sucked in a breath. He didn't get it. I'd been holding this in for hours, and I had to tell someone before I freaked out.

I'd already explained to Mom that Gray and I were having a movie night, and she was more than happy to let us eat in my room. Two plates filled with food waited for us on the kitchen island while Mom, Dad, Pop, and Lyn ate at the table.

My sister was pissed. Like, downright seething. She'd spent an hour crying after Mom told her she could only keep half the toys; the rest would be donated to the facility Mom ran. Lyn could be a sneak sometimes, so after Mom's verdict, she'd gone straight to Dad and batted her lashes. He'd stood his ground and told her to *never* disrespect Mom by going behind her back, and in return, I'd gotten punched by guilt. Because I was going behind their backs, it felt like.

I'd lied to bust Lyn out of school. I was in love with my parents' best friend. I hadn't told them about my tattoos or the fact that I was having more anxiety lately. And, last but not least, I'd bought a loft…

Well, sort of.

After five minutes of agonizing chitchat between Gray and my parents, we went up to my room with food and drinks, and then I kinda word-vomited. He sat down on the edge of my bed while I paced the floor.

My anxiety caused me to stammer a bit as I rushed to clear my head, but Gray was used to that. He let me ramble and listened calmly to my nonstop stream of consciousness about Madigan and how we'd woken up in the middle of the night, about the loft, about Casey's and Jameson's thoughts on Mad's alleged feelings; I mentioned the ink, the kinky stuff, and, and, shit. Black spots filled my vision, and I gulped in some air.

"Hey." Gray left the bed to join me in the middle of the floor, a hand going to my neck and his forehead pressed to mine. "Breathe, babe."

I nodded jerkily.

He smiled in response and eased off a few inches. "So you've had an eventful couple days."

I didn't respond, focused on calming down my thundering heartbeat, and just waited while he processed.

Gray returned to the bed and cut into his steak. "What about all this bothers you the most?"

That was a no-brainer. "What to do about Mad, and—um, thinking about the loft makes me anxious."

He nodded, then gave me a pointed look to start eating. I

wasn't hungry at the moment, but I hated food gone cold. Sitting down at my desk, I forced a forkful of steak and avocado salad into my mouth, at least a little happy the steak was still warm.

"You haven't actually bought the loft yet, have you?" he asked.

"We shook hands," I said, "and I'm supposed to sign the paperwork this week."

He offered a wry quirk of his lips and ate some more. He knew me well enough not to say I hadn't actually committed—in a legal sense—to buy the loft. If I couldn't return a sweater because of dealing with salespeople asking why I was returning it, how the crap was I going to cope with having to call the agent and say I'd changed my mind about something that came with a commission that would probably pay her bills? For the record, I hadn't changed my mind. I wanted the place—very much. It was just a big adjustment, a major deal.

"Question," he said. "If it turns out that Madigan doesn't want you—"

"He probably doesn't."

"—do you really wanna live across the street from him?"

I winced. He'd raised a good point. "Maybe not."

He nodded and reached for his soda. "Okay, so we set a deadline. Pick a day to deal with the condo, and before then, you gotta get to the bottom of what Madigan wants."

Shit, either way I went, I'd be confronting Mad too soon. "I'm gonna freak out."

"No, you're not," Gray told me firmly. "What you're gonna do is seduce him. I happen to believe Casey and Jameson, and I don't think it'll take much for Madigan to crack."

He was nuts. I couldn't seduce anyone to save my life.

"You told me you were gonna stop pretending to be all... you know, particularly grown-up around him. Did it ever occur to you that might be his downfall? You said it yourself, Abel. He's a Daddy Dom. He wants you to be however little is natural for you. He wants you to be *you*. And let's not forget that you two know each other better than most married couples do. If you fake it in the slightest, he'll sense it. He might even misinterpret it as discomfort. I don't know."

My fork clattered against the plate, and I spluttered in annoyance. "You're the one who told me to lie and claim I wasn't into him anymore!"

"That was before I had all the facts," he defended. "But think about it. Faking it—*pretending* to be more mature… around a Daddy Dom who wants to take care of his little boy? That makes *no* sense."

This was making me defensive too. "He believed I liked coffee. He didn't 'sense' any discomfort." I made air quotes around *sense* and rolled my eyes.

Gray shrugged and shoveled food into his mouth. "Whatever." He chewed some more and swallowed. "We mistake things all the time. I thought Craig didn't like me because he always grew more guarded when I was near. Like, he tensed up and shit."

I chewed on my lip, my brain switching gears. Gray had a point there. I remembered he'd called me in the middle of the night when he'd learned Coach Fuller was into him. Gray had been so shocked.

Did I tense up around Madigan? Did I do anything that made him misinterpret what I wanted?

"You think I should act more like a submissive boy around Mad?" I eyed Gray dubiously, all while my heart started racing again. I wanted this *so much*.

"I think you shouldn't act, period," he corrected.

"But I haven't this weekend—"

"You probably have." He waved me off. "On purpose or not, you've probably held back. It's what you do."

I couldn't argue there. Holding back was my default mode so others wouldn't think I was too crazy.

We ate in silence for a moment, and I mulled over everything Gray had said. I compared it to my actions, to what Madigan had told me, and everything that'd transpired this weekend. Then Gray and I talked briefly about the photo shoot; he suggested I make a genuine attempt to get Madigan to come with me tomorrow, but I wasn't sure. If there was one thing I wanted Mad to skip work for, it was so he could come with us to Seattle on Wednesday, and I told Gray as much.

He perked up at that, and he cocked his head. "Has he mentioned anything about you going?"

"No?" I didn't know where he was going with this.

He raised a brow and smiled faintly. "Aren't you supposed to *ask* him? Maybe he doesn't want you to go anymore."

"Can he do that?" I furrowed my brow.

"Um, don't you want him to object?"

Well...uh, yeah. Because then I'd have to ask him why he didn't want me to go, and in my dreams, he would get possessive of me. In my dreams...

Digging into the pocket of my sweats, I fished out my phone and sent Mad a message.

I dont know if anything has changed about this but do u care if I go to Afterfuck with Gray? Also, do I call u sir or something? I assume u dont want me to call u the other thing.

Afterfuck wasn't the type of event you attended to observe or learn more about BDSM. It was a pretty hard-core fuckfest; men went there to fuck and get fucked, end of. The club's second floor was dark in every sense of the word.

"I want him to say I can't go," I admitted.

Gray's expression softened, and he nodded before finishing his dinner. "I know the feeling."

"I'm not crying. You're crying." I looked away and wiped at my cheek.

After dinner, Gray and I had gotten comfortable under the covers to watch a movie, and the idiot next to me had picked *Forrest Gump*. He knew what this movie did to me!

"Aw, my crybaby." Gray chuckled and landed a wet kiss on my cheek. I shoved him away, to which he laughed. "Hey, this is payback for when you picked *The Green Mile*."

Oh yeah, Gray had cried then. Then again, so had I. Just not as much.

"Jenny doesn't deserve Forrest," I whispered at the TV.

"Word," he agreed. "*Jenn-ay...*"

I punched Gray's arm for mocking my Forrest.

"So violent." He rubbed his arm, down to snickers. "No response yet?"

I looked down at my phone next to me and checked it, then shook my head. There was no "read" sign either, so he hadn't seen it. "Nada."

He sighed, and we returned to watching the end of the movie.

"Look at it this way," Gray said after a while. "Madigan could've been married to a woman. At least your man isn't hiding who he is."

Madigan wasn't my man, but it didn't matter. We'd talked too much about my issues. Scooting closer, I draped an arm around Gray's shoulders and kissed his cheek. In return, Gray cuddled up against me and rested his head on my chest.

"You don't think Jameson could be anything?" I asked.

"Nah. He's in the same position, only he's obsessing over two people. I can't say I envy that."

"That sucks," I murmured. Unrequited love was bad enough with one person. I couldn't imagine falling for two. The whole concept was new to me—polyamory, that was. A friend and teammate of mine in Vancouver, Bellamy, claimed he was into that. He was the only other gay hockey player I knew of. I was sure there were others, but sports leagues weren't the gay-friendliest of places.

"Abel."

I grunted and winced, a twinge spreading in my neck as I tried to roll over. That was a no-go. I'd fallen asleep in a seated position, and now I hurt.

"Abel, wake up."

"I don't wanna." I let go of Gray and eased down the mattress to bury my face in my pillow.

"I have to go." He pinched my thigh. "I have an early class."

I groaned and stretched out. "What time is it?"

"Four."

"Christ. Get some more sleep and run home right before school." I was about to reach for him, only to notice he'd left the bed. As I squinted in the low light of the TV, I saw he was getting dressed. He said something about not wanting to rush.

"You might wanna check your phone, by the way," he added. "It was what woke me up." His knee hit the mattress, and he leaned over to kiss the top of my head. "I'll sneak out. Have fun at the photo shoot and call me later."

I yawned. "All right. Love you, jerk face."

He chuckled. "You too, dick bitch."

I snorted. That was a new one. The door clicked with his leaving, and I scrubbed tiredly at my face. Then I remembered what he'd said about my phone, so I dug it out from under the covers and squinted again as the screen lit up.

There were three messages from Mad.

I guess I had suppressed the Afterfuck event. If you want to go, you should.

The second message set off a bell in my head, a bell indicating he was struggling with how to word himself.

I'm not sure what you'll learn there, if exploring kink is what you're after, but it's your choice. I'd prefer you pick one of their official events for D/s purposes, not an orgy.

The third message made me sit up.

In the end, I can't stop you from going.

But he wanted to. I had to believe that. Or was I grasping at straws? Fuck.

He'd sent the messages ten minutes ago.

Four in the morning…

I startled slightly when the familiar dots appeared, letting me know he wasn't done typing.

What're you doing up, Madigan?

In a perfect world, I'd be your Daddy.

"Holy shit." My heart started hammering.

I screencapped the short, one-sided convo and was about to send it to Gray so he could tell me what to do. Right before I exited the window, a final message from Mad popped up.

I shouldn't have said that. I'm sorry. You can call me by my name or whatever you want, of course. Sir is always appreciated. I would never

force you to call me anything you're not comfortable with.

Yeah, sure, whatever.

I sent the messages to Gray and got up from bed, ready to pace the crap out of the floor until he replied. Thankfully, he did so quickly.

I don't know what the fuck you're waiting for. RUN, FORREST, RUN!

I was fighting off panic by the time I parked outside Camassia Ink. In my haste to get out of the house, I'd forgotten to get dressed properly, so I wasn't wearing anything under my jacket. My boots weren't laced, and there was a stain on my sweats. I was pretty sure I'd accidentally grabbed one of Dad's beanies instead of my own, too.

I wouldn't be here without Gray coaching me. I'd had my phone in my lap on the way down to the Valley, and he'd sent me encouraging texts several times.

Are you there yet?

I swallowed past the lump of nerves and killed the engine.

Yeah. Just parked

I focused on the breathing exercises Madigan and my parents had drilled into my head over the years, and I waited for Gray's response.

Text him. Tell him to let you in. If he doesn't answer, call him. He might've fallen asleep.

Good point. It was four-thirty in the morning.

I typed a message to Mad and sent it before I could overanalyze it and rethink this whole thing.

Im outside the shop, can u open pls

Gray asked me how I was faring, and I thanked him for everything. My breathing was somewhat regular now. I promised I'd call him later, to which he sent a winky emoji and said he was sure his schedule for tomorrow had just cleared up. I wasn't as confident as he was, but I hoped.

Madigan had seen my text.

"Shit." I blew out a breath and stepped out into the freezing cold, locking the car behind me. What would happen now? Gray had told me that Mad would take it from here. Though, what if he didn't? What if he only asked what I was doing here? Could I keep up the pretense and bullshit my way out of this?

A light flickered on in the back of the tattoo shop, revealing Madigan in a pair of jeans, a tee, and extra messy hair. He was the sexiest man ever, I just knew it. For whatever reason, he'd been aggravated enough to run a hand through his hair multiple times. It was too short on the sides to cause any damage, but the hair at the top looked almost like a mohawk now. The ends stood in every direction.

He didn't look too tired, and he walked with purpose. My pulse skyrocketed for every step he came closer to the door, and I didn't even notice I'd crossed the sidewalk until I was on the stoop in front of the "We're Closed" sign.

He was tense. I saw it in the look he gave me as he unlocked the door. I saw it in the way his jaw was set and the faint lines at the corners of his eyes. The door opened, and I couldn't take it. I almost freaked out. Rather than running away, I lowered my gaze to the ground and entered the shop as he stepped aside.

Oh God, now what? He was going to pretend he had no clue why I was here, wasn't he? He was going to ask if anything was wrong, if there was something he could do—

My stomach did a somersault. My train of thought drove

out the window, and I found myself yanked inside and trapped between the nearest wall and Madigan.

"You shouldn't have come here, Abel."

I gulped while he caged me in, his presence immense and intimidating, yet he touched me as if I were fragile. Hands framing my face, shifting upward until his fingers disappeared into my hair. The beanie dropped to the floor. I realized my eyes were screwed shut when I felt the ghosting touch of his lips at my temple. Heat suddenly exploded between us, causing my skin to flush.

"Why?" I croaked.

He drew in a breath through his nose, then slowly grazed his teeth along my jaw. My knees nearly caved. "Because I don't trust myself." His voice was a low, gravelly rumble and had the same effect as fire. I turned liquid, and he had to hold me up. "My sweet trouble…" he whispered against my skin. "I can't fucking stay away from you anymore."

I was done for. A whimper slipped through my lips, and I clutched at his arms. A moment later, his mouth covered mine. There wasn't an ounce of me strong enough to resist. I kissed him back tentatively, afraid I'd wake up and all this would be a dream.

When Madigan deepened the kiss, I felt him everywhere. His body pressed against mine, and he was hard in his jeans.

"I knew you'd ruin me," he murmured hoarsely.

Please let that be true.

The first real taste of him made me moan. He swept his tongue between my lips in sensual passes, ultimately coaxing me out and meeting him with the same passion. I kind of threw myself into it. Locking my arms around his neck, I pressed myself against him and angled my head to deepen the kiss further.

Stars appeared behind my closed eyelids, and for one silly

second, I thought it was because I was kissing the love of my life. Then logic kicked in, and I had to wrench away to suck in some air. Holy fuck, my lungs were burning. A gasp filled them with air, and my chest heaved.

"Mad..." I swallowed a groan and exposed my neck to him as his kisses trailed south. His hands snuck between us, and then he was unzipping my thick jacket. It was totally in the way.

I released my hold on his neck long enough so he could strip me of my jacket, and he grinned a little when he saw I wasn't wearing a shirt underneath. It was just a new gauze wrap, which didn't look half as good as when he'd done it.

"I forgot—I-I was in a rush," I stammered, out of breath.

He merely cupped my jaw and dipped down for another deep, toe-curling, hungry kiss.

I shuddered and brushed my hands over his stomach and sides. The soft fabric of his vintage tee did nothing to hide the strength underneath, and I wanted to feel him up. Kiss every tattoo, trace every dip and curve, and lick him all over.

Without a word, Madigan started walking me backward toward the stairs behind the shop. His mouth never left me, either leaving me breathless and panting or eliciting moans when he teased my neck with his tongue and grazing teeth. His hands...fuck me, they were working me just by stroking my lower spine and the back of my neck. Imagine when he did more than that...?

"Are..." I heaved a breath, a dizzy spell coming over me. Shit. "Are you a man with a plan?" I hoped he was taking me to bed.

"I'm a man defeated." With a final kiss, he turned me around and hugged me from behind instead. He guided me up the stairs, his hands wandering across my torso. "I have half a mind to inhale you."

I let out a breathy laugh, and my stomach twisted with nerves. Had I ever wanted anything as much as I wanted this? My body was trembling. If he had second thoughts later, I would break. Completely fucking shatter.

He reached around me to open the door to his studio, and he led me straight to his bed. The place was already dark, aside from a single light in the window.

Excitement blossomed within me, and I spun around to kiss him. He hummed and stroked my cheek, and my brain was reacting strangely. Most of me was ready to jump him, except another part, mostly my mind, that was cowering. Hesitating. No, wait. I frowned internally as he kissed me languidly, passionately. Definitely no hesitation. Just... I wanted reassurance. I wanted guidance. I was so tired, and I wanted to let go.

I didn't want to worry and hurt anymore.

"Lie down," he whispered.

"Okay." I touched my thoroughly kissed lips, then looked down and quickly got rid of my boots, socks, and sweats. Was he going to fuck me? I didn't know what was happening here.

Madigan shed his jeans and tee before joining me under the covers, and a burst of nervousness hindered me from ogling him. "Come here."

I inched closer until I was wrapped in his strong arms, and I practically heard the crack he made in my internal armor. Could I let go? Did he really want me? For how long?

"Are—are we gonna have sex?" I kind of blurted out. Maybe I shouldn't have.

He tensed for a second, then loosened his hold on me enough to ease off and look me in the eye. "Sure as shit not at the moment." He furrowed his brow and gripped my chin gently. I swallowed hard, struggling to maintain eye contact. Tentatively, he leaned down and pressed a kiss to my mouth. "I wanna hold you. Kiss you. All night, if you don't mind."

A drawn-out shiver traveled down my spine, and I began to relax. "I want that."

"Good," he whispered, brushing another kiss to my lips. "I can finally kiss you."

My body flushed, and I fought against a goofy grin. Kissing when smiling wasn't the easiest, and I had to keep kissing him. "You, um, *could* have been doing that for a while."

He let out a soft chuckle and touched my cheek. "There are so many things I wanna tell you."

"Like what?"

This became our position for now. I rested my head on the pillow while he was splayed half on top of me, an elbow on the mattress to keep his upper body elevated, and the kisses continued. They went from soft and barely there to deep yet unhurried. And his free hand never left my skin, whether it was tracing the curve of my neck, cupping my jaw, or stroking my sternum.

"Like I'm so goddamn doomed, it's not even funny." His mouth twisted up slightly to show he wasn't entirely serious. "I was…still am, I guess…worried. I knew that the day I caved, there would be no going back for me."

I searched his eyes at that, so hopeful that my stomach fluttered uncomfortably. "Have you caved? For me?"

He nodded once and captured my mouth in a hungry kiss. *Oh my God.* He knew how to use his tongue to reduce me to a useless puddle, a panting mess. I tried to pull him down on me, but he wasn't having it.

"Let me savor this, Abel," he murmured, breathing heavily. "Fuck…this is unbelievable." He kissed me once more, then hugged me to him tightly.

More tension rolled off of me, and I allowed myself to believe. For one moment, at least. I believed it was us now. He wanted me. He'd tried to resist, but he wanted me the way I wanted him.

"You're so beautiful. You know that?" He pressed slow kisses along my neck, his hand traveling down my side. "I don't know how many times I've wanted to tell you." Then he was back with a sweet kiss to my lips and his fingers weaving into my hair. "Sinfully sexy too."

I had to grin now. He thought I was sexy?

He smiled back.

"Don't forget I'm cute," I said.

He laughed through his nose. "The cutest."

I snickered and burrowed against his chest, my arm snaking around his middle. "You're the hottest that ever lived."

He rumbled a low laugh and gave me another squeeze. Next, he pulled the covers higher and snuggled us together real tight. It was funny how liberating it was to be restricted by him.

"My hotheaded little troublemaker," he sighed contentedly.

I closed my eyes, ignoring the burn. I didn't want to ruin this by getting emotional, but dammit if this wasn't overwhelming.

CHAPTER 10

Madigan and I dozed on and off for a couple hours, and I was super happy. He woke me up here and there with warm kisses and squeezy hugs. Those hugs were my favorite. They started out slow, with the pressure increasing, and his contentment showed the most when he held me the hardest.

I roused more fully when it was getting light out, and I got to watch Mad sleep for a minute or two. He looked more peaceful.

I ghosted two fingers over his temple, which seemed to wake him up.

He hummed and pulled me closer to his body, his eyes remaining shut.

"Do you remember the summer after you turned nineteen?" His voice was full of sleep, and he stroked a hand over my hip. "You were sick on your birthday, and then you went straight to the play-offs that spring. It wasn't until summer came around that we could celebrate you properly."

I eyed him curiously and tucked my hands under my chin.

"I had a pool party. Why?" It'd been a good day. I'd had friends over at Mom and Dad's, and we'd had a barbecue on the roof. Gray and I had delivered a piss-poor performance later that night when we did karaoke.

"You—you jumped into the pool wearing a pair of fucking Speedos." His sexy mouth quirked wryly, and his eyes opened. "I stopped seeing you as the adorable kid I was ridiculously attached to in a more appropriate way, and since then..." He blew out a breath and slipped a hand under my knee, hiking it over his hip. "That's when the fantasies began anyway."

It definitely was hard to believe. Nineteen... That was two years. He'd wanted me when I texted him, when I confessed I was in love with him.

Chewing on the inside of my cheek, I closed the last distance so our lower bodies were aligned. *Oh, fuck.* This was going to take some getting used to. I buried my face under his chin so he couldn't see my blush, and then I just focused on feeling his cock nestled against mine. I shivered as he ran his knuckles over my arm.

He was driving me crazy with his teasing touches and kisses. I'd gotten my reassurance, and we'd cuddled for hours now. I couldn't help but want more. This was the man I'd fantasized about since I hit puberty, pretty much.

"When's your shoot today?" he murmured.

"Um, at two." I didn't understand how he could pretend like he wasn't hard as a rock in his boxer briefs. Wasn't this a good time to address that? And maybe I could take care of it?

He moved like a sexy, lethal predator and rolled on top of me. I gasped into the deep, drugging kiss he took. Every shift of his body was deliberate and seductive. It felt...more. Like a buildup. Like maybe he was ready for more this morning.

He shuddered as my hands slid down his sides and settled

above his ass, and I traced dimples there with my fingers. Then he pushed his tongue into my mouth and gave a slow thrust of his hips. My breath caught as my body flooded with lust, and he hissed.

I felt small and vulnerable underneath him, and for some reason, it was perfect. Every taste of him, every move he controlled, and every touch pushed me down. My worries were temporarily silenced.

"More," I groaned weakly.

He cupped my cheek and nipped at my bottom lip. "I want to be your Daddy, Abel."

"Oh God." I sucked in a breath and blinked, startled by a wave of pleasure and relief. Was this really happening? Holy shit. "You, um—so you still want—"

"More than ever." He nudged my nose with his. "I won't have to hold back. We can both let go. How does that sound?"

"Like..." I licked my lips, thinking. "Like I wanna know what it's like. My brain is a little unsettled right now. I just want."

His mouth twisted up at the left corner. "That's what I'm here for. You leave everything to me. I'll take care of you."

It sounded good in theory—too good, even. In reality, I had no idea. I'd never been able to hand it all over to anyone before. But this was Madigan. I could trust him with my life.

"There's no pressure." He kissed me softly. "Don't force anything, never pretend with me, and talk to me about whatever you want—*when*ever you want." His message was clear, and I didn't feel the need to squash my hopes. He wasn't going anywhere. "We'll ease into things, okay?"

I nodded once and pressed my lips to his 'cause I wanted to, 'cause I could.

Somewhere, my phone started to ring; there was no way I'd get it. Crappiest timing ever.

"Ignore it." I spoke into the kiss.

"That's Lincoln's ringtone." He grabbed my jaw and angled my head back so he could suck on my neck. "You should answer."

I exhaled a moan, my abs tensing up. *Fuck*, he felt good on top of me. "Or not. I'll talk to him later."

But no. The bastard rolled off of me slightly, enough to grab my phone from my sweats on the floor. My mouth went dry at the sight of his cock straining upward in his boxer briefs, so I acted on instinct. I reached down and palmed the thick length, earning myself a gritty curse from him.

He eased back to sit on his heels in between my parted legs. "I didn't say you could do that."

"It's not ringing anymore—you can put away the phone." I followed him, acting like I was possessed, and pressed kisses to his chest while my fingers did their best to circle his cock. *Jesus.*

I had the worst luck, 'cause Dad called again.

"It better be important," I grated, frustrated and out of breath. Snatching the phone from Mad, I let my head hit the pillow again, and I pressed answer. "Yeah?"

Or maybe I didn't have the worst luck. Madigan hovered over me and started leaving a trail of wet kisses on my chest.

"Mom wants to know if you'll be home for breakfast after the gym," Dad said.

Of course, they assumed I was at the gym.

"*Ugh.*" I *knew* it wasn't important. "N-no, I don't think so."

"I'm going to hell," Madigan whispered. When he licked one of the gutters between my abs, I threaded my fingers through his hair and tensed up. It was half maddening with lust and half ticklish as fuck. "You're perfection."

Marry me.

"Right. Uh, be careful when you're outside," Dad told me. "I'm watching the news, and a kid's gone missing since last night."

Probably in Seattle and nowhere near here. Sometimes, he called me in Vancouver and told me to be careful because some old lady had been robbed in fucking Portland.

"Got it," I managed. Lifting my head, I watched as Mad nuzzled the spot right above the waistline of my briefs. They needed to come off. Now. "I gotta go, Dad."

"Gym, my ass. Say hi to Gray and wear protection." The line went dead.

I released a breath, dropping the phone somewhere, and dug my head into the pillow as Madigan finally pushed down my briefs. My dick slapped mutedly against my lower abdomen.

A flicker of self-deprecating mirth passed in Madigan's eyes. "You'll defend me the day I tell two of my closest friends I'm dating their son."

I laughed softly, more happy to hear we were dating than amused by his predicament. "I guess there's no need to tell them what I'll be calling you."

I could sense the topic change the second his features changed, going from amusement to something more serious. "No pressure there either," he murmured and crawled higher up my body. *Goddammit!* "While I have countless age-play fantasies starring you, that's not why I'm a Daddy Dom. I don't want you to call me Daddy until it's the name that feels the most right for you. Not because it's hot or dirty, but because it's who I am to you, whether it takes minutes or months. Does that make sense?"

I got it, and I nodded. I'd read enough to get a grasp of the type of Dom—scratch that, I knew enough about Madigan to know it went beyond kinky fantasies. It was a role in which he clearly felt the most comfortable. I'd yet to witness the full extent, but I'd seen glimpses, and I knew his personality. He'd always been a caregiver, one of my biggest supporters, teacher, and rock. That was why it'd hurt so much to lose him.

"Can we fool around now?" I asked.

He let out a chuckle. "Are you saying you don't want to talk more?"

"No, that's boring grown-up stuff." I pulled him down on me and kissed him before he could protest. "Or...I guess, Daddy stuff."

He hummed, letting me control the kiss for a beat. "But Daddy is a grown-up."

Oh, fuck. There was a sense of *rightness* that came with that title. It was not only hotter than hell. It was also all-encompassing and hinted at a world I was so ready to explore. Only I would call him that, nobody else. He would be *my* Daddy; it would be only for us, just him and me. Wasn't that what I'd always dreamed of?

The tension thickened as he took charge, slowing down the kiss all while deepening it. He stroked my tongue with his in those sensual swirl-like movements, and I let everything around us fall away.

"I might get possessive of you," I mumbled in warning.

"I can think of worse things." He probably wasn't surprised anyway. I'd always been territorial where Madigan was concerned. "I'll never give you reason to worry, Abel."

I was gonna respond, until he decided to steal all my air with the next kiss. The hand he wasn't using to support his weight started to wander, and his lower body pressed fully against my own. Swallowing a moan, I got lost in the kiss and the way he controlled it.

"One way or another, it's always been Abel and Madigan," he whispered. And his words made my eyes sting again, 'cause I felt the same. "I can't believe you're finally mine."

I threw my arms around him, forcing him to lower himself farther.

"I need to hear you say it, sweet boy." His kisses grew urgent and hungrier.

"Get serious. I've been yours since I was, like, twelve." I sucked in a much-needed breath and nearly lost my shit when he kissed his way down my neck. The moment he grazed his teeth around a nipple, I moaned embarrassingly loudly. "Oh my God."

"We'll work on your manners." He sucked lightly on the flesh and reached up to cup my jaw. "I'm less inclined to let you get off when you're not polite."

"Noted—I'm sorry. I'm yours, Mad." I gasped, arching into him, and was met by two fingers pushing into my mouth.

"Suck," he commanded huskily. "Show me what you'll do when this is my cock."

Fuck, he was killing me. Patience wasn't my strong suit. Luckily for him, I was competitive and wanted to be the best he'd ever had, so I obeyed and swirled my tongue around his digits. I sucked hard, using my teeth along him teasingly, and hollowed out my cheeks. I was slightly obsessed with giving head, and I hoped he replaced his fingers with his cock fucking ASAP.

In the meantime, Madigan continued driving me crazy with his mouth. He sucked, nipped, and rubbed at my nipples until the sensations were zinging and zapping straight to my crotch.

I groaned when he pinched a sensitive nipple and tugged at it. I swore my cock leaked because of it.

Mad withdrew his fingers and sat back between my thighs, and he scrubbed a hand over his jaw. "You're like a drug, you know that?" He took a calming breath and looked me over, a hand going to his cock. He gripped it through the fabric of his underwear and gave it a stroke, twisting it slightly at the head.

I couldn't stop staring, and I was sitting up before I knew it. "Let me suck you."

He cleared his throat, to which I glanced up at him in confusion. At his raised brow, I caught myself.

"Can I suck you off, please? I want it so much."

"That's much better." He pushed down his boxer briefs, revealing his long, thick cock, and I buzzed with anticipation. "Give it a kiss first."

A shiver caused my breath to hitch, and I scrambled into a better position to get full access. Then I lowered my head and swiped my tongue over the tip, wanting that little drop of precome. Madigan inhaled sharply and wove his fingers into my hair, and I gripped his cock at the base before I left another openmouthed kiss over the slit.

"Jesus fuck." He tensed up as I sucked him into my mouth.

He parted his knees a bit and guided me over him, and I cupped his balls in my hand, rolling them gently and stroking the skin. When he hit the back of my throat, I eased off and took a deep breath. *You can do this.* Then I sucked him in again, coated him in more spit, and didn't stop until he was pushing at my throat.

I closed my eyes and breathed through my nose, and I managed to take all of him. I swallowed around the head, earning myself a gritty groan from Mad. It set me off, and I got giddy and greedy and super determined.

"That's a good boy." His breathing picked up, and he thrust into my mouth. "Fuck. Goddamn perfect."

No, it wasn't. I could do better. With a frustrated noise, I released him and pushed him backward. His back hit the mattress, and I ignored his evident surprise. I was on a mission, already crawling over him. Then I gripped his cock again and swallowed him whole. *Now we're talking.* Judging by Madigan's sounds, he didn't mind I'd taken control for a beat.

In between thirsty sucks that hollowed out my cheeks, I did my best to convey that I wasn't in it for a quick release. If he was going to take care of me and allow me to let go of everything, he deserved my worship.

He groaned as I licked my way down the underside of his cock to fondle and suck on his balls. The sensitive skin became firmer with every pass of my tongue. His thighs trembled, and his fingers flexed in my hair.

"Jesus, Abel," he whispered, out of breath.

I returned to his cock, sucking him in slowly, feeling every ridge and the texture of him against my lips. I looked at him, in love and horny and happy, and I couldn't stop the grin. Or, as much one could grin with a big cock in the way. Madigan scrubbed his hands over his face, then shook his head as his hooded gaze landed back on me.

"I have no words for how sexy you are." He brushed his thumb over my cheek when I hollowed it. "Are you my baby boy now?"

I nodded quickly and licked around his head. Shifting my position, I noticed I'd left a wet spot on his leg, and I looked away, hoping he didn't notice. It wasn't my fault!

"I'm getting close," he grunted. *"Fuck."* He pumped into me once, twice, then set a steady pace to fuck my mouth.

There was no stopping my moans. He was too fucking hot, using me to chase his orgasm. I couldn't wait to swallow him down, nor did I care anymore about where I left wet spots. I pushed my cock against the mattress and groaned.

The second Madigan hissed and tensed up, indicating he was there, shock tore through me. Holy shit, the pleasure built up so fast, and I nearly blew my own load. God, that would've been embarrassing. I'd barely touched myself, other than rubbing against the mattress and his leg.

Heat rose to the surface of my skin, and Madigan stole my attention again. Faint lines appeared across his stomach, his abs clenching. He gritted another curse and called me *baby*... and then his come flooded my mouth in bursts.

The explosions made a comeback. There was euphoria fucking everywhere. I moaned and screwed my eyes shut. Could I feel him? Oh, for the—My brain short-circuited. For half a second, I thought I could *feel* his orgasm, except...I was an idiot. Shuddering and screaming internally, I fucking came. It was my own orgasm I felt. I tasted Madigan and swallowed what he gave me; his cock throbbed and pulsed, and so did mine. I pushed harder to get more friction and slid through the mess I was making on the sheets.

My climax had barely subsided before I grew hotter, this time with mortification.

"Motherfucking...*fuck*..." Madigan was temporarily distracted, trying to regain his breath.

Giving him a final lick, I eased away from him and stayed on my stomach so I could hide the evidence of my fuckup. My heart rate wouldn't go down, and my ears started ringing, to boot. This sucked!

"Why are you hiding your cute face in the mattress?" He slid down the bed until we were at the same level and dropped kisses on the side of my head. "Get on your back, baby. It's my turn."

Uh-oh.

"You can't," I mumbled into the sheets.

"Why?" He stroked a hand down my back until he

reached my butt. "Look at this perfect little ass." He totally groped me, even slipping two fingers between the cheeks, which was highly distracting. "I wanna taste every inch of you and intend to do so whenever I please."

Ugh. The humiliation burned. "But I came," I whispered.

"What was that?" He hadn't heard me.

It sparked some anger, directed at myself, and I couldn't help but snap, "I already came, okay?"

"Easy there, tiger." He grabbed a handful of my butt and squeezed hard enough for me to whine and squirm. "You want a shot at rephrasing yourself?"

Christ, just kill me and get it over with.

"I'm sorry I came," I groaned.

"Wrong thing to apologize for." He gave my ass a pat. "Show me the mess you made."

Uh, fuck no. I was more thinking he could go to the bathroom or something, and I could change the sheets. "I don't wanna."

Of course, he didn't give me a choice. With a few nudges, he had us lying side by side, and he gripped my chin so I couldn't turn away from him. Then he slipped his other hand between us and palmed my junk, to which I gulped. His eyes flashed with arousal, amusement, and something else. I couldn't pinpoint what it was.

He forced me to maintain eye contact as he fondled my junk slowly and rubbed in the fluids.

"Never apologize for coming." He leaned in and kissed me unhurriedly, and I shivered violently. "This...? This is fucking delicious." He hummed into another deep kiss, his tongue playing with mine as he brought two wet fingers under my balls. He rubbed the skin there in little circles while his thumb swiped across the softening head of my dick. Although...if he kept this up, I was gonna get hard. "Lucky for us," he murmured, nipping at my bottom lip, "I love it when little boys make a mess."

Goose bumps rose everywhere, and his words killed most of my uncertainty and embarrassment. "And I'm your little boy now, right?"

"All mine," he confirmed with a hard kiss. "My one and only."

Love and other fuzzy feelings filled every fiber of my being, and I was totally buying the loft across the street.

CHAPTER 11

The rest of the day was surprisingly boring. Madigan had a few hours of work, so I went to the photo shoot alone, and it was nothing I hadn't done before. They were pushing it so I could be on the next issue's cover—or maybe it was the one after that; I couldn't remember. And afterward, I got to gush a bit about Mad to Gray. We went to a sandwich shop, and he let me ramble until I was stumbling over my words.

I had the *best* best friend. Gray was genuinely happy for me, and he laughed and went, "No shit!" when I said Afterfuck was canceled for me.

When we parted ways, I had high hopes that Mad and I could continue where we'd left off this morning.

I was wrong.

We spent the two hours after he was off work discussing safety. He was adorably jealous when I confirmed Gray and I had shared a fuck-buddy thing, though the mildly sour look faded pretty fast. He'd suspected Gray and I had hooked up, and he told me he was proud of me for taking safety seriously. Which was one of the reasons Gray and I had entered into our friends-with-benefits thing in the first place: we didn't want to risk anything.

Besides, both Gray and I preferred sex with people we were comfortable with. Me more so than him. And for as long as we'd been fucking, we'd been exclusive up until Jameson and now Madigan.

It was Mad's turn next, and he hadn't been kidding the time he'd mentioned living like a monk. He hadn't been with anyone for over a year, and he got himself tested routinely because he handled needles at work.

I thought the boring was over once we got that out of the way, but no. Just to be on the safe side, he said, we should go get tested before the nearest clinic closed for the day. I may have groaned and stomped my foot, which didn't work for shit. He only found me *cute*.

That was how I found myself getting an unnecessary screening for all kinds of sexually transmittable diseases at five o'clock on a Tuesday afternoon.

"We could've spent this time in bed," I pointed out as we left the clinic.

He inclined his head and draped an arm around my shoulders. "Mm. But I want to fuck as many releases as possible into your sweet little bottom until Daddy's come is running down your thighs, and I can't do that with a condom."

I stopped on the sidewalk and stared up at him, eyes wide.

Daddy's come…running down my thighs…

Oh God.

"You're mine now, Abel." He stepped close and cupped my cheeks. Right there on the sidewalk. "I've wanted you since you were nineteen. I've wanted to *own* you…" He nuzzled my temple, his nose cold from the weather.

"Fuck," I breathed. "Um, can we go to your place now? If

we skip meals and don't leave the apartment, we could probably fuck a thousand times before I go back to Vancouver."

"A thousand times," he echoed with a soft laugh. "Are you trying to kill me already?" He took my hand, and we headed for his SUV across the street. "I'm afraid my plans will get in the way of that."

"Oh? More clinics you want us to visit?"

"Smartass." He smirked and shook his head, then unlocked the car. "We'll be doing a lot of talking—"

"Mad!" I complained.

"Hush, boy. Get in the car."

I huffed and got in next to him. I did not want to spend my last two days in town *talking*... "I get it, you wanna talk rules and stuff, but you could just send me away with a list on Thursday night. I'll read it, I promise."

"Not good enough." He looked over his shoulder as he backed out of the parking spot, and I removed my beanie. "You'll be on the road for most of the next three weeks. We need more than a list to establish structure, sweetheart. But don't worry—" He grabbed my hand and kissed the top of it. "Before you go to Vancouver, I'll make plenty of time to spoil you rotten." He nodded at me. "Seat belt on."

Oh, right. I'd forgotten. "You don't have to spoil me," I said as I buckled in.

"I want to. Starting right now. Let's pick a restaurant so I can take you on a proper date."

I smiled widely. I hadn't thought about it much, but I guess on some level I'd assumed we'd be in hiding before we told my parents about us. The fact that he wanted to do date stuff made me super happy.

"Stop looking at me like that," I said around a mouthful of the best fish burger I'd ever had. Sorry, Coho. The fish camp in the marina in Downtown Mad had taken me to didn't fuck around where seafood was concerned. The blackened shrimp and aioli could make any foodie orgasm. "You're making me feel self-conscious."

"Can't help it." He leaned forward and rested his forearms on the table. The round tabletop was wooden, old, and attached to a wine barrel. It went with the fishnets in the ceiling and the wall behind the bar made up of sea glass. "I don't think I can go back to pretending even if I tried. I'll be your personal stalker until it hits me that this isn't a dream."

Then he said things like that...

I grinned and took a gulp of my soda.

Unlike him, I didn't get full on one burger and a loaded baked potato, so I continued scarfing down my second burger and listening to Madigan. He was going all out. Whenever we were away from each other, there would be Skyping and frequent texting. Maybe some would feel suffocated jumping into this with a fair amount of restrictions, but it had the opposite effect on me, and he knew it. I could tell he had me in mind first and foremost when setting up rules.

Already, I could feel myself relaxing into this. It was like stepping out on a platform, ready to jump, and knowing I had the best safety net to catch me.

Having fewer worries would lessen my anxiety. Having less anxiety would improve my mood swings. In turn, I wouldn't doubt myself as much or be as angry with myself. It was one of the biggest hurdles with bipolar disorder. The ripple effect—a small stone could cause major damage over time.

"I'm happy. I just wanted to say that," I said quickly.

He stopped talking, having been on a minor lecture about

my stress levels, and scooted his chair a bit closer to me. "Give me a kiss."

I reached over the side of the table and smacked a kiss to his lips, smiling like a dork. "How long do you think it'll be until it feels more Daddy/little boy-like?"

The power was his, in that sense. It would take no effort to submit to Mad, and I could sense something else changing too. Like...my thought process? I wondered if that was what I'd read—regression and embracing a younger mind-set once I was more comfortable and settled.

"Well..." He took a sip of his beer, then returned with his forearms on the table. "You have a job where you have to be assertive—you're a dominant force on the ice. So, we'll have to find a balance. But in the end, I think it'll happen naturally. More than that, I don't think you're that little. We'll just have to see what feels right for you."

I scrunched my nose. "You don't think I'm a Little?"

"No, I mean..." he chuckled, pensive. "I think your Little mode will be special, just like you. You're a cheeky little shit, and with time, you'll let that side of you take over when you're with me." That made sense. "But, Abel, no matter how much or little you revert, we'll find our way in this. Okay?"

I nodded, hopeful and appeased. There was no switch to flip; it would happen naturally.

The bartender came over, not because it was his job but because he was a buddy of Mad's. I'd been introduced to Darius Quinn when we were seated. He had smirked and hinted at Madigan coming here with Jameson sometimes to bitch about their lack of love life.

"Just a heads-up," Darius said, handing Madigan a new bottle of beer. "Casey and Ellis got a table on the other side of the bar."

I looked across the establishment, the two dining areas

divided by the entrance and the bar, and I could see my uncles scanning their menus while chatting with a waitress.

"I appreciate it." Madigan inclined his head. "We're not hiding, it's just—"

"Not my business, buddy." Darius squeezed Mad's shoulder before taking a step back. "Whatever put that sickeningly lovesick look on your mug's gotta be a good thing."

"Fuck you," Madigan laughed.

Darius grinned, and I gave him a once-over. Was Madigan in a secret club of only gruff, stocky, tatted bad boys? I couldn't actually see any tattoos on Darius, but he fit the bill. He looked to be a few years older than Mad, and he rocked black jeans, a beater, and an open flannel shirt. Standard Washington wear.

"Go watch the news or something," Mad told him with a smirk.

"As someone who watches C-SPAN for kicks, you don't have a lot of wiggle room to bitch at me," Darius drawled. "But y'all enjoy the rest of your date." He left before Madigan could offer another dig, and I smiled curiously.

This was, after all, a new side to Mad for me. He'd always been family to me. Now I was...his boyfriend? I sure hoped so anyway. And I would be meeting people he saw outside of family dinners and holidays.

"You still watch C-SPAN?" I tilted my head. "Dork."

"Hey, it's a front-row seat to see what happens in our country's legislative—"

I cut him off by pretending to snore.

He pinched my leg under the table. "My little brat."

I snickered and shoved the rest of my burger into my mouth. It caused my cheeks to puff out, and I crossed my eyes at Mad's grin.

"Am I ffftill cute?" My words came out muffled and distorted, and he chuckled at me.

"Cuter than ever."

"Can you tell Mom I won't be home for dinner?" I placed the phone between my shoulder and cheek and kicked off my shoes. "Mad and I are gonna have a movie night, and I'll crash here." By movie night, I meant *Netflix and chill*, and everyone knew what that entailed.

"All right," Dad replied. "When do you go back to Vancouver?"

"Thursday night." I'd contemplated leaving early on Friday, but it wasn't worth it. We had practice at ten, and I didn't wanna get stuck in traffic.

"Make sure you spend some time with your sister and Mom before you go. She wants to know how the shoot went."

"It was tedious." I threw myself on the bed with the TV remote while Madigan changed into a pair of sweats and a new tee. "Do you know how much baby oil it takes to turn me into a sex object?"

Mad snorted from the entryway.

"I had to shower before I left the place." I was lucky Uncle Ellis had a dressing room and a shower for such bullshit. "At least the interview was all right. I got all the questions on a piece of paper, and the team's publicist had already 'suggested' my answers."

"Nothing like good journalism," Dad muttered. "You have more interviews, right? You mentioned something about LA."

"Yeah, for a piece on mental health in professional sports," I replied. "I'm supposed to talk about the foundation for kids with bipolar that I work with in the summers."

"Makes sense. Go see your brother in LA," Dad said. "I'm one worry away from getting on a plane myself."

I knew that. Jesse was...different. He didn't come home nearly as much as our parents would've wanted, and he didn't share much about his life. Casey and Ellis went down there not too long ago to check in on Jesse, who promised to visit more often.

"I'll talk to him," I answered. "Anything else? More disappearances or old ladies getting robbed I should know about?"

"You gotta stay awake today." There was some yelling in the background from my mom, and Dad sighed. "Right. You gotta stay woke. Because fuck grammar."

I grinned and snorted, and I didn't have the heart to tell him watching the news didn't necessarily make you woke. Instead, I let him have it, and then we wrapped up the call with I-love-yous and another promise for me to be home for dinner before I returned to Vancouver.

By then, Madigan had set sodas and a few packets of Nutella on the coffee table, and he was scrolling through the movie selection on Netflix.

"You know Netflix and chill is code for sex, right?" I sat up on the bed and yanked off my clothes, except my sweats.

He sent me a sideways smirk and sat down in his chair. "I'm not completely new to millennial lingo."

"So what're you doing?" Grabbing the duvet with me, I aimed at the available chair, but he cleared his throat and gave his lap a pointed look. *Well, okay.* Like I was going to say no to sitting on his lap.

"I'm putting on a movie, of course. Pants off."

Yes, Daddy.

When I was in nothing but my briefs, I settled carefully across his lap, my legs hanging off the armrest, and he pulled me closer. A shiver coursed through me as he tucked me in, making sure the duvet covered us both.

"There." He kissed my cheek and started rubbing the back of my neck. Meanwhile, I wasn't sure I could believe any of this was real. His shoulder was right there, waiting to be my pillow. We were *together*. We'd just been on our first date. "I'm not fucking you tonight, Abel."

Screeching sound. Hopefully it was only in my head, and what the fuck?

"You're not?"

He shook his head. "It might be a while."

This was outrageous. "But-but *why?*" I spluttered.

He found my evident horror funny enough to chuckle at. "Because I wanna take my time exploring every delicious inch of you." He leaned in and bit playfully at my earlobe, and I swore I fucking giggled. Ugh, sometimes I was embarrassing. "That's a beautiful sound, baby. Don't hide your face from me."

I hadn't been. Not really. I'd just looked away a bit.

"I like it when you call me that." I poked his neatly groomed beard. It was the one thing that never looked messy on him.

"I like watching you relax around me," he murmured. My gaze flicked up to meet his, and he released my bottom lip from my teeth. I hadn't even realized I'd been biting it. "That's the main reason I wanna wait. You know I've always been your Mad, right?"

I nodded and smiled. That was only my name for him.

"But being your Daddy will be new for both of us," he went on. "And you're not quite sure how it's gonna turn out or where you stand yet." He paused, and I hated that he was about to make a valid point. It was a gut feeling. "I've seen glimpses of that little boy lately. I see him right now."

Of course, I had to duck my head because he was putting me on the spot.

My cheeks grew hot, and I squirmed on his lap, trying to shift lower and make myself smaller. Then I sucked in a breath when his hand slipped between my legs. Not that he did much; he just rested it between my thighs and stroked my skin with his thumb. Yet, it was enough to steal my attention.

"Do you like being little around me?" he asked.

I nodded again. "More and more every minute. I guess that's the best answer I can come up with since I don't have much experience yet. My brain is…" I squinted and searched for the right word. "Quieter. I'm less frazzled."

"That's perfect." His voice drew me in like nothing else. It was as lulling and soothing as it was seductive and full of authority. "So we'll keep taking it slow, okay?" At that, I sent him a small scowl, and he laughed through his nose and pressed a kiss to my lips. "Slow doesn't mean we won't do anything, you little perv. You think I don't want to get inside you? Sometimes, it's all I can think about."

Hope sparked. "So maybe I can convince—"

His rumble of laughter cut me off.

I huffed and folded my arms over my chest.

"Sweetheart, if my goal is to be the best Dom you deserve," he said, down to chuckles, "how will it look if I obey my cock and take you whenever I'm in the mood?"

"I don't know, but it sounds very pleasurable."

"It does, doesn't it?" He snuck a kiss to my jaw. "But I can guarantee your beautiful mind won't be able to rely on me if I don't have any self-control."

Logic was so gross sometimes. I didn't want to admit he made sense, so I just kept moping to myself.

"So we're really gonna Netflix and chill?" I asked dubiously.

"We're really gonna Netflix and chill," he confirmed and reached for the remote. "If you don't pick, I will—"

"No way." I quickly grabbed the remote from him. "You like the worst and most boring movies." As I scrolled through the genres of action and comedy, Madigan finished a packet of Nutella before opening his soda. I settled for a comedy—*Anchorman*—then got comfortable against Mad's chest. "Can I have a sip?"

He held the Coke for me.

"Thanks." I took two big gulps, and the icy-cold fizziness reached my nose. It made my nose itch, so I rubbed it vigorously.

He found that amusing too.

With the movie starting, I focused on that instead, though I couldn't stop myself from constantly making sure I was really here with Madigan. Even as I sat on his lap, I had to touch him. I fidgeted with his hand under the covers, I kissed his neck every now and then, I brushed my fingers through his chest hair, and I reached up and played with his ear, tracing the shell of it, rubbing his earlobe.

I snickered at the TV. I loved this movie.

"I adore you." Madigan's murmur and his lingering kiss to my temple made my heart soar. "I haven't thanked you yet for being braver than me."

"I'm not braver." I scrunched my nose and tore my gaze from the movie.

"You sure as shit are when it comes to going after what you want."

I lifted a shoulder and stole another sip from his soda, then returned it to the table. "I guess I understand why you didn't. Just be mine forever and we're good."

Crap. I hadn't meant to blurt out the forever part, but it was kind of difficult to take back. Even more so when he surprised me by cupping my jaw and going in for a hard and hungry kiss.

It was dizzying. I moaned softly, tasting Nutella on his tongue.

He always got my body going so fast. It wasn't fair. A familiar rush of desire swallowed me whole, and it made me wanna cling to him.

"Nothing less than forever," he confirmed quietly, huskily.

I took a breath. For a second, anxiousness rolled in my stomach, and I searched his eyes. They showed warmth and something heavy, intense.

It wasn't weird for me to speak of forevers. I'd been in love with him for so long. Didn't matter that I was young, in my opinion. Him, though...? He'd only mentioned having fantasies about me since I was nineteen.

"You're everything to me, Abel. I don't want you to go back to Vancouver without knowing that."

My mind went blank, and he was lucky I could manage a nod. If I was everything to him, chances were he maybe loved me too. The *love*-love type of love.

He touched my cheek, and I kissed him. There wasn't much more I could do at the moment.

Actually, there was one thing. "I say it in my head all the time." I nuzzled his neck so he couldn't see my face. "I mean, I call you that in my thoughts."

He hugged me to him. "Call me what?"

I swallowed. "Daddy," I whispered shakily. Jesus Christ, that felt good. *So* good. My skin broke out in goose bumps, and my heart hammered.

It seemed he liked it also. He grabbed my jaw and kissed me with so much passion that it felt like my head was swimming. And it grew hotter and deeper and more frenzied. Something was threatening to burst inside me. I couldn't figure out what it was, only that I had to get closer and reach better. So I raised myself up enough to straddle him, all while he continued stealing my breath.

"*Daddy.*" I had to say it again. Or moan it, beg it, gasp it. Whatever. The chemistry messed me up. Calling him that was like twisting a valve that released a bit of pressure, yet, at the same time, the urgency kept increasing.

"That's it, baby." His callused hands roamed my back and neck in firm strokes, somehow matching the tempo of his tongue exploring my mouth. "I'm your Daddy, aren't I?"

I nodded quickly and gasped, just as rapidly diving for the next kiss. He was growing hard under me, and I was so needy-wanty that I didn't know what to do with myself. My dick strained in my underwear.

"More," I pleaded. "P-Please…"

"*Fuck,*" he growled, the sound shooting sparks through me.

I whimpered and lost control. One word went on a restless loop in my head as I kissed him wherever I could, clung to him like a desperate boy, and rolled my hips over his cock. *Daddy, Daddy, Daddy.* "Daddy… Oh God…" *Daddy, Daddy, Daddy.*

My stomach flipped violently, and I found myself airborne. Madigan was carrying me over to the bed, and he dumped me on the mattress before crawling over me.

I groaned and arched my back underneath him. He slipped a hand between us and under the waistband of my underwear, and then he was fondling my dick. Another desperate sound escaped me, and I used my feet to push down his sweats. His boxer briefs were another story, so I had to use my hands for those.

"Get on all fours for Daddy."

Yes!

I didn't dare ask if he'd changed his mind and wanted to fuck me, 'cause I had a feeling he wouldn't go back on his word. It wasn't the type of man he was. But sticking my butt in the air for him? Count me in. He could do whatever he wanted with me.

I scrambled into position once he'd eased off of me, and he slipped off my underwear in one go.

"Who owns this pretty little bottom now, Abel?" He stroked my butt firmly and spread the cheeks. It made me flush, to no one's surprise.

"You," I whispered. "My Daddy owns it."

He hummed and dropped a slow, openmouthed kiss on my left cheek. "He really does." God, he was kissing me closer toward, um, the middle, and his tongue was freaking magical. "He's gonna use it a lot too. Kiss it, fuck it...fill it."

"*Hnngh.*" I hung my head, panting already, and squeezed my cock. "C-Can I touch myself, please?"

He told me I could, and a second later, his tongue swiped across my opening in one firm, unhurried motion. The arm I used to hold myself up trembled, and I had to lock my elbow into place. Madigan didn't ease up. He had his hold on my butt cheeks while he began to fuck me softly with his tongue.

I tried not to rush it. I rubbed my dick as slowly as I could muster, shaking and whimpering every time he did something different. His fingers danced closer to where his mouth was already playing with me, and I held my breath as he pressed a digit against my hole. He licked around it, dipped inside, only to replace his tongue with the finger.

"Mad," I whined. Great, I was a fucking whiner now too. "More." I pushed back—or tried. He controlled me, not letting me move too much. "Please..." *Daddy, Daddy, Daddy.* "Daddy, I n-need it."

"Patience, little boy."

I didn't want to be patient! I made a noise of frustration and jerked my cock a little faster. With spit coating his fingers, he pushed two deep inside me and resumed using his mouth between my cheeks. Once, he licked me close to my balls, and that felt out-of-this-world amazing.

"Again, Daddy," I begged.

In response, he shifted a hand up to my lower spine, where he pushed me down slightly. I complied with the silent order and spread my legs farther, arched my back, and gave him more access.

I could hear his breathing speeding up. I felt it ghosting across my skin as well.

I clenched around his fingers and squeezed my eyes shut. A slick sound reached my ears, and on the next upstroke, I spread the fluids around my cock. But it wasn't just me. My breathing hitched. It was him too, wasn't it? It had to be. He was touching his cock too. *Daddy, Daddy, Daddy.* Now that I'd voiced the term, I wasn't sure how to stop. My Daddy was finger-fucking me, my Daddy was stroking his thick cock while licking me.

"We're gonna need to get you wetter," he murmured in his rough voice. "Lucky for you, Daddy has a special lube."

"Oh *God*," I groaned.

Mere minutes later, he grunted out his orgasm, and thick splashes of his come slid between my butt cheeks. My eyes nearly rolled back. The sensations were so powerful I lost my grasp on reality. His fingers fucked me, coated in his come, and it felt like I left one world and entered another.

One that was depraved and filthy-sweet, one my Daddy controlled.

As he finger-fucked me to orgasm, all I could think was how ready I was to be completely his.

The power belonged to him.

PART II
PLAY

CHAPTER 12

TWO WEEKS LATER

"Get the fuck out! I barely touched him!" I shouted. Tearing out my mouthguard, I skated up to the ref while the arena exploded in protests.

"Don't fucking test me, Hayes," the ref warned. "Get your ass in the box."

I gnashed my teeth together and shot him a glare. Given my recent suspension, my hands were tied. I'd returned to the NHL with a bit of a ridiculous buzz about my temper, which the media had cranked up.

I got two minutes for roughing—a fucked-up call 'cause the pussy I'd checked went down for nothing.

Entering the penalty box, I slumped down and chugged some water, and the game restarted without me. My heart was always racing during games, but this type of pressure, I reveled in. Sweat trickled down my back underneath my gear, the air was crisp and smelled of ice, and the atmosphere was electric. I banged my stick against the board when Bellamy shouted for Dusty to get his shit together and cover him, and this only pissed me off further.

Dusty hadn't earned his nickname because his skates shone and got used very often; the GM needed to trade him already. And I couldn't do shit to help. We'd been in the middle of a shift, so Bellamy was stuck with mainly slow defensemen, while he was the quick right winger to my left wing. We belonged in the first line, and we'd become a tight-knit unit this season.

"Focus, goddammit!" I yelled. "This isn't your fucking nap time, Koskinen—he's wide open!" Oh, motherfucker, they were useless.

A sharp whistle had my attention, and Coach signaled to me. I nodded in return; we were going on the offensive the last minute of the second period, and the rest of my line was getting ready to go back out there.

Looking up at the jumbotron, I saw I had another forty seconds to go. My entire being itched to play, partly because this game was such an integral piece of me. And partly because I couldn't maintain my focus if I wasn't on the ice. Focus was key, especially when you knew you were heading back to your condo later to fight depression.

As it turned out, being away from Madigan now that we were together was sucking the life out of me.

Shut up, don't think about him now. You'll see him on Friday.

I blew out a breath, chugged some more water, then inserted my mouthguard again.

Okay, game time.

I'd been allowed to avoid the press for a couple weeks, only agreeing to well-structured interviews with vetted questions, but my luck had now run out. A few of us faced a dozen reporters about the game right afterward.

When you were a sweaty, red-faced mess who just wanted strip off his gear and hit the showers, there was nothing like having a sharp spotlight aimed at you and a microphone shoved in your face.

"Congratulations on the goal, Abel." This woman was usually nice to me. Karen, I think her name was. "You've made quite the comeback recently, averaging almost a goal every game. The guys in the studio talked about this earlier—you tend to score early in the game. Is that something you've noticed?"

I removed my helmet, thinking about what to say, and pushed back my sweat-slicked hair. "Uh, yeah, kinda. I mean, I know I come out strong in the beginning, and that's something I always gotta work on." I snapped my mouth shut because otherwise, I'd say too much. I grew frustrated when things didn't go my way, and that was the main reason I sometimes lost my head later in games. My performance when I was frustrated wasn't as awesome as it should be. "I'm lucky to have Erik, Bellamy, and our defense." It was always a safe route to take, to shift the attention to the other players. "We struggled in the second today, but I think we picked it up pretty good in the third."

After the brief interview, I proceeded to the showers. The only thing that'd changed in my postgame ritual was that I checked my phone as soon as I could now.

Coach was wrapping up a do-or-die pep talk with the third line. Nothing I had to pay attention to.

There was the usual text from Mom and Dad.

We're so proud of you, sweetie! (That ref made a bad call!) Kisses and love —Mom

I snorted softly, knowing very well she had no clue about the ref's bad call. In her opinion, all calls against me were bad—well, except for the one that got me suspended.

The next text was from Gray.

Dude. You were slow.

I rolled my eyes and grinned. That was his way of saying good game.

Lastly, a lengthy message from Mad.

I missed the second period because I've discovered I can't catch your games with your folks in the same room. I had to go home before your body checks gave me a fucking heart attack. How many times every game do you have to slam into the boards or ram someone else against there? Christ. Call me when you get home.

His concern never failed to tug at my heartstrings, and I missed him so much it bordered on insane.

Five days. Five fucking days. He was coming up to see me here in Vancouver on Friday night, and he'd told me we were gonna check in to a hotel. We'd have the whole weekend to ourselves.

We still hadn't fucked. With two clean bills of health, it was a top priority for both of us—thank fuck—but I couldn't deny I needed a hell of a lot more than that. The second he arrived, I was gonna throw myself at him and ask him to never let go. Skype was nowhere near enough, only resulting in physical aches of desolation. And we'd discovered I didn't respond well to online play or phone sex. I was just a miserable person. He could get me going quickly, and then...then

I'd remember he wasn't actually here with me, and I'd lose all traces of lust.

"Hayes!"

I snapped up my head and spotted Erik, who was about to enter the shower room. "What's up?"

"We picking up food on the way home?" he asked.

I nodded. He was one of my two roommates, though most of us who weren't originally from the area—or planning to settle down—lived in the same neighborhood. In fact, Bellamy and one of his boyfriends lived on the floor below ours.

Today hadn't been a superb game, nor was it of much significance. It meant there was very little activity in the dressing room—no press, no extra camera time, and the coaches had better things to do. Tomorrow was a gym day and then practice, before we headed to California the following day for a game against Anaheim.

At least I'd get to see Jesse this time. He'd canceled on me —the dirtbag—when we were in LA to play the Kings. If he blew me off this week, I'd punch him. Or tell Dad.

"You gonna call *Daddy*?" Erik passed me in the hallway and aimed for the kitchen, and he rounded the corner before I could kick his ass. "Oh Daddy, oh Daddy, punish me!"

"Keep it up, asshole," I hollered. I dumped my gear by the door, then carried my food to the kitchen. Erik was snickering to himself as he opened his container of chicken, rice, and steamed vegetables. I'd ordered the same. "You haven't heard me say that," I told him. "Prick."

He chuckled and opened a drawer under the kitchen island. "It's what I imagine you say when you talk to him."

I accepted a fork and opened my own Styrofoam box. "Imagine that a lot, do you?"

Erik was a cool guy. Swedish player, a great center, and open-minded. He was also constantly trying to one-up Bellamy and me, so it tended to be the two of us against Erik when we dicked around. Erik was a little taller and bigger; he could handle it.

"Every night, princess." He snorted.

I rolled my eyes and tucked into my food.

"Use the fucking chair." He pointed at the stool next to me. "You are not an animal."

"Daddy says I am," I said with a wink. Then I slid onto the stool anyway and pulled out my phone. "Is Corbin staying with his girlfriend again?" It was our other roommate, and he wasn't around much.

"Probably." Erik left his seat and headed for the fridge where he grabbed us two bottles of water. "By the way, are the Rangers picking you up?"

I furrowed my brow and uncapped the water. "Uh, no? Why would they?"

He shrugged. "Rumor going around that they want you."

I narrowed my eyes at that. The Rangers were obviously a terrific team, but I wasn't gonna move all the way across the country again. The reason I'd signed with the Canucks was because it was close to home. You didn't really commute from New York.

"What kind of rumor?" I knew he was dating the GM's niece or something, so it must've come from there.

"I can ask if you want."

I hesitated, then shook my head. "Doesn't matter. Even if they're interested, I'm good here." And there was no way Vancouver would get rid of me. I'd secured my position in a short period of time and was too valuable.

"It's like you're trying not to win a Cup," he chuckled.

Yeah, I was one of those players. Vancouver wasn't the best team in the league—pretty fucking far from it—but I liked it here. I was hoping to make this my team permanently. Right now, my contract was for two years.

We ate in silence for a while, and when he started texting his girlfriend, I figured I might as well call Mad. Except, before I could, I got a text from Jesse.

You flying down tomorrow?

I wasn't planning on it, though I could.

I can if u take me to dinner

I actually hoped he would. I missed him a lot. And if I flew down early, I could crash at his place.

Jesse's response made me happy.

Buy a ticket. I'll even pick you up at the airport.

I grinned and immediately called Dad 'cause he had all the status and knew what airline was best. When we traveled with the team, we usually went the chartered route, meaning I never got into the whole thing of booking tickets. It made me anxious to even try to understand the systems the airlines used.

"What airport you going to?" Dad asked. "Never mind. Jesse picking you up?"

"Yeah." I shoveled chicken and broccoli into my mouth. "Are you by the computer?"

"Yup, in your room."

"Uh, why?" I didn't like the sound of that at all.

"Because I was putting Lyn to bed. Yours was closest."

Okay, next time I was home, I was changing my password. It wasn't secret anymore.

"Nice background..." he muttered.

I smirked around another mouthful of food. If he didn't wanna see three men grabbing their junk, he could use his own fucking computer. He should count himself lucky I didn't have a picture of Madigan there.

"When do you wanna go?" he asked.

"Afternoon, if that works," I replied. "I have practice before."

As Dad took care of things, I gestured to Erik I was gonna finish dinner in my room. He nodded absently, busy with his girlfriend, and I left the kitchen.

Both Corbin and Erik had been on my ass to do something with my room, yet the reluctance kept me from going there. Clothes and shit were unpacked, but I didn't have much furniture. The walls were empty. I had three photos on my nightstand, that was it. One of Jesse, Lyn, and me. One of all of us, including Ellis, Casey, Mad, and Pop from Christmas a few years ago. One of Mad and me from my high school graduation.

"Okay, all set," Dad said. "I'll send you the details."

"Thanks," I answered, getting comfortable on the bed. I turned on the TV and placed the food on my lap. "Did you put me in first class?"

"Yeah, unlike your brother, you don't fly economy to make a political statement."

I snickered. Jesse didn't reject Dad's money as much as Dad would think, but yeah...my brother was stubborn. Before —like, way back—Jesse and I came from absolutely nothing. My brother said first class was wasteful.

After promising I'd do my best to "talk sense" into Jesse, we hung up, and I called Madigan right away. I found a music station on the TV and bobbed my head to the beat of some Taylor Swift while waiting for him to answer. Music was a last resort to keep my mood where I wanted it. Well, extra medication was the last resort, but music was just as temporary. Both wore off quickly.

The second Mad picked up, my stomach dropped and my chest constricted.

"Hey, trouble."

I miss you, I miss you, I miss you.

"Hi," I managed. It wasn't fucking fair. We'd gotten a few days together, nowhere near enough to keep me satisfied until Friday. "I got a small bruise on my leg today. You should come up here and take care of me."

"Thank you for confirming that my boy engages in a lethal sport," he started by saying, and I *almost* rolled my eyes. "And if I remember correctly, I've offered to come up for the night, oh…about half a dozen times already?"

Yeah, maybe. I was the one who said no, because it would be wonderful for five minutes before I had to say goodbye to him again and go back to suffering. It legit felt like my heart was going to break.

No longer hungry, I set the container on the nightstand and fidgeted with one of the drawstrings of my sweats.

"Abel?" There was concern in Mad's voice, and I chewed on the inside of my cheek. The pressure kept building in my chest. I hated it. "Tell me what's wrong."

I lifted a shoulder, even though he couldn't see me. "I feel like we got interrupted. And this isn't even about the sex that much. It was just so soon, only a f-few days, and then—"

"I know, baby," he murmured. "We didn't get enough cuddles."

That was it. I wanted him to give me those superhard Madigan hugs, like when he held me all night and kissed me and stuff. That was what I ached for.

"Distance makes the heart grow fucking miserable," I complained. My eyes welled up, which only angered me. I couldn't do what I wanted here. Not when I was alone. If I'd had Mad here...I could've cried or bitched or... I didn't even know, but he would've taken care of me. "I *hate* this. And I know I'm selfish and a pain in the ass—"

"*Hey.*" The warning in his voice wasn't lost on me, and I shut my mouth and glared at nothing. "What have I told you about berating yourself, Abel?"

My shoulders slumped, and I sniffled. "That I'm not supposed to."

"That's right. Now, do you trust me?"

I blew out a breath. "You know I do."

"Good. Then be strong for me until I see you this weekend. I'll fix this, okay?"

How the hell was he gonna do that? He had a business to run, one he was very passionate about, and I was on the road so often. No matter what, I wouldn't get what I wanted until the off-season. Shit, I was gonna end up hoping we never made it to the play-offs.

Even so, I trusted Mad. If he thought he had a solution... perhaps he did. "Okay," I whispered. "I'll be strong."

"That's my boy. And hey, you're gonna have fun with your brother, aren't you? You'll see him before the game?"

His attempt to brighten my mood warmed me up, and I smiled a little. "Yeah, I'm flying down tomorrow. I'm gonna make him take me to my favorite place with the fried chicken."

"That sounds fun. Much more fun than getting punished by me anyway."

I scrunched my nose. "Punished?" I hadn't done anything wrong, though. Was he being silly? He was silly sometimes.

He chuckled. "Funished is more like it, but we can save that for the weekend." Now he was a damn sadist! The anticipation was going to bug me. "I want you to have a good time in LA with Jesse first." He paused and cleared his throat. "Do...do you want me to transfer some money that you have to spend on something fun?"

What? I cocked my head. Wait... "Oh," I mouthed to myself.

Madigan knew very well I had my own money, and no shortage of it. No, this wasn't about that, was it? He was testing the waters, and this was all about our relationship with him as the Daddy and me as the little boy. And I'd read about allowances in D/s arrangements.

The gesture was not only symbolic, but it made my eyes water again. I fucking *yearned*.

"Yes," I admitted, feeling weirdly vulnerable. I couldn't understand my body's reaction, only that I had the biggest urge to hide my face in that warm curve of his neck and burrow in real close. "I've, um...I've read about it." I fidgeted with my earlobe and forced out the rest of the words. "There was a Daddy who gave his girl a weekly allowance, and she spent it on toys and ice cream and stuff."

"Yeah?" His smile was unmistakable. I didn't need to see his face to know it was there. "You wanna do that, baby?"

Jesus Christ, I really loved it when he called me baby. It was one of the most common terms of endearment, but I'd dreamed about being his this way for so long that it was exactly what I wanted. That, and being his trouble and sweetheart and little hell-raiser.

"Yeah." I smiled to myself and wondered why I felt so... so...*shy*. It was the best word to describe it. "And, like, I can buy you a present."

He laughed softly, and the sound was the best. It was comforting. Falling back against the pillows, I closed my eyes and pretended he was right here next to me with his warm chuckle tickling my ear.

"You have no idea how happy you make me, Abel." He let out a sigh of contentment, and it sounded like he was getting comfortable in bed too. "I completely zoned out today at work. Jameson had to kick my leg."

I giggled under my breath, picturing him messing up a tattoo or something. Of course, knowing him, he would never do that. Still, it was a funny thought.

"I think about you a gazillion times a day, so I win." I spoke through a yawn.

"I think I won already," he murmured. "Did you have dinner tonight?"

"Yessir." I bunched up my pillow a bit and snuggled into it.

"Tired?"

"Mmhmm, but I wanna hear your voice."

"That can be arranged, but you gotta brush your teeth first."

Ugh. "I can wait till tomorrow, just this once."

"You can, but you won't." An ounce of Daddy sternness seeped into his tone. "You'll be a good boy and obey when I tell you to do something."

It was possible I may have whined. Whatever. "It's so nice here, though—"

"Abel."

"Jeesh!" I moped and dragged myself out of bed. "Daddy Buzzkill."

The bastard laughed.

CHAPTER 13

It felt *so* nice to be met by heat in LA. It was hot compared to Vancouver anyway. It was T-shirt weather for someone from the north, and I didn't even wear sweatpants today. I'd dug out a pair of cargo shorts that ended mid-calf, 'cause they had lots of pockets. I didn't like traveling with too much luggage. Other than my wallet and passport and phone and whatnot, I'd stashed a pair of clean briefs, my toothbrush, and fresh socks in my pockets.

My earbuds hung out from the inside of my T-shirt, and I'd tied my hoodie around my hips.

"I can't see you." I held my phone to my ear as I scanned the crowded street for signs of Jesse. "Should I walk closer to—"

"Driving up behind the cabstand in about thirty seconds," my brother replied.

That was what I was gonna suggest, that I go closer to the cabstand. Easier to swoop in for a two-second parking spot there. Sidestepping and dodging the sidewalk that was flooded with travelers and their house-sized luggage, I made my way over to the cabs, and I told Jesse I was ready to jump in.

He ended the call right as I spotted his car, an SUV I was pretty sure Mom still didn't know that Dad had given him.

I smiled widely at the sight of my brother behind the wheel. We shared the same traits that we'd gotten from our biological father—mops of unruly brown hair with natural highlights, blue eyes that somehow were always popular with girls, and straight noses. Only, mine had been broken a couple times, and my two front teeth were implants.

All my life, people had said I was the boyish version of Jesse, but that was just 'cause he walked around with a permanent scowl. Even when he was happy, there seemed to be something wrong. He was only eight years older than me, yet he brooded like he was sixty.

I stepped out and gave him a two-finger wave, and he nodded and pulled in.

I figured I had ten seconds to hug the crap out of him since I didn't have to waste time stowing away luggage, so that was exactly what I did. I got in the car and threw my arms around him, catching him off guard, and earned myself a surprised laugh.

"You're a douchebag," I said lightly.

He knew why I said it too. He didn't suck at texting me, but calling and coming home? Nope.

In response, he hugged me harder for a quick beat.

It was a good time to notice there was a child in the back seat. What the fuck? The shock came to me slowly, as if I couldn't believe it at first. There was actually a kid there. A little girl was strapped in tight, watching me with a curious expression.

"Dude." I eased away. "I don't wanna alarm you, but there's a little person in the back seat."

Jesse cast an amused look over his shoulder. "That's Avielle." He gripped the wheel again and pulled away from the sidewalk. "Avielle, this is my little brother, Abel."

This cleared up absolutely nothing.

"Hi," the girl said shyly.

"Hello." I kept looking between her and Jesse.

"Jesse say you play hockey," she revealed. "And you're superfast."

Well, Jesse's said nothing about you.

She couldn't be more than four or five. Her eyes were an incredible emerald color, and her hair was messy and dirty blond. She wore a pink tee with the words "Don't Kiss Me. I'm Irish, and I'll Knock Yer Teeth Out."

My mouth twisted up.

"You wanna eat, honey?" Jesse asked Avielle. He was watching her in the rearview.

I realized I hadn't responded to her, though it was too late now. Maybe because I'd been fucking railroaded by this whole thing. Instead, I faced forward and put on my seat belt.

"Mommy promised me bacon," Avielle replied frankly.

Jesse chuckled. "I'm aware." He smirked faintly and addressed me next. "Girl's obsessed with bacon."

"I don't know who you are," I said.

That sobered him up, and he cleared his throat. "I'll explain everything, okay?"

Looking forward to that.

Jesse lived in a nice neighborhood in Santa Monica, only a few blocks away from the beach, but before we headed there, we picked up food and dropped off the girl. I stayed in the car while Jesse knocked on the door to what looked like a shut-down bar, and a woman opened it. They exchanged words, and it looked like they knew each other well. And whoever she was, she made my brother smile. In fact, he couldn't really tear his gaze away from her.

She was obviously Avielle's mom. Short and very, very curvy, with a cheeky grin. It was too dark, so I couldn't see much else.

Jesse nodded at something and stepped back, then extended the bag of food he'd bought. He said something else and jerked his thumb my way, at which the woman squinted toward the car.

Why wouldn't he tell us he had a girlfriend? It had to be serious if a kid was involved.

Mom would be fucking ecstatic.

Jesse seemed to hesitate about something for a second, which wasn't like him at all, and then he dipped down and kissed the woman's cheek. His hand went to her hip quickly before he backed away. It was a sweet moment, one that was totally foreign to me. Where he was concerned, that was.

I was gonna grill the fuck out of him.

After ruffling Avielle's hair, Jesse returned to the car, and he probably saw all the questions written across my forehead.

"So...are you gonna tell Mom and Dad they're grandparents now, or...?" I lifted my brows.

He frowned and started the car. "What? I babysit a friend's kid and suddenly I'm a dad?"

I laughed. "That's funny."

"I'm not kidding." The crease between his brows deepened. "Cass—Avi's mom—is a friend. She's also my girlfriend's baby sister."

"Oh," I mouthed. If possible, my eyebrows went even higher.

The plot thickens.

Jesse thought we were done there. He said he assumed I was hungry—accurate assumption—and promised he'd take me to my favorite place tomorrow. It was getting late, at least too late to go far, so I agreed to our regular tradition.

Tradition might be a stretch. We didn't see each other often enough, but we'd done it a handful of times. And that was to hit up a pizza place and eat on the beach. Said beach was only five minutes away if you avoided traffic, and our way to do that was by skateboarding.

Once we were at his house, we parked in the garage and grabbed our boards.

I didn't have one at home, saving it for whenever I was here. Better streets and weather for it.

Jesse put on a baseball cap too, twisting it backward.

"They've collected dust," I said. Expected with mine, though I'd thought he still used his.

"Yeah, it's been a while."

Disappointing. He used to do awesome tricks. He'd take me to a skate park sometimes and show me.

I emptied my pockets of luggage items, making Jesse chuckle, and then we left again. I was rusty, but it came back pretty quick.

There were no cars around. Closing my eyes for a couple seconds, I breathed in deeply as the street slanted into a hill.

"It's good to see you, Abel."

I opened my eyes again and nodded with a dip of my chin. I knew I'd told Dad I was gonna try to get Jesse to visit more often, yet now that I was here, I couldn't. It would be the same old song and dance. Jesse would swear he'd do better, something that never happened. He ventured up to Washington maybe twice a year. I saw him a bit more frequently because I had games here, either against Anaheim or the Kings. Dad saw him on the rare occasion he had business in LA, and he usually brought Mom along, and Madigan had met up with Jesse for dinner once or twice too.

Ellis and Casey had checked in on him after the holidays. Once again, Jesse had made empty promises.

"I wish we could have what we used to," I settled for saying. "I wish Lyn could see..." *what an awesome brother you used to be.*

Jesse didn't answer. The only indication that he'd heard me was the trouble lines in his forehead and between his brows.

At the next turn, we reached a more trafficked street that led straight to 4th Street, and conversation was impossible for a bit. We navigated between cars and the evening crowd, never really stopping. When the light turned green for pedestrians, we skated through the walking herd before reaching the next street.

Jesse took the lead, and it didn't take us more than a few minutes to arrive at the best pizza place in Santa Monica. They had all kinds and sold them by the slice. I stayed outside while my brother filled a box to make up a large pie we could share.

As I waited for him, I decided to send Madigan a message —except, he'd already texted me, and I reread it with a puzzled expression. It just said "Stoked and missing you," and there was a picture of what looked like a hotel keycard trapped between his fingers.

Stoked about what? Where was he? My stomach twisted with butterflies; was he in LA?

I quickly typed a response, hopeful as hell.

Where r u? I miss u! are u at a hotel?

Holy crap, it would make my day if he came down to watch the game tomorrow night.

Madigan answered as I spied Jesse paying for the pizza inside the shop.

It's a secret. You'll see this weekend.

Dammit.

I jutted out my bottom lip and sent him a picture of my pout.

For a second I thought u were here :((((

That was a good caption, I thought. Friggin' secrets... I *hated* secrets. I could keep them well, but this kind was torture. Now it was kept from me. Not cool. Besides, we'd already made plans to spend the weekend at a hotel, so what was so secret about this? Though...it was strange he already had a keycard...

I made a confused face. If he had a key—which was completely blank—he would have to be in Vancouver already, and that made *no* sense.

His response popped up.

You are too fucking cute for words. Sorry I got your hopes up, but trust me, it'll be worth it. Can't wait to see my troublemaker.

"Evidently you *can* wait," I mumbled to myself. From the corner of my eye, I saw Jesse grabbing the pizza box and pocketing his credit card. Oh...credit card—I looked around me for an ATM. Then I typed a quick text.

Daddy = meanie and sadist

I pocketed my phone after sending it off, and Jesse joined me on the sidewalk.

"Oh, man." Even from here, I could smell the cheese and spices. My stomach rumbled in response. "Can we go to the ATM before the beach?" There was one across the street.

"Uh, yeah, sure." His forehead creased in confusion.

"People still use cash sometimes," I defended.

"If you say so." He grabbed his board.

There was fifty dollars from Mad on my debit card, and I grinned as I slipped the bills into my wallet. Despite his abhorrent behavior of keeping secrets from me, I was going to buy him the *best* gift before I went home.

Jesse and I hit our boards and went down along Santa Monica Boulevard until we reached Ocean Avenue and the bridge to get to the pier. It was impossible to skate there, so we had to join the gazillion tourists and walk for a minute or two. Then we took the first set of stairs down to the beach, at which point I was almost nauseated with hunger.

"So, does the team bring your gear or something?" Jesse asked. "For tomorrow, I mean."

Who cared? "Yeah. Pizza, pizza, pizza. Gimme."

He chuckled, and we found a place to sit that wasn't too far away from the lights of the pier.

"Will you come to the game?" I asked as he put the box between us.

He nodded while I got busy. There was a thick slice dripping with cheese and pepperoni that had my name on it, and he grabbed a slice with what looked like peppers and mushrooms.

"I was gonna ask," he said. "Think you can get me an extra ticket?"

"Sure." I crammed the tip of the slice into my mouth, and I groaned in pleasure. The hot cheese burned my tongue, and I couldn't give one fuck. "Is that for the not-stepdaughter, the not-girlfriend you were eye-fucking, or the girlfriend?"

He sighed and extended a napkin. "Don't eat too fast. It upsets your stomach."

My brother could be cute. He walked around like he didn't care about the world; he was rough around the edges and shrugged more than...someone who shrugged a lot. But he fucking *loved* to take care of people. More than that, he loved kids. When I was little, he was always there. The second I had a panic attack or fell into depression, he was at my side. And I was the reason he ultimately went off to college to become a social worker. So, he cared. He cared a lot. I just...I didn't know why his family was an exception.

"Thanks." I used the napkin and wiped my mouth. "Well...?"

He sighed again and made it obvious by the look in his eyes that he didn't like my question. Tough shit. "It's for Avi. I thought I'd take you both to dinner after the game. Unless you're flying out right away."

I wasn't sure, and it didn't matter. I couldn't come to LA without visiting the place that had the best fried chicken on the West Coast. Worst-case scenario, I took a later flight.

"Babysitting again?" I bit into the rest of my slice.

He was quiet for a beat, mulling something over as he ate, and I waited him out. He had to say *something*. He couldn't completely shut me out.

"I lost my job."

I coughed, half choking on a piece of pepperoni. "Wh-what?" No way. "How?"

Jesse returned his half-eaten piece to the box and removed his cap to run a hand through his hair. "I've fucked up a lot, Abel. The only reason I haven't told you guys is 'cause I've been so goddamn embarrassed. Still am." He paused and brushed some sand off his leg. "I don't wanna get into it too much right now—I'm working on getting through shit, but I used to drink."

My appetite was effectively ruined.

"What?" My voice was all but dead, and I was flooded with fear and anxiety.

"I don't anymore." He was quick to reach out and squeeze

my shoulder in reassurance, though it didn't help much. I'd been shielded from a lot of problems growing up, but I could remember some of it. Mom used to have a problem with addiction—from before our biological father died and Jesse and I were adopted. Dad—Lincoln—had struggled with alcohol like forever ago too. Though, I had no memories of that. Only of Mom, right before she got help. Because her stepdad had been an abusive asshole.

If she knew Jesse was addicted, she'd be crushed. So would Dad, and I... God, I didn't know how I felt, only that it hurt.

"You're—" I swallowed heavily. "You're an alcoholic?"

He winced and let his arm fall. "Technically, yeah. But I haven't touched a drop in four months. It's gotten a lot easier."

My eyes welled up rapidly, and my brain started spinning. This wasn't fucking okay.

"This has been g-going on while none of us knew?" I croaked.

His lips parted, only for him to close his mouth just as fast.

"Answer me," I demanded.

"Yeah." Suddenly, he looked a lot older than twenty-nine. "I'm so fucking sorry, Abel. I know I've handled this wrong, but I'm fixing it, okay? I'm gonna fess up to Mom and D—Lincoln, too."

I made a noise of anger and frustration and punched his arm. "He's your goddamn dad, you stupid asshole!"

I was so sick of this. Both Mom and Dad—mainly Dad—had told me to stay out of it and not be too hard on Jesse, but fuck it all. I could understand that it was difficult to come into a new family, and there was a man taking on the father role, while the previous dad was dead in the ground. I *understood* that. I'd been there. Only, I'd been much younger. It'd been easier for me to adapt. But Jesus Christ, it'd been almost fifteen years since Morgan died. Closing in on ten years since I hyphenated my name to take Hayes too.

Dad had earned his title ten times over; he'd put Jesse through college and currently paid for his fucking house. I couldn't *believe* Jesse still struggled to accept Lincoln, and before I even knew it was happening, the words tumbled out of me.

I ranted to Jesse about his stupid hypocrisy. He couldn't accept this and that, yet he had no problems letting Dad buy him a house and maintain his lifestyle in LA. Jesse drove around in a nice car Dad had paid for, but coming home occasionally and, oh, I don't know, showing some motherfucking appreciation was too much to ask?

Jesse took my angry assault like a champ. He sat there and listened, every now and then offering small nods and "I know, little brother."

"You have to fix this," I gritted.

"I *will*. I'm done making promises. I know they don't mean anything anymore, so I'll show you instead." He shifted a few inches closer and rubbed my neck. "This is all on me, and I'm gonna make things right with him too."

I shook my head. "Cop-out. Him, who? Say it."

He blew out a breath. "Dad. I'll make things right with Dad."

My shoulders sagged, and I looked down at my lap, still too anxious.

"I fucked up a long time ago," he said quietly. "And instead of working it out then, I chickened out and started drinking. I hid."

"What do you mean?" In my opinion, he continued to fuck up.

"I mean that I've been wanting to come home for years."

His jaw tensed as he averted his gaze, and he gathered his hands in his lap and cracked his knuckles. "I've just been a coward."

So he wanted to move home to Washington? I could work with this. I sniffled and perked up slightly.

"Did you lose your job because you drank?" I asked.

He nodded. "That was how I met Cass. It was literally the day she arrived here to move in with Laura—that's her sister. We didn't even get through introductions before she asked if I was heading into work while drunk. And I guess Laura had told her I worked with kids."

It dawned on me, and this Cass woman suddenly became my favorite person in LA. "Cass reported you, didn't she?"

Another nod. "She called my boss, and I was fired on the spot."

"Wow."

I hadn't met the woman, yet I felt enough relief to believe that maybe, just maybe, she would make sure Jesse followed through on his not-promises. He was gonna show me instead.

"You're not allowed to drink," I stated. "Seriously, if I hear about you having a single beer, I'll freak the fuck out."

He smiled faintly. "I'm not gonna drink, Abel. That's one promise I'm never going to break. Avi made me pinkie swear."

Babysitting, my ass.

I couldn't be sure how much that kid meant to him, but it was more than babysitting for a friend. Knowing him, he missed working with children.

"Can you keep this between you and me until I'm ready?" he asked hesitantly.

Great, that put me on edge again. "It's not gonna get easier, Jesse. What're you waiting for?"

He should be on the first flight home to tell our parents everything.

"It's...it's complicated. It concerns Cass and Avi—partly, anyway—and..." He struggled to find his words. "I have some things I gotta work out before."

That didn't appease me for crap, so I would need something. Narrowing my eyes, I thought of progress—baby steps he could take. Maybe he didn't have to tell Mom and Dad yet. There were others. Actually, he didn't have to tell anyone anything, but he did have to start treating us like family again.

"I have conditions," I said.

"Great," he muttered. The small twist of his mouth showed he wasn't entirely dismayed. "Let's hear 'em."

"You have to come up and visit me in Vancouver." I figured that would take some pressure off. Partly, I would see him more often. Partly, it would prepare him for the next step. "Yeah—that's it. You gotta come to two of my games this season." What was left of it. "And you gotta call more often."

"All right," he replied slowly.

He was right to look cautious, 'cause I wasn't done.

"We have a charity game in three weeks against the Caps. You gotta be there, and you have to bring a guest."

That made him suspicious. "Why a guest?"

Because it was a great opportunity to get parts of the family together for one day, without our folks being there. "We don't know anything about you, bro. That's gotta change." I shrugged. "Dad's taking Mom to Rome that week, so they can't make it. But Mad and Lyn will be there."

I had no idea why Jesse felt the need to think it over. If he didn't agree, I was gonna snitch.

"I could bring Avi." He put his cap on again. "All right, we'll be there."

Feeling marginally better, I picked up another slice of pizza. "You seem awfully invested in the kid you babysit."

He chuckled under his breath. "Yeah, maybe. It'll be good

for her, though. I want her to spend as much time as possible with you."

"Huh?" I cocked my head and chewed on the delicious barbecue chicken piece. "Why me?"

Jesse followed suit and grabbed a slice. "Because she was recently diagnosed with cyclothymia, and it's made her insecure."

"I don't know what that is."

He half smiled. "It means she has a lot in common with you. It's on the BPD spectrum, a milder case." Oh, damn. "She's a little too young to understand it, but she knows she's different."

"That sucks." For her to have been diagnosed early meant the symptoms were clear enough. It meant she had medical trials to suffer through, and I didn't envy her that, no matter how mild her disorder was.

"I told her a lot about you," Jesse said. "She soaks it up."

"Really?" I perked up more.

"Of course." He nodded. "I think it matters to her to know that different doesn't mean bad. She struggles the most with her depressive episodes, and seeing you on TV is a comfort."

Now I felt bad I hadn't talked to her in the car. Thankfully, I'd see her again tomorrow. Since I knew firsthand how alienating it could be to have a mental disorder, the last thing I wanted was for someone to feel like I didn't care.

"Anyway," Jesse said, "enough about me. How are you? You seeing anyone?"

Thank fuck the beach was dark and he couldn't see my cheeks heating up. Did I have to tell him? He'd been secretive for so long. Surely, I didn't owe him anything yet.

"Um, everything's good." I nodded slowly, picking a piece of chicken from the pizza.

The biggest problem right now was that my brother knew

I was into BDSM. I'd told him about it once, and he'd been concerned. So...I'd elaborated quite a bit in order to ease his worries. For instance, he knew this wasn't merely something I got off on. It was the D/s lifestyle, which meant that whenever I introduced him to a boyfriend, Jesse would know the dude was a bit more than that.

"Abel...?"

"Maybe I'm dating someone." I spoke in a rush, then quickly filled my mouth with pizza.

He chuckled. "And? Tell me about the guy. He better be treating you well."

"I don't wanna." My words were muffled.

"Why? Is there something wrong with him?"

"No!" I scowled and swallowed the doughy lump. "He's amazing and perfect."

He both smirked and scrunched his nose. "Then what's the problem?"

I huffed. Did I tell him now or when he came to Vancouver? Ugh. Maybe I should get it over with. Like Jesse, I had to take baby steps before I fessed up to Mom and Dad.

"You know him," I mumbled.

"Oh." His brow furrowed. "It can't be Gray. He doesn't strike me as...uh, what you want."

Blurt it out, blurt it out. I screwed my eyes shut and hoped for the best. "It's Madigan."

Silence.

For a drawn-out moment, I only heard the background noise from the pier. People shouting and laughing, music playing, and mechanical sound effects from the arcade games and joyrides.

"Say something." I cracked one eye open, then the other.

Jesse was staring at me with a blank expression, and since he was facing away from the pier, his features were darker. I couldn't tell if there was any anger or disgust or…whatever.

"Madigan," he said. "Our Madigan, the Madigan you said you were gonna marry when you were a kid—*that* Madigan?"

"Yes." I found myself holding my breath and watching him warily.

The way I saw it, Jesse's reaction would set the tone for how the others would react. Maybe not Casey and Ellis; the former probably already knew, and the latter was kinder than Santa Claus without a Naughty list. Mom and Dad, on the other hand… They would react twenty times worse than Jesse.

"*Jesus.*" The word left him in a whoosh, and he ran a hand through his hair, knocking off his cap in the process. "Are you —you're actually—I mean—*Madigan.*"

I quickly grew antsy and impatient. "*Yes*, Jesse. Are you gonna say something or just sit there and stutter?"

"I'm gonna sit here and stutter," he snapped. "Christ, Abel. You gotta realize this is a shock."

"Yeah, but are you mad at me? Do you think Mom and Dad will hate me? Or worse, hate him?"

That seemed to take the fight out of him, if there ever was one. "I…I don't—" He sighed heavily. "I can't picture them accepting this right away, but they would never hate you. Or Madigan, for that matter."

I wasn't comforted by that, despite that I knew it was going to be rough.

I hated, hated, hated when people argued and got upset. It made me very anxious, and I *felt* emotions from others. I could pick up the tension in a room crazy easily, and it was suffocating when that tension was filled with anger and pain. It landed like a heavy blanket over my chest.

"I love him," I said quietly. "This is serious. And he's so good to me. He knows me better than anyone."

He scrubbed a hand over his face. "How long has this been going on?"

"Not long. Just a few weeks. It took for-fucking-ever to wear him down."

He gave a tired chuckle. "Believe it or not, that's a good thing."

Oh, please. I rolled my eyes. Why were people so damn concerned about my "virtue"? How about caring about my happiness first? No, they had to make sure an experienced man hadn't preyed on me.

"It'll take some getting used to," he admitted. "But when push comes to shove, you know I'm on your side, right? As long as he's good for you and you're happy, I've got no complaints."

"Thank you." I took a breath and nodded. Mad and I had to face the biggest obstacles yet, Mom and Dad, but I was glad Jesse knew.

CHAPTER 14

The next forty-eight hours were a whirlwind. Between the game against Anaheim, dinner with Jesse and Avielle, and flying back to Vancouver and spending nine consecutive hours in the gym, I was so beat.

Friday arrived, and I didn't think I was going to pull through. With Mad's permission—and Coach's—I slept in and skipped morning practice, and then I had to have Erik's help to get me mentally ready for the game. We played against Edmonton, and it was my fault we sucked the first period.

I was frazzled and unable to stop looking at the clock. My diet hadn't been the best today either. I'd missed two meals, so my stomach was a little upset. I could sense my own despondency growing, and I hadn't been completely honest with Madigan. Every time I told him I missed him, it was a shot at him. I felt it. He hated it when I was sad. As a result, I'd fronted and told him I was somewhat okay.

The good thing was that personal failures made me angry, and I could channel that. During the second period, I pushed Madigan out of my head—and the fact that I'd see him in less than two hours—and I became worthy of being on the first line again.

By the third period, the game had swallowed me whole.

I winced, then gritted my teeth as an Oiler got away with boarding, and Bellamy, standing next to me, shouted to the ref in outrage. Our guy got up and rolled his shoulders, to which I glanced at Coach. Was it our turn yet or what? I'd rested enough. There were a couple Oilers I'd like to send back to Edmonton with bruises.

The signal came after icing was called, and I adjusted my mouthguard and hit the ice with Bellamy and Erik.

"Thirty-six!" Erik yelled at us over the music.

We already knew. The Czech player with thirty-six on his jersey was gonna be my snack.

I got into position on the left, and Erik skated up to the center to take the face-off. Way behind us, we had our goalie hollering warnings, and Bellamy adjusted his position accordingly. The second the puck was dropped, the music died, and I flew toward Thirty-Six.

Erik passed the puck to me, and I spun around, skating backward to cover myself from the two players approaching. Where was he—? There. Thirty-Six got closer and closer, and I narrowed my eyes. *Come at me, needle dick.*

"Ready!" Erik shouted.

"Got you." Bellamy skated up behind me to assist.

Right as Thirty-Six made a move to check me, I flipped the puck between my legs to Bellamy, and he fled with it. The arena exploded. Then I quickly shot my elbow up into Thirty-Six's chin and laughed my ass off, 'cause all the refs saw was him ramming into me.

"Son of a bitch!" he growled and tumbled over.

I'd already forgotten him, racing past the defense line to join Erik and Bellamy.

I got the puck again when Erik circled the net, and I passed it swiftly to Bellamy.

"Back now!" Erik's command rang higher than the background shouts from the other players, and Bell got him the puck. Exchanging a look with Erik, I deked left and found an open spot. A second later, the puck was mine, and I shot it straight between the goalie's legs.

The familiar goal horn sounded, followed by the heavy drums of Green Day's "Holiday," and I found myself smashed by my teammates.

My name was blasted across the arena.

I grinned and knocked gloves with everyone as the huddle dissolved, and I made sure to skate past a pissed-looking Thirty-Six.

"I'll get you next time, Hayes," he growled.

Unable to help myself, I skidded to a stop and circled him. "Promises, promises. Why don't you just go home and eat your mom's ass? Fuckin' inbred." I skated away from him and his yelling, awfully pleased with myself.

I was out of the arena first chance I got, "forgetting" the press interviews and dodging the fans outside. While I was in the shower, Mad had texted the directions to the hotel we were staying at, and I wasn't too surprised he'd picked one near the harbor. Our first weekend together in ages—we were gonna do it up in style.

I drove home quickly to drop off one bag and pack another, and then I was gone again. It was a wonder I didn't get caught by the police, 'cause I broke like four traffic regulations. My heart rate had barely slowed down, and my body reacted as if I was still in the middle of the game.

"Come on, shithead!" I punched the wheel, stuck behind someone who clearly shouldn't be on the road. My breathing picked up. I'd run out of patience a long time ago, and I knew I didn't have long before I'd be fighting a rage fit.

The frustration was at an all-time high.

And a Friday night in the harbor in Vancouver…? Fuck my motherfucking life. It was a tourist trap surrounded by skyscrapers and a glittering marina.

When I finally arrived at the waterfront hotel, I breathed a sigh of relief at the sight of the valet. I wouldn't have to drive myself crazy looking for a parking spot.

I rolled up to the lavish entrance and happily handed over the keys.

"Welcome to the Seaside V Suites, sir. Checking in or—" He paused and eyed my car. "Abel Hayes, by any chance?"

Shit. "Yeah," I replied warily. I was too anxious and strung tight to deal with Canucks fans.

The man retrieved something from his pocket and smiled. "Mr. Monroe told us you were arriving soon and wanted me to give you this."

Madigan was a goddamn angel. I exhaled heavily and accepted the room key. Now I wouldn't have to stop by the check-in desk. "Thank you."

"Seventeenth floor, suite 1706. Any luggage you'd like for us to bring up?"

I shook my head and opened the back to grab my duffel. "No, I'm good. Thanks." After getting a ticket for my car, I entered the hotel and went straight for the elevators.

My entire being buzzed with anticipation on the way up. The elevator was made of glass and offered a more spectacular view of the harbor for every floor I ascended.

Halfway up, I glanced down and opened my hand. The keycard was completely white, had no text on it whatsoever, and matched the one Madigan had sent a picture of when I was in LA.

Had he been here already this week?

The elevator dinged and slowed to a stop. My stomach flip-flopped, and for a second, my legs were frozen. *What's wrong with you? Go to him!* I was such a loser. But I just knew I was going to embarrass myself when I saw him. I could feel the emotions bubbling up already, putting pressure on my chest and making it difficult to swallow.

Suite 1706 was easy to find and faced the same side as the elevators. I'd only passed a couple doors and a nook with an ice machine.

I knocked on the door twice before swiping the card over the sensor thing, and I noticed my hand was trembling.

The first thing I saw was a living room area with huge windows and a view of the marina that probably made this suite incredibly costly. The floors were covered in soft carpet, and the sofa and two chairs looked super comfortable and plush. Rustic red met pristine white.

I dropped the bag on the floor, and as I kicked off my sneakers, I poked my head farther in to see a kitchenette to my left. Only, it was a little larger than expected. No table and chairs, but a bar with two stools. Small fridge—even a freaking stove and oven!

"Mad?" I called.

Scanning the open space again, I noticed the lights were dimmed, and there were two candles on the coffee table.

I blew out a pent-up breath, weirdly nervous. There was a door to my immediate right, which I assumed led to the bathroom, and there was a hallway of sorts after that. Just as I was about to go that way, Mad appeared and kind of knocked the air out of my lungs.

He'd showered recently. His hair was a little wet. And he

looked sinful in a pair of ratty jeans, a vintage tee, ink on display, and bare feet.

"There's my boy." He smiled.

My eyes watered rapidly, and I rushed forward to throw myself at him. Literally. I flung my arms around his neck and screwed my eyes shut, then climbed him like a tree. I couldn't get close enough fast enough. Not even with my arms and legs wrapped around him was I anywhere as near as I wanted to be.

Madigan steadied himself and let out a raucous chuckle, quickly tightening his arms around my middle. He gave me a special Madigan hug, and I almost broke. In the best ways. Fuck, I couldn't believe how long it'd been. This wasn't okay. We couldn't go almost three weeks in between visits.

I sniffled and buried my face in the warm, delicious-smelling curve of his neck. "This has been t-torture," I croaked. "I can't—not again—"

"I know, baby." He stroked my back and kissed my shoulder, and I couldn't hold back the tears. "Shh, I've got you. I know." He huffed a breath and walked us...somewhere. "You're like one of those mouse-sized mutts who weigh a ton 'cause you're all muscle."

"Sorry—"

He cut me off. "Don't even. It'll be a long time before I let you go." He shuffled around a bit and loosened my legs, and then we dropped. Into a chair, I think. "There we go." He hugged me impossibly harder and breathed me in.

I was gonna do that too, when my nose wasn't stuffy.

"I missed you so much, Abel."

"Me too." A whimper slipped out, and I could feel wetness against his neck. I just couldn't hold it together, could I? "I hope this weekend never ends."

He hummed and brushed back my hair. "Actually, I think a weekend's only supposed to last a couple days."

Jerk! Now was not the time to be funny. "Why do you have to be a fucking dummy—"

His low growl and swift grip on my jaw made me freeze in place. *I'd crossed a line, I'd crossed a line, I'd crossed a line.*

I was forced to face him, knowing I probably looked wide-eyed and intimidated. Not to mention my face was wet from crying like a bitch.

He cleared his throat and, surprisingly gently, wiped my cheeks. It was then I saw that his eyes were a teensy bit red too.

"Did you call me a fucking *dummy*?"

I instantly lowered my eyes. "I'm sorry, but that wasn't very nice. You want our weekend to be over fast."

"Was that what I said, Abel?" He dipped his chin to capture my gaze with his again. "I was teasing you about the length of a weekend." At the quivering of my bottom lip, and maybe because I was the idiot who couldn't stop getting emotional, he cut me some slack and brought me into his embrace. "My little hothead. The only reason I said that was 'cause, come Monday, I'll still be here."

"Wh-what?" I eased back enough to look him in the eye.

He stroked my cheek. "Being apart doesn't work for either of us. These past few weeks have been fucking excruciating."

Hope got stuck in my throat. Or maybe it was my heart. "Really? But—"

"Before your brain starts spinning, let me explain." He chuckled quietly and stole a quick kiss. It was enough to remember that we hadn't actually kissed until now, and that little peck was far from satisfactory. "This hotel has rooms for extended stays. That's the kind of suite I rented. This is ours for two months."

I dropped my jaw. Two months! Holy fuck.

In two months, the season would likely be over. I honestly didn't see us making it far in the play-offs, if we made the cut at all.

"When you're on the road," he continued, "I'll head home and work with clients there. Then I'll be back by the time you land."

Wait, wait, wait. "That can't be enough," I protested. As much as I wanted this—fucking craved it—I couldn't let him neglect so much of his job. "You work full time, Mad."

"Who says I won't do that now?" He smirked and tapped my legs. "Stand up. I'll show you."

So I rose from the chair, and he grabbed my hand and led me down the hall. There was not one but two doors. One was open and revealed a nice bedroom. Madigan went for the one across the hallway, and I stopped short. I guess it had been another bedroom...? But now it was...something else. Empty, except for a big desk taking up one corner, the type of tilted desk he had at home in Camassia. There were also a handful of moving boxes, all of them labeled. "Kitchen," "Clothes," "Work," "Bathroom," and "Play."

Play...

I swallowed. "P-Play?"

Madigan chuckled under his breath and walked over to the box, flipping it open. "A lot of it, I hope. I went shopping when you were with your brother."

I walked a little closer and peered into the box, then promptly took a couple steps back. Um. Yeah. Play. There were *toys*. Brand-new stuff. *Sex* stuff.

My face caught on fire, and I shuffled where I stood and tugged at my earlobe.

Mad continued as if this was normal. "I'll work from here too, baby. I'll work on my sketches and arrange to have a few clients come up. I've already made some calls, and I'll be renting a chair at a local shop." He paused. "I've spoken to Jamie too. Since living in Vancouver isn't temporary for you, I don't want my plans to be temporary either."

I furrowed my brow.

"We'll expand in the near future," he said. "He'll continue running Camassia Ink, and we'll open Vancouver Ink up here. I can keep my station in both shops but spend most of the time with you."

An invisible whoosh went through me, and I nearly staggered backward. I felt light-headed with the possibilities. This meant…this meant…oh God.

"You're s-staying?" I stammered. "You're really staying? We'll see each other often?"

"I'm really staying. Once the season is over, we'll find a place that's just ours." He closed the distance and dipped down and kissed me. I shuddered as his arms snaked around me, and I melted into the kiss. "I think we both need this," he whispered in between soft yet deep kisses. "You won't be able to fully let go until we have stability, and I can't be the Daddy I wanna be unless I can be there for you."

I lost the last shred of composure I had left and locked my arms around his neck. I couldn't form words; my head was too jumbled, but I could kiss him for all I was worth. Because he was right. I was never gonna be normal, and for as long as I wasn't absolutely certain and secure, I'd hold myself back.

It was the last thing I wanted.

Now, though… We could have everything.

Jesus Christ, I… "Love you. I love you, I love—" I froze. Oh my God, I couldn't believe I'd blurted that out! And so soon! Shit, shit, shit, he was gonna—

"Abel, sweetheart, I love you too." He cupped my cheeks,

a firm expression on his face. I focused on that and sucked in a breath. "I love you so much. Stay with me."

I nodded jerkily. *Don't freak out, don't freak out.* Maybe I hadn't messed up.

"I've got you, yeah?" he murmured. "It's you and me. I'll take care of everything."

I blinked rapidly and managed another nod. "You—you love me also?"

"With all that I am." He pressed his forehead to mine, a small grin tugging at his mouth. I licked my lips, still discombobulated. "I wouldn't mind hearing that again, though."

Hearing what? Oh, that... "I love you. I'm like...heels over —I mean..." *Stupid!* I groaned. "Head over heels, I mean."

His smile grew, and he kissed me hard. The entire moment was a mindfuck. I had no problems throwing myself into the kiss, because it seemed it was all I could get right.

As the seconds ticked by, I began to lose the tension in my shoulders, and slowly but surely, the fog in my brain cleared. *He said he loves me.* I tilted my head and moaned breathlessly, tasting him on my tongue. *He loves me.*

"Head over heels sounds accurate." He gripped my hips and walked me backward until I hit the wall. "No one's owned me the way you do, Abel—or nearly as much. I want you to know that."

I closed my eyes and exhaled my relief. "Daddy..."

"Always."

It went without saying that I was ready to be mauled by him, but he had other plans. He was full speed ahead now, and there were rules. I had to eat, he said. Sure, I was hungry—I was always friggin' hungry. Sex with Madigan, *my Daddy,* though...? Yeah, priority!

While he got started on dinner, I was told to change into something comfortable, so I stripped off one pair of sweats to go with another pair. They were old, threadbare, and the softest in the universe. Then I took a seat at the bar that separated the kitchen from the living room and merely watched him cook.

"It's been forever since you kissed me," I said.

He chuckled and checked on what I thought was pasta. "You'll get all the kisses you want later. Now I wanna hear about your game."

"Good. Same old." I slumped my shoulders. "I was sucky in the beginning and awesome at the end. I couldn't stop thinking about you." I shook my head at myself for having been so distracted. It was his fault. "Hopefully, it'll get better now because you're here."

He nodded. "Now I can come to more games too."

That would be *awesome.*

"I caught your goal on TV. It was fucking stunning."

"Thank you." I grinned, happier than ever, and enjoyed the silence for a bit. This was going to be hard to get used to. It was almost too good to be true.

Daddy, Daddy, Daddy... I loved watching him. Most of all, he seemed really at ease. More than I'd sensed in the past. I prayed that meant he was as happy about this as I was.

My mind wandered while he prepared something. I spotted olives, avocado, spicy sausage bits, and bell peppers. He was sexy when he chopped the peppers superfast like it was nothing.

He should've had a bigger kitchen from the start. Not that sad excuse for a kitchenette in Camassia. All he had there was

—oh! I sat up straight and remembered my gift. Then I was in motion, hurrying out of the kitchen.

"What's the rush?" he hollered.

"You'll see!" I called from the hallway. Other than some clothes and stuff, the only thing that filled the duffel was this huge bucket of Nutella. An actual bucket. It was *nuts*. Hazelnuts. I snickered to myself and lifted it with a grunt. "Look what I got you!" I appeared in the doorway and held up the bucket with both hands.

Mad did a double take, which made me laugh, and then he was smiling really big and shaking his head.

"Sweet fucking Jesus, boy, are you trying to kill me?" He let out a laugh and stepped closer to inspect the bucket.

"Isn't it huge?"

He snorted and eyed the label. "Uh, it's a hundred and five ounces, Abel. Yeah, you can say it's huge." Eyes brimming with laughter, he cupped my cheeks and pressed a firm kiss to my forehead. "Every day, I think you can't get any cuter. Every day, I'm wrong. Thank you, trouble."

"Welcome." I willed away my blush and set the bucket on the bar. "You'll share it with me, right? I think Nutella is delicious too."

"If I ate that by myself, soon you wouldn't want me." He winked and returned to the stove. "Same rule as always. The equivalent of one to-go packet a day."

"But sometimes, a little bit more." I squinted and held up my hand, pinching my thumb and forefinger together. "Sometimes, maybe two spoons. Or three."

He shook his head in amusement again and rinsed the pasta. Spaghetti, more correctly. "I reckon I'll have to hide it where you can't reach."

Buzzkill.

Eh, at the end of the day, even though I was a brat, I was gonna obey him. Mostly.

After a delicious dinner, we moved to the comfy couch in the living room, and we brought the Nutella monstrosity. Madigan went to the bedroom and grabbed a rolled-up duvet as well. It wasn't big enough to fit the king-size bed I'd spotted earlier, so maybe it was a spare.

I was ready to dip my finger into the Nutella when he uh-uh-uh'd me and muttered something about hygiene. Boring. Instead, he gave me a spoon.

"Just one."

"Just one," I mocked and crossed my eyes.

He only grinned.

During dinner, he'd told me how he "fucking loved" seeing me relax, seeing the little boy in me make a reappearance, that he thought it'd be hard to be strict. At least, right away. I was okay with that. Maybe I could rack up an impressive tally of sexy spankings.

He scooped up a generous serving for himself and stuck the spoon into his mouth. He kept it there as if it were a lollipop. In the meantime, he turned on the TV and settled for the late news.

"This isn't very fun to watch," I pointed out.

"It is for me." He spoke around the spoon and held up an arm. "You can come cuddle with Daddy while he watches the news."

Yeah, okay. Luckily, he'd changed into comfier clothes too. Cuddling with jeans in the way was *not* pleasant.

Tugging on the hem of his tee, I made it abundantly clear

he should take it off. And he obeyed like a good Daddy. I snickered, glad he couldn't read my mind, then dove into his arms and pulled the duvet over us. His chest was as perfect as always.

"I can't reach my spoon…"

He leaned forward and grabbed it for me, and then chocolate exploded in my mouth. He was already done with his spoon, and now he was sipping gross coffee.

"My brain is quieter now." Having a mouth full of Nutella made the words come out thick and garbled.

"That's the way we want it, isn't it?" He dropped a kiss to the top of my head before he started playing with the hair at the back of my neck.

"Yeah. But I still have questions," I said. "Like, how long have you been here? You sent me that picture…"

"Oh, just since this morning." He set his coffee mug on the table. "I drove up on Tuesday to look at the suite and sign some papers. I got the key then. The desk was delivered here yesterday."

After leaving the spoon on a napkin, I cuddled closer and kissed his chest. "You're the best thing that's happened to me."

"Funny, I was just thinking the same." He landed another lingering kiss in my hair, and he gave me a squeeze. "Did you by any chance tell Jesse about us?"

Uh-oh. "Um…maybe? He was shocked but said as long as I was happy…"

"It's okay. I got curious because he suddenly joined Facebook yesterday and friended me before anyone else."

"He's on Facebook?" I lifted my head, fucking offended. "He hasn't friended *me*."

My entire family was boring on there. It was mostly Casey and me who used Facebook. Mom uploaded pictures sometimes, and Dad dutifully liked them. Madigan was even worse. He used Facebook to read articles.

"Maybe he's in the process of it." He tapped my nose. "He and I haven't been close in years, so it stood out. He asked how I was doing and if I traveled much."

I scrunched my nose. Why would Jesse ask that?

"I think he was feeling me out—to see if I had the time to be there for you."

Oh. I chewed on the inside of my cheek and rested it on his chest again. That was nice. It mattered a lot that Jesse was making an effort. He'd texted a lot more this week, and after the game when we went out for dinner with Avielle, he'd stopped pretending about the girl. He acted like a dad and seemed to be wrapped around her pinkie, and he did nothing to hide it. It was sweet.

I told Madigan about everything I'd learned, except the part where Jesse had struggled with addiction. It was a scary topic for me, but I felt I could trust my brother better now. When he was ready, he would tell everyone.

Last but not least, I explained that Jesse and Avielle would come up to see the game in two weeks.

"I think that's a good idea," Mad replied. "What do you say about inviting Casey and Ellis too?"

"But they don't know about us. Well...Casey probably suspects."

"Maybe it's time we tell them," he murmured. "We still have a couple weeks. Then it's only Lincoln and Ade left."

"Only..." I muttered.

He chuckled quietly. "It'll be fine, baby. Somehow."

I hoped so.

CHAPTER 15

I woke up disoriented, my face pressed against the back cushions of the couch. A shiver ran through me as I registered kisses along my spine.

"I didn't mean to fall asleep," I mumbled groggily. "Bedtime?"

"Not yet." He hooked a couple fingers inside the waistband of my sweats. "Lift up."

Awareness shook me, and I obeyed quickly so he could pull down my pants. Was this it? Finally? Oh God, I hoped. Even as sleep continued to grasp at me, desire slithered into my bones and made me needy.

"Mad..." I pushed out my butt.

"Hmm?" He continued his kissing, up my neck where he grazed his teeth along my skin. "I can't wait any longer." Fuck yes, I was so ready. "Can you hike that leg over the cushion?"

Yes, Sir, right away. I remained lying on my side and lifted my leg to rest it along the back of the couch. My eyes fell closed, and I reveled in every touch. His hands were warm and kneading my flesh, and I could feel his big cock pressing against my leg. He was kissing his way down when I wanted him way up.

When he pushed away the duvet, a cool blanket of air covered me instead. I shuddered. Farther down, farther down, he spread my butt cheeks farther and licked the length of my ass. I yelped, only to moan and melt into the couch.

My dick got harder and harder, and my belly tingled.

He traced a finger over my opening, causing me to meet his too-gentle touch. "Such a beautiful little bottom... And it's all mine."

I let out a whine. "I need you, Daddy. Please? We've waited *so* long."

"We have, haven't we?" He gave me an openmouthed kiss, right where I wanted his cock, then slowly pushed his tongue inside. I groaned and felt the pleasure spreading like wildfire. "No more waiting for us." With that, he finally crawled higher, and I heard the unmistakable sound of a bottle opening.

He handed me a small towel too. Slipping it between my stomach and the cushion, he wrapped my cock in it.

"So you can make a sticky mess." He kissed my neck and groped my dick in perfect strokes that couldn't be played off as "adjusting the towel." Next, the only sticky thing I felt was in my butt. He teased me with two wet fingers, circling me, then pushing inside.

I exhaled noisily and white-knuckled the cushion.

He fingered me long past my begging for his cock, and I cursed how unwavering he was.

"I have to prepare you, baby boy." He sank his teeth into my shoulder, and I hissed at the sting. "Daddy won't go easy on you. He can't."

"Is that—*ungh*, 'cause you're also needy-wanty?" I sucked

in a breath and forced myself to accept three fingers. "Like, desperate?"

"So fucking desperate." His breath was warm against my neck, eliciting another shudder. "It might hurt a bit in the beginning."

"That's okay," I said quickly. "I wanna hurt for you. I like it, I promise."

The more it hurt, the more I lost control. I couldn't go so far as to call myself a masochist, but it did serve its purpose. And I needed a generous dose of it.

"We'll go with safewords. You know the color system?"

I nodded. "Yes, Daddy. I like saying stop, so it's good that it doesn't mean anything. If I'm too hurty, I'll say yellow or red."

"That's a good boy." He grunted as he slipped his thick erection between my legs, rubbing it against my cheeks and balls. "Fucking perfect... Christ, I just wanna take you until you scream. Until you don't know if it's too much pleasure or too much pain."

I gulped and instinctively grabbed my dick. I had to rub it quickly and hard to relieve some pressure. If only that actually worked.

He must've noticed when I was ready, because he withdrew his fingers as soon as I started bearing down on him every thrust. I made a noise of complaint, which I shouldn't have. *Nothing* could've prepared me for how fast he was going to replace his fingers with his cock. The wet, blunt head pressed against my opening, and then he gripped my hip and thrust inside in one sharp push.

My mouth popped open, though no sound came out. The pain was blinding and robbed me of air. And in that moment, he had only one name. Daddy became everything, and I needed all of him. He'd shocked me, shocked my fucking system. I felt him throbbing deep inside of me.

"I warned you." He let out a harsh, shallow breath and bit my shoulder. "Oh God, Abel."

Eventually, I let out a choked sob and just barely managed to utter a broken, "M-More." Because if he mistook my reaction for something bad, I would've freaked out. Holy hell, I had no word for this sweet agony. The pain kept me in a death grip, clearing my head, wiping away any coherent thought, and chained me to the moment.

"*Ow...*" It hurt to move, it hurt to breathe. Instead, I focused on him completely taking ownership of me. His rough hands were everywhere, his mouth breathed of his own bliss—uncontrolled and unsteady—and his every action pushed at my mentality.

I wasn't some hotshot hockey player with a big chip on his shoulder. I was a blubbering little boy getting ravaged by his Daddy.

He started fucking me in long strokes. His energy was intoxicating and consuming, and it made me doubt there was any being on this planet he couldn't seduce.

"You'll take it for me, won't you?" he murmured, out of breath.

"An-anything," I gasped. "K-Keep loving me, Daddy. Promise, promise."

He slipped out slowly, then pushed in once more. "I promise, sweetheart. I'll always love you. I'll always need you."

When he slid a hand along the backside of my thigh, the one that was hitched over the cushion, I exhaled a high-pitched whine. I felt like my brain had short-circuited. I was ticklish and supersensitive, and my skin wouldn't quit breaking out in goose bumps.

The euphoria was beginning to flood me. My cock strained uncomfortably, but before I could do anything about it, Daddy reached for it and smeared the fluids over my skin.

"Look how hard you are," he whispered between thrusts. "Already leaking too."

His touch wasn't enough. He wasn't stroking or rubbing me, he was just ghosting his fingers alongside it, tracing the ridges, and it was gonna drive me to tears if he didn't give me more.

He cupped my balls gently and fondled them as if he was getting to know them.

"You're being mean again," I whimpered. I bucked into him, back and forth, rolling my hips. "Please, Daddy!"

"Patience, boy. I've waited too long to rush this." He drove in hard and deep and set a faster pace. Then...as soon as I was shaking and pleading, he slowed down, and the sadist chuckled darkly when I accused him of enjoying my misery. "Or maybe I love hearing you beg for me."

"Or maybe both," I moaned. "Oh fuck—yes, right there, please don't stop, please, please." I begged shamelessly and reached behind me to grab at him. My fingers dug into his firm buttock, and I met every thrust like a greedy whore. "I want you so much."

Daddy shuddered and held me tighter to him, and his movements picked up more speed. I could feel how tense he was, his muscles flexing and rippling. It was so goddamn hot.

"Fuck, you feel incredible," he groaned. "Tightest, most fuckable little boy ever."

I flushed all over, and then he gave me exactly what I'd begged for. He fisted my cock and swiped his thumb over the slit, then stroked me firmly and expertly. My breathing hitched, and I went rigid.

"Please, please, please," I heard myself chant breathlessly.

"So good, Daddy, so good, ohhh—" I gasped as he hit a different angle, and I almost came right there.

"I think that's it." He kept hitting that spot, and his upper body inched away a bit. "If you could see this... I'm gonna get this on film. Just like this, legs spread, your pretty little ass taking Daddy's cock."

"Daddy, I'm..." I mumbled like a drunk. The orgasm was coming at me from every direction, and I couldn't turn away from it. "I'm, I'm..."

"I've got you, baby boy. You can come."

I was already gone. I exploded within and let the tremors shake me up.

My ears rang, and Daddy fucked me brutally through my climax. Through the rushing sounds and skin slapping, I heard his gritty curses and how he was going to come in his little boy, how much he loved me, and how he loved that I made such a big mess for him.

I was a whimpering, squirming, sweaty, thoroughly used boy by the time he slammed in once more and came in me. His hand was still rubbing my dick, coating me in my come, causing me to squirm more. He'd stopped breathing. He rocked lazily, fucking his release deeper inside me.

I couldn't have asked for anything better than the silence that followed. He didn't let go of me; if anything, he hugged me to him impossibly hard, neither of us caring that my belly got wet from his hand.

The soreness was already making itself known, but it only made me sleepy-smile. It was perfect. I hoped he'd stay inside me all night. And maybe wake me up and fuck me some more to see how many of Daddy's orgasms I could take. Like a game.

"I love you," I whispered.

He released a breath and kissed my neck. "I love you more, Abel. You have no idea."

The next morning, I was in for a rude awakening. Clearly, I'd only played with amateurs in the past because Daddy's brain was some next-level, evil mastermind bullshit.

"Why are you whining?" he asked.

"Because it's embarrassing!" I wanted to throw him a glare over my shoulder, but I was too mortified to look him in the eye. "And I'm not whining," I grumbled. "I'm protesting."

A bead of sweat trickled down my temple, and I gripped the grab bar tighter. Four people could easily fit in the fancy, mosaic-decorated shower; there was even a built-in bench in the back of the space. It was where he sat and had fun at my expense.

"It sure sounds like whining." The sound of his zipper had my attention, and I clenched harder. He removed his belt next, by the equally recognizable sound of it. "You can leave the shower at any moment, Abel. You know what to do."

I huffed and looked up at the showerhead. If I said or did the wrong thing, he could turn the water on. Cold. Right now, the shower was as dry as a desert.

This morning was supposed to have been amazing. I thought we'd wake up, eat breakfast, and spend the day fucking and cuddling. Instead, he'd run out and gotten us breakfast that I hadn't been able to enjoy because he'd informed me I was gonna get punished. And after *that*...he'd fucked me quickly, only finding his own release.

I gnashed my teeth together.

"You better clench, boy," he'd advised afterward. "If you

lose a single drop of Daddy's come, you'll get the belt. Now, go into the shower. Remember...clench."

Problem was, I didn't know what I'd done wrong, and his way of helping wasn't fucking helpful!

"I need another hint," I gritted.

"Of course. You know the drill."

I held my breath and closed my eyes. Then I carefully widened my stance a few inches. It was the price to pay for a hint.

"A bit more, Abel."

Dammit.

When I'd spread my legs to his satisfaction, he ran a finger along the inside of my thigh. Making sure I was still dry, maybe. What I knew for certain was that he was a sadist. End of discussion.

"The punishment is twofold," he revealed. "One is an actual punishment. The other is mostly for fun."

"That's not a hint," I complained.

"I wasn't done speaking," he responded irritably, and I gulped. "Are you gonna behave?"

"Yes, Sir. I'm sorry."

He took a breath. "Before you left Camassia, you promised me to always be honest. Do you remember?"

I nodded hesitantly. I'd been honest with him. "I remember."

"You also promised you'd share your days with me," he went on. "If something significant happened, you were gonna tell me."

And I had! Sharing during a long-distance relationship had nearly done me in, and it hadn't even lasted more than a few weeks. So, of course, I'd shared stuff with him. If I hadn't, there wouldn't have been much to bond over.

"I've—I've told you everything." I became instantly aware

of his presence. A moment later, something cold touched my hip, and I realized it was his belt. "I haven't kept anything from you," I insisted. Glancing down, I saw he'd folded the belt and that he was dragging it slowly down my thigh. "Was it because I didn't tell you about Jesse right away?"

"No." He pressed a soft kiss to my neck. His breathing was strangely labored. If I didn't know better, I'd say he was trying to get off. "This is why this part's only funishment. You kept something from me before you made that promise, and..." He laughed through his nose. "To be honest, I thought it was hysterical when I found out."

Okay, he was gonna be the death of me. Frustration built up rapidly. *Not the bad kind*. I cocked my head briefly at that thought, and it was true. This kind of frustration was different. My anxiety was nonexistent, thank fuck.

Focus!

Right. I blew out a breath. All right, so it was something I'd kept from him before. That didn't narrow it down much!

"God, my asshole is killing me," I groaned. He had no fucking idea. I'd been tensing up and bearing down for the better part of an hour, and it was goddamn painful. "Can you just tell me, please?"

He hummed and stepped closer, the warmth of his chest touching my back. And he was hard. Rock fucking hard, and definitely stroking himself. To make my suffering even worse, he rubbed the head of his cock over my hole, which I was fighting desperately to keep clenched.

The belt hit the floor with a thud and a clank.

"Did you," he whispered, "or did you not...buy a loft in the Valley?"

My eyes grew wide. Oh my God, I'd totally forgotten—"Fuck!" I cried out. Without any warning, he forced his cock inside me aggressively, breaching the tight rings of muscle.

The shock mingled with pain and a weird rush of exhilaration.

It got weirder. And hotter. And mind-blowingly humiliating. My Daddy wasn't fucking me. He was coming. He rocked deep into my butt and groaned out his release, effectively using me as a come hole.

I whimpered, speechless and stunned. My face burned hotly, and the embarrassment pushed me to the ground mentally.

"Tighter than ever." He smacked my butt, panting, and withdrew his cock. I quickly hauled in a breath and clenched down once more. "You actually bought a condo," he said heavily as he zipped up his jeans. "Then you enlisted your best friend to pick up the key for you. Only, he called us at the shop and said he was running late after a class. He asked if I could go across the street and meet up with the real estate agent."

It seemed all I could do lately was whimper. He'd shaken me up, and I didn't know how to divide my focus. One part of me demanded I listen to what he was saying; the other was still reeling from what he'd done. A single thrust. He'd stroked himself until he was right there, then pushed inside to empty himself.

"You neglected to tell Gray that I didn't know about the loft," Daddy whispered in my ear.

"I just wanted to live close to you," I croaked.

He hugged me from behind and kissed my shoulder. "I know. One of the many reasons I adore you. But in the future, this is one of those things I shouldn't have to tell you to give full disclosure about, understood? Buying property is a big deal."

I nodded obediently. "Yes, Sir. I'm sorry I forgot."

"You don't have to apologize—"

"I want to," I said, sniffling. "I don't care about technicalities. I should have told you—oh, no." I screwed my eyes shut and felt myself slipping. "Daddy, I can't hold your come in much longer." My thighs were on fire from the effort, and they strained painfully.

Daddy's fingers brushed over my opening, circling in the wetness slowly seeping out.

I was failing.

"You can let go any moment, sweetheart."

"But y-you said I'd get the belt!"

He joined me at my side so he could face me better. "Twenty lashes," he confirmed, to my horror. "That's for the actual punishment I'm doling out today, Abel. I'm very disappointed that you've lied to me this week." I opened my mouth, and he wouldn't have that. He didn't let me speak. "Do you deny that you've minimized your struggles with being away from me?"

Oh, shit. I promptly snapped my mouth shut again.

He eyed me grimly. "You seem to forget that I've known you since you were a little boy. I know every tell. I also know *why* you feel the need to downplay your hurt, and it ends now." As he moved in and cupped my face, I gripped the grab bar so tightly my knuckles turned white. If I didn't, I was gonna throw myself at him and cry like a baby. "I love every part that makes you who you are, Abel. You're one hell of a fighter, and I couldn't be prouder of you. But I will never tolerate you keeping something from me to spare my feelings, and if I don't know how you're faring, I can't make informed decisions." He paused and leveled me with a serious look. "When I tell you you're everything to me, it means I'm with you through every bout of depression, every episode of mania, and every moment in between."

I sniffled some more, and my eyes watered.

He leaned in and kissed me on the forehead. "The damage is greater when you withhold things from Daddy, so this punishment *will* hurt. Because I don't want you to forget it anytime soon."

That frightened me, and I practiced full disclosure by saying it. "I'm a little scared."

"Of what?" His eyes flashed with concern.

I swallowed audibly. "Will everything be okay after the punishment?"

"Definitely," he said firmly. "Once a punishment is over, all is forgiven. That's the rule."

Okay, then. I nodded jerkily and exhaled shakily. "I won't lie. I won't try to shield you from my psycho personali—" I realized my mistake when his eyes turned downright livid. Oh God, oh God, oh God, oh God. "I'm sorry, I'm sorry, I'm sorry!"

It was of no use. He disappeared behind me and picked up the belt.

"Bend over," he ordered. "Right fucking now. You thought twenty lashes would be harsh? Let's go higher."

Tears sprang to my eyes in a heartbeat, and I started shaking. Shame flooded me as his come trickled down the insides of my legs.

Nothing happened, though. I stood there bent over, waiting for the pain, and nothing.

I'd fucked up badly. I knew it.

"D-Daddy—"

"Gimme a minute." He was not in a good mood at all. "I'm reminding myself that it's second nature for you to be your own worst bully."

"I'm so sorry," I cried.

"I know, baby, but you crossed a big line. You've lied, and

you've called yourself horrible names. Now, I want you to count."

Two fat tears rolled down my cheeks as I screwed my eyes shut super hard, and I steeled myself.

This hurt. This hurt so badly. I'd disappointed him, and it crushed me.

One.

The belt gave off a resounding whack at the back of my left thigh.

"T-Two," I gasped.

Three, four, five...

He did not hold back.

He beat me without mercy, the heavy leather belt smattering against my thighs and bottom. But the worst part was his words. In between blows, he told me that it hurt *him* when I called myself bad things. *Seven, eight, nine...* Oh fuck, my skin was burning.

"Ten," I choked out.

"Remember your safewords?"

I could only nod.

I knew I could stop and this would be all over with in a second. If I wanted to, I could be cuddled up in his arms, and we would forget this whole thing. But I needed this. I'd given him the power over me, and it meant I wanted things done his way. I took the pain, even as it made me sob and tremble, because I had a feeling forgiveness would send me flying when I'd earned it.

"T-Twelve—owww!"

By fifteen, I no longer cared about his releases coating my legs. I was damp with sweat and come, and the pain was becoming unbearable.

By twenty-five, I could barely breathe.

Daddy went rough. He kicked my legs farther apart so he

could belt the sticky parts of my thighs. That stung much worse. I tensed up with each hit, and after having worked my muscles for so long, it intensified the ache.

By thirty, I was a mess. My knees gave out, I had to gasp for air, and tears streamed down my face. I couldn't see, and I didn't know what was happening. Only that the beating seemed to be over.

Strong arms circled me before I felt lukewarm water. It rained down on us, and it was only then I noticed we were on the floor. Low murmurs caressed my ear, though I couldn't make out the words.

I hadn't felt this weak in years, yet, at the same time, I felt undeniably safe. Daddy cradled me between his legs, swaying us gently, and turned the water a little warmer. Next, he began soaping me up in soothing strokes with a soft sponge. He didn't shush me or tell me everything was okay yet; he merely let me cry it out.

I hadn't expected it to feel so cathartic. As my cries lessened and my breathing regulated, I was sure I'd never experienced this level of peace inside my head. It was as if only he and I existed in the whole world.

"Your jeans," I whispered hoarsely.

"Will make it," he whispered back.

The pain got easier to ignore as his comfort continued. Aftercare, I realized. He washed me all over, kissed me on the forehead lots, and massaged my scalp. At the same time, he forgave me for my mistakes and promised he'd be there for me so we could tackle my behavior. The part of my behavior, anyway, that led me to be mean to myself.

He mentioned it would be a good idea if I brought his up with my therapist as well, and I agreed with that. I guess I hadn't paid attention to how often and how easily I slipped into those self-destructive patterns.

"You have your appointment next week, don't you?" He pushed back my hair and used the showerhead to rid the shampoo suds. I only nodded in response, too comfy and content where I was. "I'll take you to your doctor soon too."

I grimaced, then closed my eyes as he let the water wash down. "I have a doctor thing?"

"Mm, your annual checkup."

Oh, man. Those were a drag. Mostly, it was to check my lithium levels, but also to see how everything else was going. I'd been through it almost all my life.

I tilted my head back and smiled. "I like that you know all those things."

He chuckled quietly. "That's good. I'm glad someone benefits from my being a control freak."

I giggled, 'cause of course I benefitted from it. Weren't all Doms control freaks to a degree?

"You feelin' better, trouble?"

I nodded and yawned. The physical pain was going to keep me in suffering mode a while longer, and I no doubt had red marks all over my legs and butt. But it paled next to the mental bliss.

"Am I really forgiven?"

"Absolutely." He kissed the side of my head. "In fact, I think you handled your first punishment very well. What do you say we order up some ice cream and cuddle in front of a movie?"

Yessssss.

CHAPTER 16

There he is.
I stepped closer to the sidewalk as Gray pulled up outside the hotel, and I waited somewhat patiently while he handed the keys over to the valet and grabbed his bag.

He looked...like a mess. Like he hadn't slept in days. Yet, he had a bed head and sweats I knew he often slept in. Matching hoodie. They were from our high school days.

"Hey." I wanted to touch him, hug him, but settled for giving his arm a squeeze. "You look like shit."

He laughed hoarsely. "Feel like it too." Oh man, he was sick, to boot. I could see now his nose was a little red, and his voice was barely there. "Thanks for letting me come up."

I hadn't exactly given him a choice.

We talked on the phone yesterday after I got home from a game in Detroit, and he'd told me that Coach Fuller—supposedly the stupid love of Gray's life—wasn't gonna divorce his wife because she'd been diagnosed with cancer.

I wasn't surprised for crap that he wasn't divorcing her—and seriously doubted he would have even if the wife had been okay. Even so, cancer sucked, and it put Gray in a horrible situation. After all, he'd been good. He'd stood his ground. He'd confessed his feelings but hadn't started an affair or anything; it was Fuller who'd been a prick. He'd made empty promises and often wanted to meet with Gray, who had been blinded by his feelings and believed him.

"I've made plans for us," I said.

"Oh?"

I nodded, and we entered the first elevator that opened. "You said you haven't been eating well, which I can fucking see, you skinny—"

"I'm bigger than you are," he huffed.

"Whatever. You've lost weight, so we're gonna do meal prep." I'd bought a ton of chicken, fresh vegetables, and rice. And Daddy had picked up like fifty Tupperware containers after work yesterday.

"All right. Anything, just no talk about Craig."

"He can go fuck himself," I retorted. "He's lucky I haven't smashed his face in. I even told D—um, Madigan, and he got angry too."

"You told who?" Judging by Gray's sly little smirk, he'd caught my slip. In response, I scratched my eyebrow with my middle finger. He chuckled tiredly. "Chill. You've already called him Daddy half a dozen times when we've been on the phone."

Oh, shit. "I have?"

"Uh-huh. You don't even notice it."

I winced, thinking of the disaster it would've been if I'd called him that while talking to Mom or Dad. It seemed two weeks of living with Mad had all but erased his actual name. Madigan, in particular. I did still call him Mad often enough, but most of the time, it was Daddy. Funny how things worked.

We rode in silence the rest of the way, and I took Gray's

bag, feeling helpless. I wanted to do something and didn't know what. Before I got together with Mad, it would've looked a lot different. Gray and I would've been in bed, holding each other tightly. I couldn't exactly do that now.

"Did you swing by my house?" I asked as we exited the car.

I'd asked if he could bring me some stuff from my room at Mom and Dad's—only if he had the energy.

Gray nodded. "It's all in the bag. Your mom gave me cookies."

"Of course she did." I smiled and held up the keycard in front of the door. "I tried calling her earlier, but I guess they're in the air by now." I'd get my Rice Krispie treats another time.

Today I was looking forward to a chill Friday. This week in particular, I'd been on the road a lot, and it'd be nice to have some low-key fun before everyone came up tomorrow for the charity game and stuff.

"Your uncles were picking up Lyn while I was there," Gray said with a nod.

Made sense.

We entered the suite, and Mad was on the phone in the kitchen, so he nodded hello to Gray, then mouthed "room service" to me.

"Order a lot," I whispered.

He grinned faintly. "Sounds good, and a couple snack plates and sodas with that." He raised a brow in question to us.

"Diet Coke," I supplied.

"Regular Coke, thanks," Gray said.

Daddy relayed the information and hung up shortly after. "Lunch will be here in half an hour," he told us. "How you feelin', Gray?"

Gray lifted a shoulder. "I'm okay, I guess."

"Uh, he doesn't need his bullshit radar to detect that lie," I muttered to Gray.

Mad chuckled. "Well, I have work to do, but you boys get comfortable. They're bringing up a bed for the spare room later."

I nodded and set down Gray's bag, and Mad passed us with a kiss to my forehead and a squeeze to my friend's shoulder.

At that point, Gray had spotted the mountain of food on the kitchen bar, and he walked closer to peer inside the bags.

"There's no dairy whatsoever."

"Um, no." I joined him and began hauling out the vegetables. Two big bags of chicken breasts were already defrosting in the sink, and I had three whole salmons in the fridge that Daddy had promised he'd gut for me later. "Actually, there's sour cream in the fridge. It's vegan—"

"Then it's not dairy."

I shoved his shoulder. "Shut up. It's still awesome, and a teammate gave me a recipe for sour cream, lemon, and some spices. It'll go with the salmon. And, and, and baked sweet potatoes with spinach and mushrooms." I patted his firm stomach. "You'll thank me, I promise."

He was eyeing the netted cache of avocados. It was possible I'd gone overboard when I'd bought twenty of them, but let's be honest, seven meals a day made food disappear like magic. Between the two of us, nothing would go bad.

"Hey, have a seat. I'll fix this." I pulled out a stool for him, but before he slid onto it, I had to pull him in for a hug. "You'll get over him, Gray."

"I don't know how." His voice broke at the end, and he buried his face against my neck. "I've fucking tried."

I knew he had. It all sucked.

I wanted to suggest he switch hockey teams. Scouts didn't

show up at the other team's games at the same rate; it was located in Camas, not the best neighborhood, and they mainly recruited from the local high school, but he'd be away from Coach Fuller. Maybe it would be easier for Gray to get over him if they didn't see each other almost every day at practice. Besides, Gray had repeatedly stated he only played to stay in shape and because it was fun. He didn't need to be on a team that flirted with talent scouts.

"Tell me what to do," I whispered.

It physically pained me to see him hurt. Gray was more social and outgoing than I was and had more friends. I mostly just had him, and he'd done so much for me. From the moment I moved to Washington, he'd been there. Through school, through hockey practices, through my draft, and through both of us coming out. I guess I'd always been out, though there was a cycle to go through when you were new in a town and played a sport that was so drenched in masculinity and stereotypes.

Gray had made all those transitions easier for me.

"Just...distract me." He blew out a heavy breath and eased away, scrubbing his hands over his face.

I swallowed hard, unsure what that meant. Guilt struck me the second I realized what I wanted. Getting him under the covers and holding him and telling him everything was going to be okay...which could be very misconstrued.

I would have to think of new ways to convey comfort and support. It was a bit confusing.

He mustered a weak smirk. "Cook for me."

"I can do that."

When lunch arrived, we all ate in the living room because the kitchen was full of meal prep stuff.

I devoured two servings of pan-fried halibut and a big salad while Mad and Gray ate tastier treats. Sometimes, like now, I envied regular people. Hockey was more than a job. It was a way of life, and there were plenty of sacrifices. Hell, I couldn't go anywhere without having a food plan mapped out. The glove box in my car was where I kept my stash of meal bars, and one of the cabinets in the kitchen was overflowing with powders, shakes, and pills.

Most days, I didn't think about it. It was second nature. Like a background buzz that was simply there.

Today wasn't most days, though, and I chewed around a mouthful of kale and arugula while I watched Daddy tuck into a piece of steak and a baked potato. He was a medium-rare type of guy, and if it weren't for the daily trips he took to the hotel gym, I'd freak out about his health. The steak gushed pink and was bathed in gravy, and...it looked so fucking delicious.

He noticed my gawking and lifted a brow, a smirk playing on his lips. "I probably shouldn't count on you picking me over this steak, should I?"

Gray looked up from his plate of nachos, first eyeing Mad in the chair, then me.

"You probably shouldn't, no," I grumbled and stabbed a forkful of greens. "Christ, Gray, I can fucking smell the cheese."

To be a dick, he dragged a nacho through the queso and closed his mouth around it with a bunch of yummy noises.

"My poor baby." Mad was failing at showing concern.

I scowled at him and stuck some fish into my mouth. My own meal was good, great even, it just wasn't greasy and perfect.

"Thanks for the grub, Madigan." Gray piled his nacho plate on top of the other dishes he'd finished, then sat back on the couch and pulled up his legs.

It tugged at me to see him so defeated. Needing to offer at least a semblance of comfort, I reached out and put my hand on his.

"Anytime, kid." Actually, Daddy had no issues showing concern for *Gray*. It was clear as day in Mad's eyes. "Are you sleeping okay? Abel mentioned school's rough."

At first, it looked like Gray was gonna shrug it off, which wouldn't have been strange. Up until now, he'd only been "Abel's buddy." Gray would have to get used to at least some fussing from Mad, though. It came with the Dom territory.

"Finals coming up. That's gonna suck, but..." Gray lifted a shoulder and pinched his bottom lip. I drew mindless patterns over the top of his hand. "I think sleep is the only thing that comes easily. I can get twelve hours and wanna go back to bed."

I could definitely relate to that. It was how I felt whenever I was depressed.

Mad knew that part of me very well, and it probably explained the furrow of his brow. He was realizing the damage. He cleared his throat and cut into the last of his steak. "I trust you'll come up here when your schedules allow it." He gave us both a look that brooked no argument.

I smiled. Fuck, how I loved that man.

"Are you getting domly with me?" Gray's mouth twisted at the corners, and I gave his hand a squeeze.

"Get used to it," was all Daddy said. "Does your mother know you're struggling?"

"Hell no. She'd worry herself to death," Gray replied.

Mad huffed. "Then, yeah, you're definitely coming up

here more often." He started grumbling. "Fucking kids and their hiding. Abel's just the same."

Gray side-eyed me and spoke under his breath. "Should we remind him we're not kids?"

"No, he's on a roll now." I grabbed my soda and took a sip. "You're lucky he won't turn your ass red for downplaying anything."

Gray lifted his brows, the silent question written across his face.

I nodded. Oh yeah, Mad had definitely turned my ass red for that. And my thighs. It'd taken days for the welts to fade.

"Damn," he mumbled.

I snickered.

"Dude, you're using too much salt." I nudged Gray away from the stove so I could protect the steamed vegetables. "The nachos were bad enough. Leave this to me." I patted his cheek.

He grunted something and returned to the bar where he cranked up the volume on the Britney song that started. My docking station was one of the things he'd brought up from Camassia, along with some video games and clothes.

Daddy emerged from the room he'd turned into his study, looking like he was mildly grossed out. "What the fuck is that smell, boys?"

Gray and I shared a grin, and he said, "Is it wrong I think it's hot when he calls us boys?"

I shook my head.

Daddy found the source of the less-than-awesome smell: a pile of chopped vegetables, mainly broccoli, on the kitchen bar. It was the third batch getting steamed as soon as the one I was working on now was done.

"Still doing meal prep, huh?" He picked up a piece of broccoli, only to toss it back in the pile.

"Yes, Sir." I nodded and opened the oven to pull out the chicken. Bobbing my head to the beat of the song, I put one piece of chicken in each of the containers on the counter.

Daddy cleared his throat. "Can I assume changing this bullshit music into something better is outta the question?"

What. The. Fuck?

"It's Britney, bitch," Gray and I barked out, insulted. Gray added, "All due respect, man, but she's a fucking goddess."

Daddy snorted and shook his head in amusement.

"What he said." I bumped my hip to Gray's and set the empty pan next to the stove. "She's an old-school icon."

"Old-school... Oh Jesus fucking Christ." Daddy looked at us in disbelief before stalking back to his study. "You two wouldn't know old-school if it bit you in the ass."

Despite his earlier non-stern reaction to our outburst, I wanted to make sure he got it right, so I excused myself and followed.

I knocked twice on his door, then opened it enough to poke my head in.

He looked up from his drawing board. "What's up?"

"I, um, I just wanted to make sure you knew I wasn't calling you a bitch," I said. "It's part of a Britney song."

He chuckled and rolled out his chair a bit. "Come here."

I grinned unsurely and walked over to straddle his sexy self, and to remind him I was cute, I gave him a loud kiss.

He smiled and groped my butt. "I've been subjected to your awful taste in music for years, so I've heard the song before."

I dropped my jaw. "It's not awful!"

"It's *horrible*." His smile widened, and he leaned close to nuzzle my cheek. "Have I told you today how much I love you?"

"Yes, and I love you a gazillion times more, and it's *not* horrible." Why the hell couldn't I keep the whine out of my voice when it was just him and me?

He looked pleased as punch. "Give Daddy a kiss," he whispered.

I sighed, always caving in so easily to him, and kissed him. Lots of little pecks grew into a perfect, unhurried make-out session.

"Thanks for letting Gray crash here," I mumbled against his lips.

"Of course, baby." He touched my cheek and slowed down the kiss. "I'm glad you have each other. It's fun to see you goof around—now that I don't have to be jealous."

I grinned and ducked my head, fiddling with his tee. "You never did. Hell, even Gray would rather have a round in the sack with you than me."

He hummed, turning pensive rather than finding my joke funny. "We haven't discussed this. Perhaps we should."

I quirked a brow, confused. "Discuss what?"

"Monogamy."

"Um, I'm a thousand percent monogamous with you." I hoped this wouldn't be an issue. In fact, discussing it was plenty uncomfortable. "I don't want anyone else. Do, um—do you?"

"That's the last thing you have to worry about where I'm concerned." He nudged up my chin. "I'm just putting this out there, okay? You're an affectionate boy, and I don't wanna change that. I know what you and Gray shared was special for you."

That made me frown. "You're doing it wrong. You're supposed to get superpossessive and growl that I'm yours."

He laughed a little and gave me a squeeze. "Sweetheart, all I'm saying is I want you to be able to keep your relationship with Gray the way it was—if that's what you want." He quieted down and connected one of my hands with his, palms open, fingers lined up. "You've always spoken through touch. When you were younger and couldn't find your words as easily, you had your own tactile language to convey what was wrong and how you felt. I don't know if you remember, but when you were sad and emotionally spent, you would crawl up into the nearest lap and tuck your freezing hands under their arms."

I scrunched my nose and smiled curiously. I didn't remember that, nor did I know I "spoke through touch." However, it didn't feel foreign one bit when he told me.

"You can kiss for many reasons," he went on, threading our fingers together. "I kiss for one reason. While I'm a blessed bastard to have many great friends, none of them is welcome for a cuddle on the couch." I spluttered a snicker and covered my mouth with my free hand. "I guess I'm more black and white with affection. Mine is reserved for you and you only, and it's because it's intimate on a romantic and personal level for me."

"And it's not for me?" My discomfort was gone. It was as if he were physically prying my eyes open to see more, to understand more, and I wished I could roll around in this feeling. It was one of the reasons I loved him so much.

"When it's me, I sure hope so." He smiled and brushed our noses together. "Then there's Gray. You miss being near him, don't you? Something's missing."

I lowered my gaze at that, the guilt making a return. "I

don't want him, Daddy. I don't know how to explain it. Is something wrong with me?"

"Absolutely not," he murmured and nudged up my chin again. "Remember, you can kiss for more than one reason, and I think Gray's very much the same with you."

"I don't get it." And it was getting frustrating. "Weren't you jealous of him like five minutes ago?" Because I hadn't forgotten when I admitted that Gray and I used to sleep together and how Mad's features had drawn tight.

"I had something to worry about then." He shifted back a piece of hair from my forehead. "Now I know the love you have for each other is very different. I believe you when you say you're not interested in each other romantically, but that doesn't mean you don't miss touching him, does it?"

I scratched the side of my head. "I guess I haven't thought of it that way." Was that it? Was my being with Gray part of how we…I didn't know how to put it…communicated? It did make sense. "I wanted to hold him earlier," I admitted. "It makes my stomach hurt to think about it, because we used to be…you know, intimate."

"And there's nothing wrong with that."

That refused to settle in my head, and I looked to him dubiously. "Really?"

"Before you and I got together, did being with him mean you wanted to go on dates with him?"

"Well, no."

"Has that changed?"

"*No.*" Gray and I weren't like that. "It's just…I mean… I don't know what I mean." I huffed and gave up as the aggravation built.

Daddy chuckled and made me look him in the eye again. "Is it possible that when you and Gray are together, it's comforting?"

I nodded hesitantly. Was that okay?

"And touch gives you energy, doesn't it?" He knew it did.

"So basically, you're okay with me, um..." I flushed uncomfortably. "I don't know, snuggling? With him, I mean."

"This is what I'm talking about, Abel. It can be more than snuggling if it's with the right person." He cupped the back of my neck, his thumbs drawing soothing patterns. "Gray's been in your life for years, and it wasn't until today I really saw how close you are. I'm not sure you even realize how you gravitated toward each other during lunch. And before that...I saw you guys in the kitchen." He leveled me with a serious look. "I don't want our relationship to censor you with him, understand? I know my position in your life, and it lets me enjoy watching you and how you express yourself instead."

"Perv," I whispered.

He smirked and poked my nose. "Pretty sure you're the little perv for immediately making that about sex."

Chewing on my lip, I mulled over his words and wondered where my issues lay. "Why do I feel guilty?"

"I don't know," he replied honestly. "Social standards, probably. I'm not a man without limits, and this would've been a completely different conversation if it were someone else. But with you and Gray? I trust you, and I trust that he won't take advantage."

"He wouldn't," I said quickly. "But I wanna make sure this isn't some precursor to an open relationship or anything. I don't think I can handle that."

"Fuck no." He finally gave me that low rumble of a growl that set me on fire. "To each their own, but I'm kinda addicted to what we have. It's Mad and Abel against the world, isn't it?"

"*Yes.*" And I joked, "With a small window open for Gray?"

"Very small," he said and kissed me, "but significant nonetheless." Another kiss. "Speaking of, you should go to him. Maybe make him something that isn't steamed broccoli."

"It's healthy," I argued. "I can't believe you, of all people—"

"He's not a full-time hockey player in the biggest league in the world." He cut me off gently but firmly. "He's the type of guy I'd give two spoons of Nutella."

Un-fucking-fair.

I did my best to scowl at him, though when he peppered my face with kisses, I didn't stand a chance.

"Fiiine," I groaned through a giggle. "I *guess* I can make his meals more interesting."

"Attaboy." He smacked my butt as I stood up, then checked his watch. "You boys have three hours until I'm starting dinner. I want the kitchen free of broccoli steam by then."

"Yes, Sir."

I was reeling from the conversation as I returned to the kitchen, mainly because I literally couldn't believe my luck. There was no way most people would understand the difference between what I had with Daddy and what I had with Gray.

It wasn't a free pass to be sexual with Gray whenever I felt like it, which...well, that wouldn't be often anyway, but regardless, it did let me relax. I wouldn't have to worry about those little touches. I could hold him, he could hold me, I could reach out and rub his neck, he could slip his leg between mine on the sofa. *That* was our language, and Daddy had made me understand it; he'd put it into words.

Gray was slowly and clumsily chopping carrots when I got back to him.

"I told you to relax." I took the knife from him and pointed at the stool. "Sit down."

He sat down. "I lowered the heat. I think the broccoli is done."

"I'll save that for me," I said, taking over the task of chopping. "I was thinking maybe we could add some gravy to your meals."

He perked up at that. "Who are you, and what have you done to my best friend?"

"Jerk." I smirked and, because I felt like it, I leaned over and kissed his cheek. "If you agree to a gym session downstairs later, I might even add some salt to your vegetables."

He finally gave me a real smile. "Okay."

Okay.

CHAPTER 17

The morning after, I was nervous as shit. I *shouldn't* be. After all, Jesse knew, Casey supported me, and I couldn't see Uncle Ellis being bothered by Mad and me. We were gonna be discreet since my little sister could be the worst snitch, same with Haley, Casey and Ellis's daughter. So why did I feel like we were about to take a turn for the worse?

The charity we were playing for today was a foundation for families who couldn't afford cancer treatment for their children, and the event included a morning practice. It was the reason I'd wanted to watch Lyn while our parents were in Rome, and she happily donned a pair of skates to show her moves.

It was eight in the damn morning, and the rink was packed with players and kids. Parents and some selected press members stood on the sidelines and took pictures.

"Wait for me!" Haley yelled. "Abel! Okay, Daddy, watch me go."

I grinned as she cautiously skated toward Lyn and me, while Ellis brought out his camera.

"Careful, sweetheart," he called.

Jesse arrived some twenty minutes later with Avielle, so I made my way over. Lyn and Haley stayed close but were distracted by the marks in the ice. Truly fascinating stuff.

By then, Mad and Casey had migrated higher up the stands to sit down, and they were drinking coffee and laughing about whatever-the-fuck.

"Hey. Did you guys check in at the hotel?" I asked Jesse. The cacophony and subsequent echo forced me to raise my voice.

He nodded, helping Avielle with her skates. "I wanted to nap. Guess who didn't."

Avielle smiled cheekily and raised her hand.

I figured it was a good time to introduce—

"Jesse!" Lyn shrieked. Okay, so she'd spotted him now. "Oh my God, you're here!"

Jesse's face lit up.

It was sweet. He didn't have to hide anymore.

Minor mayhem ensued because Jesse was such a rare sight, followed by us introducing the girls to one another, followed by me catching sight of Gray, followed by us bitching at each other because I thought he should stop being mopey and join us on the ice.

"I didn't bring any gear," he defended.

"So? Borrow a pair of skates—Christ."

It was a fight I eventually won, and then it was the two of us and three squealing girls. We goofed around, tutored them in slap shots and skating backward, as well as joined the other teammates—and the Capitals guys—in a shootout competition.

Lunch was on the agenda a few hours later, and since everyone was staying at our hotel, we decided it would be more comfortable if we went with one of the two restaurants there.

With Jesse in Vancouver this weekend, I doubted I was gonna see much of our sister. I should've anticipated her wanting a "sleepover" in his suite.

"I'll head down to the restaurant, guys," Gray announced.

"Okay, we'll be right there," I replied. Disappearing into the bedroom, I picked out a pair of jeans and a long-sleeved sweater that was fitted as hell. Maybe I should change—

"You're wearing that."

I glanced over my shoulder, spotting Mad in the doorway.

"Yeah?" Or perhaps it wasn't too tight. I was just happy it was soft. I couldn't stand scratchy fabrics.

"Definitely." He came over and kissed me on the forehead. "Still nervous?"

Yes and no. Casey had given me enough sly looks that I understood he was onto us. And if he knew, he'd probably told Ellis already. "A little," I settled for saying. Because, in the end, it was a big adjustment, going from yearning for Daddy in secret to holding hands in public.

His strong arms came around me, and I sighed contentedly. I almost wished I didn't have the game tonight. This morning's hoopla had been draining enough.

"You look tired," he murmured.

"I am." I smiled sleepily and tilted my head up for a kiss.

Rather than being a good Daddy and kissing the ever-loving crap out of me, he cupped my face and pressed his forehead to mine. "How can you be so fucking gorgeous?"

My cheeks heated up, and I ducked my head to nuzzle his neck. "Am I the most gorgeous ever?"

I felt his grin in the kiss he landed at my temple. "By a mile, at least."

I couldn't help but beam up at him, even as self-consciousness flowed through me. "Ditto—by two miles."

He chuckled and finally gave me a deep kiss. "Tonight—goddammit." His phone rang, and I huffed. I would much rather hear the end of his original sentence and find out whatever tonight might entail. "It's Casey. I guess we should head down." He muted the call before pocketing his phone again.

On the way out the door, my phone rang too, and it was Gray. What was the rush? I didn't answer. We'd see them in two minutes.

"Do you have a key?" I asked, stepping into my shoes.

He nodded, and then we left hand in hand and took the elevator to the second floor where the restaurants were.

"So what about tonight—*seriously*?" It was my turn to be cut off. This time, Gray had sent a text.

PICK UP. *Your parents are here, dude!*

"Oh, no. Oh, shit. Oh, fuck. D-Daddy," I said shakily.

He frowned, instantly alert, and eyed the screen. "Goddammit. Case must've tried to warn us. All right—" He scrubbed his hands over his face roughly. "All right, it'll be okay. We were gonna be discreet during lunch anyway, yeah?"

I nodded hesitantly as my anxiety spiked. He could be quick on his feet. I was another matter, stuck on wondering why the hell they were here when they were supposed to be on their way to Rome.

Mad's nod was firmer. "We'll get through lunch, and then we'll invite Lincoln and Ade up to our suite for a talk."

Oh God, I knew what that meant. It didn't ease my fears at *all*. "We're t-telling them *today*?"

"Yes, baby." He remained resolute, only pausing when we

reached the second floor. He ushered me to the nearest nook where we could get a semblance of privacy. "If you think about it, this is a good thing. With them pushing the date, there's no excessive waiting for you." It was possible I didn't handle anticipation very well, yes. "It'll all be over with today, and isn't that what we want?"

I twisted a piece of hair at the back of my neck and chewed on the inside of my cheek. "You're way ahead of me. I hate hiding, but we haven't planned on-on what t-to s-say—"

"Easy, sweetheart," he whispered and hugged me to him. I swallowed against the nerves and clenched and unclenched my fists. "We're realistic enough to know your parents probably won't be fully on board at first, aren't we?" I managed a jerky nod. "So if we get this over with today, we can get started on making it okay. It'll give us something to work with, yeah?"

I screwed my eyes shut, imagining Mom's and Dad's reactions. I *hated* it when they were upset and angry. Partly because it didn't happen often, so when they blew, it reverberated through me. And partly because, this time, it would be about Mad and me. It wasn't like seeing Dad yell at my doctor for not "knowing his shit," nor was it like Mom when she caught me cheating on a math quiz in high school. She'd been furious. But I could cope with that. For one, when Dad shouted at my doctor, it wasn't directed at me. For two, when Mom was angry, I'd usually done something wrong.

I was innocent here. It was gonna hurt because they were gonna get upset with me—and Mad—for who we happened to love.

"We haven't done anything wrong," I gritted in a quick burst of anger.

"I know." He smiled ruefully and touched my cheek.

"They'll see it too, Abel. Just give them time, and remember their intentions."

"Ugh, don't come here and be all reasonable, Daddy. It's gross." I broke the hug and took a deep breath. "Okay, I'm ready." I wasn't ready.

He chuckled and pressed a kiss to my forehead. "Let's go, then."

The restaurant was some trendy Italian-style place with a spectacular view of the harbor. It was big and open, and we spotted our family at a large, round table near the windows. Most of them hadn't taken their seats yet. Mom was beaming and talking to Jesse and Avielle, Dad and Ellis were standing a few feet away, Gray and Casey were obviously on the lookout for Mad and me, and Lyn and Haley were inspecting the menu.

When Gray spotted me and I subtly nodded, hoping to convey I knew what was going on, he looked relieved and nudged Casey's arm.

"We've got this, baby," Mad murmured before we reached them.

"I hope so." I held my breath as Dad's gaze landed on me.

His regular smile that bordered on a smirk was a familiar sight. He couldn't know anything, could he? Not yet. Something else must've brought him to Vancouver instead of Rome.

"You don't look surprised to see us here, kid." He cocked his head before pulling me in for a quick hug.

"Gray warned me." I could say that, at least. I patted his back, and then Hurricane Mom was all over me. *That* was a surprise. What the hell? She wrapped her arms around my midsection and hugged me tightly, and I looked to Dad over her head, confused.

"Yeah, have fun with that," he said. I lost him after that as he took a seat between Lyn and Mad.

Mom looked up at me with a pleading expression. "Am I a good mother, sweetie? Have I been neglecting you? You gotta tell me."

"What the what?" I had *no* idea where this was coming from. "Um, yeah. You're great. What's going on? I thought you'd be in Italy."

She eased off and waved a hand. "Italy will always be there. They canceled our flight in New York, and I took it as a sign. I'm supposed to be here." The worry was back, and she grabbed my hand in both hers. "Do you have time to talk before you head back to the arena? I have to get something off my chest."

"Like what?" Alarm trickled through me, and I stiffened. "You can't say that and expect me to keep my cool."

"I'm sorry, you're right." She ushered me closer to the windows while the others started ordering food. I exchanged a quick look with Mad, who was saving me a seat. He mouthed that he'd order for me, as if that was my biggest concern. "The advanced copy of *Men's Health* arrived at the house before the weekend."

I blinked and gave Mom a blank stare.

She wasn't done talking in riddles. "If you feel like you can't talk to Dad and me, I have to know, and we'll make changes. I don't want you to feel like we're not here for you."

I puffed out a breath, frustrated all of a sudden. "I'm so fucking confused right now. I've never felt that way. I know you guys are there."

A crease appeared in her forehead, and it was her turn to be confused. "But the cover—your tattoos." Oh... Oh, hell. Oh, for fuck's sake. "You've chosen to express yourself in a way that... I mean, a mother has to ask and worry that her son can't come to her when you turn to, um, alternative ways."

I barely refrained from rolling my eyes. Either she was the

most ridiculous fusser on the planet, or she was funny and adorable. Maybe a combo. "*You* have ink, Mom. Dad's fucking covered, and so is Jesse. The idea that you have to worry is nuts! Fine, if you wanna ask, just ask. But you definitely don't have to jump to conclusions and skip your vacation because you learned I have some tats."

I could admit, I was relieved it wasn't worse than this. And at least that little truth was out now.

Her mouth tightened, and she let go of my hand. "Your father may have said something similar, but I say, better safe than sorry. I won't apologize for caring and worrying."

I did my best not to smirk.

She huffed. "Abel, we're not talking tattoos of bunnies and unicorns. Barbed wire around a broken hockey stick raises red flags."

I chuckled quietly and hugged her to me, and I dropped a kiss in her hair. "You're sweet, Mom. I'm fine, though. Is there symbolism? Sure, you of all people know what I've been through, but next time, pick up the phone and ask. Don't cancel your entire trip to Italy and fly up here. Okay?"

"Oh, you think you get off the hook that easily?" Now she had attitude. "Don't lecture me, son. Not when you've kept this from us. Tell me instead why you felt the need to be secretive about this. Right now."

"I'm a grown man." I widened my eyes. "I don't see why I have to—"

"Semantics. You'll always be our little boy." She waved a hand, and I tried not to cringe. She better not see me as a little boy when Mad and I told her about us. "You still kept it a secret."

I sighed and ran a hand through my hair. "You kinda answered your question. You'd think with a girl who hasn't even started first grade in the family, I'd stop being the baby." I lifted a shoulder. "I thought you'd freak out if you knew, though certainly not like *this*. Christ." I breathed out a laugh, thinking back on the past five minutes. "I'm fine, Mom. Okay? Can you chill now?"

"I'm the chillest mom ever," she said.

I snorted and put an arm around her shoulders to guide her back to the table. "Sure you are."

CHAPTER 18

Lunch was uneventful, other than when we poked fun at Mom a bit for her fussing. Dad had some funny stories to share about how she'd inspected the magazine cover and my tattoos for a solid two hours during their flight to New York. Then how she'd hemmed and hawed and fretted once they'd learned their flight to Rome was canceled.

Dad also mentioned that it was "fucking obvious" that Mad had worked on me, at which point Mom had tried to make a thing out of it. Like, why hadn't Mad told them...? But he shut that down swiftly, stating with a smirk that I was an adult. It wasn't his place to snitch.

I was seated between Mad and Casey, so I'd managed to tell him we were planning to talk to my parents after lunch. Casey helpfully offered to take the kids to the indoor pool, something Ellis, Jesse, and Gray were on board with as well.

I'd rather go to the pool too. Mad could handle the discussion with Mom and Dad, couldn't he?

It was a good thing the game later was for charity. I had to be back at the arena in a little over two hours, and no matter the outcome, my stomach was gonna be unsettled and my anxiety brimming. In other words, my performance was gonna blow.

After the check had been settled, Mom wondered if it was too late to get tickets to the game. I listened with one ear and answered on autopilot because, on the other side of me, Mad was speaking quietly to Dad, asking if they'd come up to "his" suite for a chat.

This was it. His suite would, in a matter of minutes, be ours—publicly, officially.

I was gonna die.

"Yeah, sure." Dad's brow furrowed, but he agreed nonetheless. "You got coffee up there, or should we get some in the coffee shop in the lobby?"

I had a feeling coffee would be the last thing on his mind soon.

"I've got it covered," Mad chuckled.

Doomsday arrived some twenty minutes later when it was just Mad, Mom, Dad, and me up in what I'd grown to call home. As temporarily as the suite would be ours, it felt more like home than the condo I'd shared with Erik and Corbin. I liked it more than Mad's studio back home too.

"Oh, wow." Mom smiled curiously as she peered into the kitchen. "You went all out, Madigan."

Sure, because, according to them, he was only here for a weekend.

Dad stuck his hands into the pockets of his jeans and migrated to the closest comfortable spot: the couch in the living room. "So, what's—" He stopped talking, and just as he sat down, I caught him looking stricken by something. Legit,

I'd never seen him with that expression before. For that one or two seconds, he looked shocked, angry, and pained.

It was enough for me to be on full alert, except we hadn't even said anything yet.

"Ade!" he bit out. "Come here. Madigan and Abel wanna talk to us."

The way he phrased that...

I scanned the living room, only to do a double take at the TV stand. The heavy oak top had nothing but the flat screen on it...and one picture. Nausea crept up in my throat. *Fuck, fuck, fuck.* I'd forgotten about it. It was the only picture we had of Mad and me since we got together, and he was holding me and giving my cheek a kiss while I was crossing my eyes and making a face at the camera. For as tight as Mad and I had always been, no one would believe that was platonic. We looked every bit a couple in love.

So Dad knew, and now he wouldn't look at me.

Sending Mad a panicked look did nothing. Once Mom had passed me toward the living room, Mad merely gave my hand a squeeze, probably thinking I was nervous.

Try terrified.

I swallowed hard and followed him reluctantly. Mom and Dad occupied the couch, so I slumped down in a chair. Mad could've gone with the one across from me, but he chose the footstool next to the TV instead and moved it closer to me.

Dad clenched his jaw and looked out the window.

"We have some news." It was Mad who spoke, and his words caused my pulse to skyrocket. Holy hell, this was gonna get bad.

"More tattoos?" Mom teased wryly.

Dad let out a bitter chuckle. "Read the room, Ade."

That made her frown, and I averted my gaze.

Next to me, Mad cleared his throat. He was gonna say it, I

could tell. His face was unreadable, though the severity of the situation was unmistakable. "You guys know Abel and I have always been close. And lately, that's changed. Our relationship has changed," he elaborated. "What we wanna tell you is that we're together."

And so it was out in the open. No taking it back. Mom and Dad knew, and I couldn't for the life of me look them in the eye.

Mom made a noise, like half a laugh. An unsure, choked sound.

"We're not kidding, Adeline," Mad said quietly and firmly. "I fully expect this might be hard for you."

Oh God, I was gonna vomit. Like a coward, I couldn't form a fucking word, and Mad deserved better. All I could do was extend a shaky, clammy-as-fuck hand and squeeze his tightly. *I'm with you. I'm gonna vomit, but I'm with you.* He threaded our fingers together and even had the balls to press a kiss to my hand.

I tightened my hold to reach death-grip level.

"No," Mom whispered. Yet, she might as well have shouted it. "This isn't—you can't."

The rejection burned hotter than I thought it would. My parents were no saints, didn't give a shit about social standards, and gave hell to those with narrow minds. I *needed* them to extend open-mindedness to me too.

Out of the corner of my eye, I saw Dad adjusting his foot over his knee. The worn leather, pointed dress shoes were just so him, so typically old-fashioned rocker-like. He always wore that kind, or All Stars. But all I could focus on now was how that foot tapped restlessly. He was pissed.

The silence was suffocating me, so I chanced a glance at him, only to find him staring directly at me. I flinched.

"How long has this been going on?"

"I—" Fuck. I cleared my throat. "Um, a-a m-month and a half?"

I didn't need to see Mom to know she was crying. It fucking tore at me, and my eyes watered in response.

"This isn't something we jumped into, Lincoln," Mad told him. "I've been fighting this for over a year. And, Ade...? You know me, honey. I would never—"

"I thought I knew you," Mom spluttered, wiping at her cheeks. I kept her in my periphery 'cause if I faced her fully, I'd fall apart. I was already heading in that direction anyway. It felt like someone was standing on my chest. "You're supposed to be our friend, not our son's—I can't even say it. With the history we share, with *my* history—how the *fuck* could you do this?"

"Stop it!" I exploded without warning and stood up, fists clenched at my sides. "Just s-stop it." My blood pressure went up fast, and it got difficult to breathe. "I love Mad. I've *always* loved Mad, but you fucking joked about it because I was young, but I love him. He's everything to me. He's a good man. He knows me better than anyone, and he always wants what's best for me, and I want you to leave now be-because you're pissing me off, and I'm upset."

Mom looked up at me with wide, tear-filled eyes.

I stared at the floor instead, boiling, seething, shattering.

Mad rose to a stand too, and for the first time ever, I didn't want him to hold me. Because I always came unglued when he put his arms around me, and I didn't wanna break down until Mom and Dad were gone.

Standing there, stiff as a stick and with Mad's hold on me, I waited in a painful silence while Mom and Dad got up too. Mom's whimpered "This is wrong" on the way out nearly did me in. It was a physical blow.

Dad wasn't as quick to leave, and a second after Mad's

arms disappeared, I felt another hand squeezing the back of my neck.

"Look at me, son."

I blinked away two tears and tensed up, then forced a glare on him.

He had nothing to say. I didn't know what he found when studying me, but he only clapped me on the shoulder before walking out of the living room.

Fuck, fuck, fuck. The panic set in, and I sucked in a shallow breath.

"Make sure he knows we'll be back later. I gotta calm down Ade. You know what this is about." It was the last thing he said—to Mad, I assumed—and then the door clicked.

My knees gave in a beat later, but Mad caught me.

I heard my muffled sobs before realizing I was even crying.

My mind was blank for the most part, except for a crippling grief that told me I'd just lost something.

I became aware we'd moved to the bedroom at some point, and Gray had arrived. They exchanged words too quietly for me to hear while I was trying to calm down. Numbness had started seeping in, and it was a welcome break. I needed it. *Anything* to escape the hurt. I could still feel Mom's horror and Dad's anger. It was embedded in me along with their expressions.

Gray closed the curtains and joined us in bed, smelling of chlorine from the pool and body wash from his recent shower. His hair was damp as his head hit the same pillow I used, and then I was distracted by his arms coming around me. Until I was met with the loss of another set of arms. *No!* He couldn't leave me.

"D-Daddy?" I croaked.

"I'll be back soon, baby boy. I promise." He kissed my temple and pushed back some hair from my forehead. "I gotta talk to Lincoln and Adeline, and then I'll be right with you. Okay?"

What was the point?

"I'm gonna fix this," he whispered into another kiss. "Trust me?"

I nodded and sniffled. "Hurry."

"I will. You boys rest." He left after a last kiss, and it halted the numbness for a beat.

My face crumpled, and a fresh round of tears streamed down my cheeks.

"Abel." Gray stroked my cheek. "Lift your head so I can turn the pillow over. You've cried all over it."

"Don't be a dick," I complained.

"I'm not. I'm just saying you've cried all over it." There was a smile in his voice that I could've smacked him for, if it weren't for the fact that it was how we functioned. "Come here." He pulled me into his arms, and I came a lot willingly. I wanted skin-on-skin and warmth.

I knew Daddy had stripped me of everything but my briefs earlier, and I was content to find out Gray wore as little as I did. It made it more comfortable when I slipped my leg between his and rested my head on his chest.

"Your folks will come around," he murmured.

I hoped he was right.

Today could've been perfect, with my whole family in town for the game— "Shit!" Alarm shot through me, and I started scrambling out of bed. "The game, what time is it?"

"Hey, hey, get back here. Madigan called your coach."

Gray yanked me down again, and I huffed in frustration. "You're not playing today. They agreed it was better you recovered and focused on your next game."

Oh.

I bit my lip, unsure, though it made sense. Today was just a charity game. The one on Tuesday against Calgary, we had to win.

Fuck it, I'd be useless on the ice today anyway.

I woke up when Mad returned. He crawled under the duvet with Gray and me but wouldn't let me untangle myself from my sleeping buddy. Instead, Mad embraced me from behind and murmured in my ear that everything was going to work out.

I was too emotionally and physically spent to quiz him on details, so I let my eyes flutter closed once more, and I fell asleep with the love of my life and my best friend holding me.

I roused every time someone shifted, yet it wasn't a fitful rest. Every movement from Daddy and Gray was only a reminder that they were here with me.

Blurry images of family, work, and memories filled my dreams. One second, I was teaching my sister how a goalie should stand. The next, I was skateboarding down the promenade in Santa Monica with Jesse. He laughed at something that drew an instinctive smile from me. Then the images morphed again, and Daddy was kissing my neck and slipping a hand down my tight briefs.

"Mmph..." I grunted as he got annoying. He wanted me to move in order for him to remove my underwear, and I thought he should get rid of them with magic. It wasn't rocket science.

That's not a dream! My eyes flashed open when I felt two cold, wet fingers between my butt cheeks, circling my hole.

"Shh. Daddy needs to be inside you."

I shuddered and clutched Gray's arm, my face pressed to his chest. Daddy fingered me softly and teasingly at first, only to push three digits inside to stretch me and elicit the pained little gasps he'd come to be ridiculously hooked on. Truth be told, I was hooked on them too. Nothing was more arousing than Daddy needing me so much that his little boy just had to suffer a bit because he couldn't wait.

"Daddy, I'm gonna get hard," I whispered anxiously. I could already feel the desire swirling and fighting against the cobwebs of sleep and drowsiness. And it wouldn't be a problem if my dick hadn't been pressed against Gray's thigh, and now I wasn't wearing anything either. Oh God, I was going to make a fool of myself.

"It's okay, my lovely little boy." Daddy groaned softly in my ear and rubbed the head of his thick cock across my opening. "I've talked to Gray."

Another shudder ripped through me, and at the same time, Gray shifted and made a sleepy noise. Part of me waited for jealousy to rise, or for thoughts of how inappropriate this was to appear, but nothing showed up. There was only this blanket of comfort and love and white-hot lust. I didn't need to know the specifics of their conversation. I trusted them both and could count on them to speak up if anything was wrong.

Daddy wouldn't break any promises or do anything that made me insecure, nor would Gray push boundaries and make me uncomfortable. And right now, I really fucking wanted them here with me. I needed Daddy's indecency, and I needed Gray's easy affection.

An arm slid under my neck, and Daddy moved me closer to the middle between them. His hand covered my mouth as he forced his cock inside my bottom, stifling my sharp gasp. Next, he shushed me gently and told me I was so good for taking all of him.

I understood why he'd lifted me away from Gray's chest when Daddy gripped my hip and fucked me quickly. Sometimes, he needed a quick release, and I was his perfect little come disposal. He'd told me so lots.

All I could do was take it. I remained as motionless as I could on my side, Daddy's chest hair tickling my back, and three sets of legs tangled.

"Have you been—*hnngh*—frustrated, Daddy?" I whispered behind his hand.

It was when he was frustrated that he often needed something quick and hard.

He grunted and slammed in faster, sending zings and zaps of pain and pleasure through me. "You can say that. It's good that I have you. I'll feel better in a minute."

That was good. It was less good that I was flushed and needy and horny now, but I could deal. Daddy emptied himself inside me shortly after, and I felt the tension in him fading until he was relaxed and cuddled up securely behind me. I grinned sleepily as he peppered my shoulder and neck with tickling kisses.

Maneuvering his arm under the pillow, he let my head land on the soft down instead, and I wrapped his other arm around my middle. Okay, I tried to push his hand on my cock, which he only found funny.

"Please?" I pouted.

"Later." He shifted inside me, intent on staying, and let out a contented sigh when he rested his head on the pillow. "We can have more fun when Gray wakes up. You gotta rest, and Daddy's beat."

I can wake him up, was on the tip of my tongue. Luckily, I stopped the words from coming out, and I bit down on my lip. My eyes had adjusted to the darkness, and I could see Gray's handsome face mere inches away from me. Only, he was lying a little higher up.

Technically...Daddy didn't say I couldn't wake Gray...

CHAPTER 19

While Daddy's breathing evened out, I discreetly placed a hand on the inside of Gray's bicep. I scratched him softly there with the tip of my finger, hoping he'd at least stir. When that didn't work, I pretended to get more settled, and I moved my hand to his hip. I knew he was sensitive there to light touch.

I drew patterns across his skin, and he got cute. His nose twitched, and he frowned. Finally, progress. He mumbled some nonsense and scooted closer to me, and I took advantage and cupped his butt through the soft cotton of his briefs.

We were almost nose-to-nose, and it was easy to close that little distance and kiss the corner of his mouth. *Come on, wake up already.* Trapping his bottom lip between my teeth, I gave him a quick nip that seemed to do the trick.

He hummed and kissed me before he blinked drowsily and squinted at me.

"Oh good, you're awake," I whispered.

"Um..." He rubbed his eyes and lifted his head, first

glancing behind me and then at the alarm clock. "I wouldn't go that far. If I'm up, it's because you woke me."

I gave him my most innocent smile.

He chuckled quietly and rubbed his nose to mine. "How you feeling?"

"I'm okay." And it would stay that way as long as I didn't think about my parents. "I'm glad we can still do this stuff." To emphasize, I gave his butt another squeeze and nuzzled his cheek.

His smile widened a little. "Me too," he whispered. "Madigan gave me a spiel on how we apparently speak through touch."

That made me laugh under my breath. "Same here. I hadn't really thought about it before."

"Me either." He threaded his fingers through my hair and smoothed out the spot between my eyebrows. And I could see it now. This was how we conveyed things. By paying attention to my frowny lines, he acknowledged my worries and wordlessly told me he was here to comfort, to listen, or whatever I needed.

I kissed him. *Thank you for being the best friend I could ever ask for.*

He grinned a little, the tip of his tongue teasing mine, then pressed our foreheads together. That could mean...*anytime, buddy.* Or maybe...*I could really go for a steak right now.*

"When did you get naked?" he wondered.

"Um." I blushed. "When a certain someone decided to fuck me?"

His brows went up, and he lifted his head off the pillow. He lifted the duvet a bit as well. "Bro. Is he—"

"Yeah." I pushed down the duvet again, my gaze flickering. It was embarrassing, even when it was undeniably dirty.

"That's so hot." Gray got a dark glint in his eye and

cuddled up against me. "You want me to lose my underwear too?"

I nodded quickly, still struggling to make eye contact. This was new to me, being in my now-normal Little mode and having Gray with me at the same time. Granted, I got littler when it was only Daddy around, but I'd be a liar if I said everything was normal, like how I used to be when it was just me and Gray.

"So he's filled you up already, huh?" He squirmed out of his briefs as his teeth grazed my jaw. "Ass full of cock and come."

I shivered and closed my eyes. "Daddy says it's how it's supposed to be."

"I think he's right. You're cute as a little slut."

"Jerk."

He chuckled and kissed me. "Am I wrong?"

"Yes. Maybe. I don't know." I couldn't think anymore, and I wanted Daddy to wake up so he could tell me—or us—what to do. "I'm always cute," I decided. "Sometimes I just have to remind people."

He smiled into the kiss, then deepened it and stayed in control until I felt light-headed and needed air. When he pressed his lower body against mine, I moaned and cupped the back of his neck. We kissed hungrily, riling each other up, and rubbed our hard dicks together. Well, he moved more than me because I couldn't, unless I wanted Daddy's cock to slip out of me. And I definitely didn't.

"I wanna blow you," he murmured, breathing heavily. "Can I?"

I sucked in a breath and stopped caring about friggin' naps. "Daddy." I slipped a hand behind me and shook Daddy carefully. "Daddy, wake up. Gray's up now."

Gray smiled affectionately and traced a finger along my cheek.

Behind me, Daddy let out a yawn. His hand trailed up my chest. "You woke him up, didn't you?" His sleep-husky voice turned me on further.

"It was best that way," I giggled through a groan. Fuck, when he pushed deeper inside me, it was easier to feel him thickening. "You didn't say I couldn't."

"Brat." He nipped at my shoulder. "What did you wake me for?"

"We wanna do stuff," I said.

"*Actually...*" Gray kissed my sternum and brushed a thumb over my nipple. *Ungh.* "I think I said I wanna blow you."

"I'm not always as blunt as you, okay?" I griped.

He snickered.

Daddy seemed to find humor in that too, but then he helped me out, thankfully. "In the future, baby, this is how you respond to that question." His fingers disappeared into Gray's hair, cupping the back of his head, and Daddy guided him to meet me in a kiss. I caught on and angled my head, slipping my tongue into Gray's mouth. "Fuck, you're beautiful together." The fact that Daddy really felt that way—judging by how increasingly aroused he became—was exhilarating.

With Daddy in charge, Gray's kiss soon trailed lower. I felt his soft lips moving wetly down my neck, down my chest. I gasped as he closed his mouth around a nipple and sucked lightly.

Daddy yanked away the duvet before returning his hand to the back of Gray's head. At the same time, Daddy's cock had grown hard enough that he wanted to fuck me again, though he was in no rush. Lazy thrusts only served to make me feverish with horniness. He was the worst tease *ever*.

Gray licked the valley between my abs, causing them to tense up.

"Suck me," I gasped.

Daddy responded by replacing his hand with mine so I could control Gray's pace, and I was more than happy with that. Then there was a loss of warmth across my back, and I glanced behind me to see Daddy reaching for the nightstand.

Gray's tongue snaked around my dick before I was engulfed in wet heat.

"Oh, fuck," I breathed.

For several minutes, I got to fuck his mouth, and it was so, so good. Fuck, so good. Oh fuck, fuck. I groaned, fisting his hair tighter, and rammed my dick down his throat. I knew he could take it. Heck, he lived for this.

"We shouldn't neglect Gray's little ass." Daddy's chest connected with my back again, and I caught sight of the toy in his hand. I licked my lips, excited. He was putting a condom on a prostate massager, so I tugged on Gray's hair.

He released my cock with a wet pop and eyed the toy with lust written all over him.

"I know you're not a sub," I told Gray, "but you're gonna wanna thank Daddy. That toy is fucking amazing."

Daddy let me use it on him often too, and he loved it as much as I did. It was shaped like a regular vibrator, only the end was thicker and curved.

"Just tell me when and where to bend over," Gray said with a smirk. "*Sir*."

I grinned. He called Daddy Sir!

Daddy chuckled and jerked his chin. "I want you both on all fours." Ohfuckmeyes. "Clench," Daddy murmured in my ear. "Don't lose a drop." That was enough warning. I clenched down hard, and he pulled out from me. *Wince*. "I'll go get you some cock rings."

This shit kept getting better. Gray and I quickly scrambled into position, and because we were both horny as all fuck, we immediately started making out.

"Are you sure you're okay with this?"

I nodded. "Because it's you. You're my jerk."

He smiled and took a deep, wet kiss. "You're my idiot."

"Yeah, but I'm cute." I sniffed and wriggled my butt.

Daddy returned with two silicone rings, and we rolled them onto our dicks.

"You boys can do whatever you want, but neither of you is getting off until I say so." Daddy climbed onto the bed and positioned himself behind me. "We clear?"

"Yes, Daddy."

"Sure thing, boss." Gray leaned closer. "Is it just me, or is your Dom a control freak?"

A resounding smack filled the air, and I went rigid out of reflex. But it wasn't me who'd gotten spanked hard as hell; it was Gray, and he gasped and let out a loud groan. With a look over my shoulder, I saw Daddy's hand was still firmly attached to Gray's butt, fingers digging in.

I raised a brow at my friend. "You can call this a lesson."

"No shit," Gray wheezed. "Jesus fucking Christ, I'll behave."

"Attaboy." Daddy guided his cock to my butt again, and of course, he had to tease me. "Sweetheart, there's some of Daddy's come running down here. What did I tell you about that?"

I winced. "I'm sorry, Daddy. I really tried. But don't you like seeing it coming out of my bottom?"

He hummed and kneaded my butt cheeks. "I really fucking do." Inch by thick inch, he slowly stretched me to accommodate him until he was buried all the way in. "I'll let it slide this time."

"Thank you, Daddy. You're the best." I shuddered violently, bordering on shaking, as I got re-used to his size.

At first, when he didn't move, I thought he was only being a sadist. Then I heard Gray's gasp and realized Daddy was pushing the toy inside him.

Gray didn't know the half of it yet. What I hadn't told him was that Daddy had the remote...

"Christ, that feels good," Gray breathed. He hung his head and arched his back, pushing back against the vibrator.

The second the toy began vibrating, I felt Gray's reaction because we were close enough that our bodies touched. He moaned loudly, and Daddy twisted the massager until it hit the right spot and Gray cried out.

"There we go." There was an evil smirk in Daddy's voice, one I was intimately familiar with.

Gray and I got fucked after that. Literally. Daddy played us expertly, and I didn't understand how he managed. Then I didn't care because he railed me like a savage, one hand gripping my shoulder for leverage, one foot planted firmly on the mattress so he could push harder, and one knee to support his weight. My string of moans and sharp gasps was constant, as was Gray's.

Daddy didn't fuck him as quickly with the massager, because the vibrations and the rubbing against his prostate handled the rest. Gray was a pleading mess by the time I reached the same state, and my dick fucking *hurt*. I pulled at it, hoping it would relieve some pressure, which it never did.

My balls churned uncomfortably, and Daddy said they were perfect when they were "full of boy come."

"They feel very full already, Daddy," I whimpered.

"Not yet." His breathing grew choppy and gritty. "I wanna see big, big messes from you two."

"Oh God, I need to come," Gray groaned. "Please, Madigan—or Sir, fuck. *Fuck.*" He stroked his cock desperately and screwed his eyes shut. Out of nowhere, the buzzing stopped. "No! Fuck!"

Daddy traced my spine with a firm hand, and he was pushing me down. My elbows shook, and I let them fold. Back arched, ass out, face down, I jerked my dick and tugged at my balls as Daddy fucked me deeper and longer.

"What a fucking sight," he muttered, out of breath. "Two slutty little boys aching to come."

I moaned into the mattress, sweaty and past desperate.

Gray whimpered, and it was a sound I'd never heard before. It was so hot. My Daddy was making him that way. Using him, playing with me, turning him to mindless pleas.

Daddy's cock slipped out of me after a while, and he commanded us to lie down on our backs.

We had less strength at this point, but we obeyed and let out matching panted breaths as our backs hit the mattress. Daddy arranged our legs, spreading them wide, which meant my left leg and Gray's right leg crossed. His went over mine. Arms aligned, our hands quickly found one another, and we threaded our fingers together.

Not one but two buzzing sounds danced in the heavy atmosphere, and Daddy revealed another toy. A J-shaped massager that he quickly lubed up and pushed inside me. There was no time to protest, to say I wanted his cock instead, because the forceful vibrations shoved all the air out of my lungs. My eyes flew open, and I started shaking.

The pressure on my prostate was continuous. Daddy had positioned Gray's toy in the same way, and he'd stopped touching us. Instead, he kneeled between my parted legs and stroked his heavy, hard cock and watched us.

I squirmed as I rubbed my dick, having the strongest urge to curl into a little ball. I didn't know what to do with myself. The buildup was gonna fucking crush me.

"Man, he's sexy," Gray whispered breathlessly.

I'd lost the ability to speak, but yeah, Daddy was out of this world. All muscle and ink and chest hair and dominance and filth.

"*Please.*" My mouth merely formed the word; no actual sound came out. It was becoming unbearable. The orgasm was *right there*, yet it was stuck.

"You can remove the rings, boys." Daddy shifted closer, the tendons in his arms visible. He was close. "Let me see those beautiful cocks come."

I ripped off the tight silicone ring with a shaky hand, arched my back, closed my eyes tightly, and let the pleasure blaze through me. Someone cried out—could've been me, could've been Gray—and then I was completely gone. Soaring, flying. Daddy applied pressure on the massager inside me, and I came with a choked sob. It was too damn intense. Rope after rope of hot come splashed across my torso, and it took me a moment to realize it wasn't only my own release.

Daddy was coming on me. "That's it, baby. You're Daddy's filthy little come slut." Then he lowered himself and sucked my cock into his mouth to get the last of my release.

I couldn't take it anymore. It was too much. I curled in on myself and shifted onto my side, burying my face in the crook of Gray's neck. I blindly reached out for Daddy, and he let me pull him down on me. Tears sprang to my eyes when I became too sensitive, and luckily, he could sense it. He removed the toy and grabbed my jaw, kissing me stupid.

Daddy pulled Gray close too, and one mouth left me to be

replaced by another. Gray and I made out as we rode out the final waves of our orgasms, and in the meantime, Daddy kissed my chest and rubbed our bellies.

"I can't fucking breathe," Gray gasped.

We collapsed in a tangled pile when Daddy decided we were sufficiently covered in come.

"Thank you for sharing this with me, pet." Daddy gave Gray's forehead a kiss, which I thought was supersweet. Next, I got a big smooch before he left the bed to get towels.

Gray's smile was uncharacteristically shy, though it lasted only a few seconds. Then he blew out a breath and tilted his head to me. "How can he move?"

"Dude, I ask myself that almost every day." I pushed away a piece of sweat-dampened hair from his forehead. "I hope we can nap again. I'm spent."

"Me too." As if on cue, he let out a yawn that triggered my own. "I'm glad you two got together. Your folks can say whatever they want. You're perfect for each other."

I smiled, half sad, half overjoyed. I prayed Mom and Dad would come around. Daddy seemed to think they would.

CHAPTER 20

Despite the shit that happened after lunch, I couldn't have asked for a better evening. Daddy was in a next-level doting mood. Gray and I repeatedly told him to please just relax and watch a movie with us, but he wouldn't have it. Every twenty minutes, he'd find a reason to leave the awesome Abel sandwich on the couch to go get something.

It wasn't an Abel sandwich if it was only Gray and me, okay?

Dressed in comfy old sweats and one of Daddy's big tees, I occupied the middle of the couch with Gray on my left, and Daddy came and went with dinner, snacks, and drinks. He checked his phone often, too.

I didn't ask. To be honest, I didn't wanna know. I assumed it had to do with Mom and Dad, and in my opinion, it was they who should come to apologize. They definitely didn't deserve Daddy's worry, and I told him so. Over and freaking over.

I also told him that no matter the outcome, it was him and

me. He always had been—and always would be—the love of my life.

In response, he draped an arm along the back of the couch and pressed a kiss to my temple. "This is my job, sweetheart. And what I live for. Your happiness means everything to me."

I looked up at him as I found his hand under the blankets. "Ditto," I whispered. "I love you."

"Love you too." He smiled and gave me a kiss. "Let me get you boys some more ice cream."

And there he goes again...

"Strawberry ripple, please," Gray said.

I scowled at him.

"Coming right up." Daddy brought our bowls to the kitchen.

I elbowed Gray. "We're supposed to tell him to chill."

"I'm changing strategy," he whispered back, keeping his gaze on the movie. "I think he needs to do this. It makes him feel useful."

Leaning forward, I peered into the kitchen and tugged at my ear. Was Gray right? It did make sense, but—

Two firm knocks on the door interrupted me—and the whole evening.

After a shower earlier, Daddy had given me half of an anxiety pill, and now I was glad for it. My brain stayed clear, and my moods were stabilized. While I couldn't say I was happy about the interruption, I wasn't flipping out either.

"That's my cue to leave." Gray kicked off the blankets and got up from the couch.

"What, why? You don't have to go anywhere."

"Oh, but I want to." He smirked a little and tightened the drawstrings on his sweats. "Besides, your uncles invited me over for postgame movies and snacks if shit hit the fan." Next, he pulled on a hoodie. "And babe, the air around the fan is starting to smell like shit."

"Fine, just leave me," I bitched.

"I'm going to." He chuckled and leaned over me to kiss the top of my head. "You've got this, Abel. Text me when it's safe to return. I like your niece, but I heard Casey and Ellis spent the whole game explaining to Haley that no, that player on the ice wasn't you."

I did my best not to show any amusement.

As Gray walked toward the hallway, Daddy opened the door, revealing my parents and their grim expressions. Mom looked...pitiful. She was usually so put together, so it was weird seeing her in yoga pants and one of Dad's hoodies. Her hair was piled atop her head in a chaotic bun, and she wasn't wearing any makeup.

Dad looked tired.

"Hi, Mr. H. Still gorgeous. Hi, Mrs. H," Gray said in passing. "Bye, Mr. H. Bye, Mrs. H."

Dad mustered a little smirk at that, and then he refocused on my mother. He was in protective mode, which I guess I could understand. She was clearly the one who was the most upset about Daddy and me.

Mad. Mad and me. It felt weird to use the term Daddy around my folks. Too intimate.

"I'd like to speak to you in private," Mom told Mad, her voice hoarse.

"Sure." Mad nodded with a dip of his chin and gestured toward the hallway between the bedroom and his study. But before following her, he came to me to set down two bowls of ice cream. "I'll be right back, okay?"

I nodded and chewed on my thumbnail. "Love you," I whispered.

Behind him, Dad was walking over.

Mad straightened. "Love you more, trouble. Have some ice cream."

I wasn't in the mood for ice cream, though it beat sitting here fidgeting. So I snatched up a bowl of strawberry ripple as Dad sat down in one of the chairs.

When it was just the two of us, I had no idea what to do or say. I kept my eyes fixed on the TV and pretended to enjoy the ice cream.

I didn't know what the movie was about. It flew right by me.

"I won't allow anything to come between us, Abel." Dad's low tone would've sounded threatening if, when I faced him, he didn't look upset. He had his signs, the visible restlessness, tension in his jaw, and…it was hard to explain the most telltale sign. He wasn't a crier, and he rarely overreacted in serious situations. It was something else. His face just looked older when something was really wrong. Like it did now.

I swallowed hard, a small spoonful of thick strawberry ice cream sliding down my throat. "Mad and I haven't done anything to risk that. You and Mom are the ones freaking out."

He sighed and leaned back. Fingers drummed on the armrests, one foot over his knee. "Madigan's one of my closest buddies. Learning that he's shacking up with my son isn't something any parent would take lightly."

"I'm not telling you to take it lightly!" I argued. "What about trusting me? Or trusting the guy you call one of your closest friends? You guys couldn't even give us the benefit of the doubt."

That irritated him. "That's a naïve outlook. You gotta give people a chance to process."

I gnashed my teeth together but said nothing. If he was right, I wasn't gonna admit that—not right now. He sucked. He and Mom hurt me. Actually, there was one thing to say.

"It's not wrong," I said, and fuck me if my eyes didn't sting. "Mad's and my relationship. It's not wrong or gross or shameful." *Fuck.*

A lot of emotions flickered past in his eyes. Pain was one of them. "I'm aware," was his sober reply. "We never wanted you to feel that way."

"Mom said it was wrong." And that fucking killed me.

He dipped his chin. "She's gonna explain that." He paused. "I won't apologize for how we reacted, Abel. When you have the whole story, I hope you'll understand. Maybe then you'll also understand why I've spent the day helping your mother through back-to-back panic attacks."

"What?" Dread flooded me.

Dad leaned forward and rested his elbows on his thighs. "You're too young to remember, but Ade once escaped her stepfather." Maybe I was too young to remember, but I knew about this. He'd been an abusive dick.

"Yeah, he hit her and stuff."

He nodded and looked down and cracked his knuckles. "He did more than that. He forced himself on her for years."

I pushed away the ice cream bowl and set it on the table.

Dad blew out a breath, looking over his shoulder toward the bedroom and study. Perhaps debating something internally, I didn't know. What I did know was that I got angry. I hadn't known this, that Mom's stepdad had gone that far. It was sickening.

"And because we're so close with Madigan," Dad continued, "we know the gist of his, uh, lifestyle choices."

Oh no, my fucking hell. I slapped my hands over my face, legit horrified. I was embarrassed, mortified, beyond uncomfortable. At the same time, it pained me that they'd go there. There was no comparable equivalency. What Mom had gone through was vile. What Mad and I had was based on trust, respect, and love. It was, most of all, consensual.

"It's not the same," I said in a strangled voice.

"I know," he was quick to respond. "Mom knows that too. Well, she's getting there. She always knew it was different, but she didn't know enough that it wouldn't hit too close to home. Does that make sense? It's been a fucked-up day."

I understood him. It was all kinds of messed up, but I understood him. "I get it."

And given how protective my folks tended to be of me, reluctantly, I could see how easy it would be to overreact when drawing the conclusions that I might call Mad, well, what I actually did call him.

"We want what's best for you, buddy. You know that, right?"

I nodded once and let my hands fall to my lap. "He's what's best for me, though."

"And we're with you. Just…give Mom some time." He cleared his throat. "I mean, she and I get kinky too—"

"Dad!" Oh my God, I did *not* want to hear this!

He let out a low whistle. "Especially her… Christ. She's creative—"

"I'm fucking serious!" I yelled. "Why do you wanna gross me out?"

At that, he smirked. "Mom and I are gross?" Oh, motherfucker. "Look, son, I get it. I suspect none of us wanted anyone's bedroom activities to come out. But since they did, it's okay to be uncomfortable. You gotta accept that it'll take us a minute to process this."

He'd fucking played me. I walked right into that, and I couldn't fucking believe it. Ugh, I was so pissed.

"Don't tell me you would've been okay with us if you didn't know about the BDSM," I said irritably.

"No," he conceded. "But it made things a lot more vivid, and with your mother, especially. You know you're her baby. Now she's gonna have to come to terms with you dating our friend—one who happens to be older than her."

I averted my glare to the window and bit my nail, hating that he was right. Mad had said the same over and over, that we'd have to let them come around.

"I'm sorry we made you feel like you'd done something wrong, though. You didn't deserve that."

I met Dad's somber gaze and nodded once. I appreciated the apology.

A door opened down the hall, and Mad came out with Mom, who'd been crying. It snuffed out my rage in a heartbeat, and all I could think about was what Dad had told me. And like Mad had *also* reminded me, intent mattered. Mom wouldn't hurt a—actually, she hated flies, but she wouldn't hurt an innocent human being.

I left the couch to go to Mom, and her face crumpled the instant I wrapped my arms around her.

"I'm so sorry, sweetie." Her words came out thick and muffled, and she hugged me back as hard as she could. "Madigan's explained things to me, and what I said was so wrong. Can—can I talk to you—"

"Dad's already told me," I murmured. "It's okay. I get it. I'm sorry too."

She shuddered and sniffled. "Oh."

"I'm sorry that happened to you." I kissed the top of her head and embraced her a little harder as she tried to calm down. "I hate that it happened. I hate it."

I guess the time Mad told me there were things about their past I wasn't gonna like, he hadn't been kidding. He knew a lot more about my folks than I did, because he'd been there. He understood more.

Mad passed us with a kiss to the side of my head before he took a seat on the couch. "Don't worry, Lincoln. I won't start calling you Dad."

"I fucking dare you," Dad grated. Looking over my shoulder, I was relieved to see some humor behind his glare.

"Maybe we hold off on the jokes for at least a week or two?" Mom suggested and wiped at her cheeks.

"Weeks? How about *years*?" Dad scoffed. "This ain't gonna work for me. Madigan's been an equal for too long. He's not gonna show me respect or call me Mr. H like Gray does. That shit matters to a father. Makes me feel important."

I stifled my smile and exchanged a look with Mom, who, thankfully, looked to be struggling withholding some mirth too.

"How about I spend the rest of my life keeping your son happy?" Madigan replied.

There was no holding back the smile any longer, and even Mom mustered one, along with squeezing my hand. I got it; it was too soon for her to be all cheerful, but I could see the light at the end of the tunnel now. One day, I had to believe, she would agree with me. She'd know there was no better man for me than Mad.

"Won't make me feel very important," Dad muttered, "but I guess it'll do."

I snorted.

Mom being Mom, still wanted to talk to me in private. She didn't know exactly what Dad had told me, so it was my turn to go into the study with her.

The details didn't matter in the long run. They were gonna piss me off, yet make me more thankful her stepdad was dead. What really mattered was that this was gonna be okay.

Later that night, I stood in the bathroom and brushed my teeth when Mad paused in the doorway and told me Gray was crashing in Casey and Ellis's suite.

"Yeah, I know," I said around the toothbrush. "We've been ditched."

He chuckled and joined me to brush his own teeth.

"I don't mind, though." I spat out some foamy toothpaste. "I just wanna cuddle the hell out of you tonight."

"Me too." He smiled at me in the mirror. "So, I was checking your work schedule in the kitchen, and it looks like you have a few days off in a couple weeks. Wanna go somewhere?"

Yes...but no. "Sorry, I already have plans for us."

"Is that so?" He cocked a brow, and I nodded and rinsed my mouth. "Come here."

I dutifully opened wide so he could make sure I'd done a good job.

"Beautiful boy." He kissed my nose, then stuck his toothbrush between his lips. "Tell me about your plans."

"We have a loft to move in to!" I smiled happily and sat down on the closed toilet. "I was thinking we could buy furniture and maybe a pet."

He was totally on board, judging by the fondness in his eyes, until I mentioned the pet.

I flashed a toothy smile. "You could consider it?"

He huffed, amused, and pulled out the toothbrush. "You've never once talked about having a pet before."

"I know." The idea was perhaps twenty minutes old. Didn't matter. "But think how cool it would be to have a puppy or a kitten or a ferret—"

"We're not getting a damn ferret, boy." He laughed and

paused with his toothbrush in midair. "Who's gonna walk the dog when you're on the road and I'm working?"

"A dog sitter? Or we could get a cat. They can be alone more. I've googled."

"I'm sure you have." He finished the brushing and bent over to rinse. "I'll think about it. In the meantime, I'm all for shopping for furniture with you."

I handed him a towel, excited. Before the year was over, we'd have one place here in Vancouver and one back home. We were officially together; everyone we considered friends and family knew, and maybe we'd get a pet. This day couldn't end on a better note.

"Should we have a playroom?" I asked as we left the bathroom. "We don't really use the bigger kink equipment, but it could be fun."

He hummed, starting to undress me. "A whole room for it might be unnecessary. A bed, though. A big, sturdy four-poster one with hooks and a built-in cage under the mattress."

"A c-cage?" I gaped at him.

He grinned faintly and folded my tee. "I have a buddy in San Francisco who makes BDSM furniture. Cade. I should give him a call. You'd like him and his Littles, I reckon."

"You're not putting me in a cage, Daddy!" I batted away his hands and shed the last of my clothes before getting under the covers.

He laughed and completely ignored me, instead continuing his musings. "Think of the possibilities. A nice X-cross on the wall to strap you to when you're a mouthy little shit. Or maybe an exercise bike with a dildo—"

I squeaked and dug my head underneath my pillow, which he found funny as hell. He even tickled me! I hated tickles! I giggled and cursed, doing my best to shove him away.

"Fuck, you're adorable." He stopped his assault and

pulled me to his chest. "Did you know that hearing that sweet giggle of yours always makes my day?"

I puffed out a breath and reached up to Eskimo him.

"Are you feeling better?" He stroked my cheek. "It's been a rough day."

"Much better," I promised. "What about you? You did all the heavy lifting. I just panicked like I—" Whoops. Yeah, I shut my mouth before I could say something that would earn me a punishment. I'd been doing better, I thought.

"Nice save," he said. "I knew Lincoln and Ade would come around, so my main concern was you. You're my little worrier."

"You worry lots too."

"Not as much about this." He tapped my nose.

"Whatevs, Daddy-o. I feel good. Mom and Dad know, everyone knows, and you're stuck with me forever and ever." I let out a huge yawn and hitched a leg over his thighs. "Can we sleep in tomorrow?" Because as happy as I was right now, today had been a roller coaster, and I was exhausted.

"Afraid not." He pressed a kiss to my hair. "I told your parents we'd have breakfast with them before they head back to Camassia. We can nap afterward, though."

That was so not the same thing, but I'd live. "'Kay." I tilted my face up and puckered my lips. He smiled and kissed me, lingering with a few soft pecks.

"Sleep, my little love."

"Mmmm, love you, Daddy."

"Love you too. Always."

EPILOGUE

A FEW MONTHS LATER

Sometimes, it still surprised me how attuned I was to Daddy. If he wasn't around, I sensed it. Even in my sleep. I mumbled a protest and felt blindly along the sheets, and no, he wasn't in bed with me.

I was naked, for goodness' sake. He should be all up in my butt business.

Lifting my heavy head off the pillow, I squinted in the low light and saw it was almost four in the morning. It was the middle of summer, which meant there was no reason for me to be up now. I could sleep till nine, and Daddy could sleep till noon if he wanted.

"Daddy?"

"Right here, baby."

I found him by the window, seated in the rocking chair, feet perched on an old-fashioned chest—one we happened to keep sex toys in—and a sketch pad in his lap. My head hit the pillow again, only this time, I was facing him, and I tucked my hands under my cheek.

He wasn't naked, sadly. Evil boxer briefs. I cursed them.

"Can't sleep?" I asked.

He smiled faintly, focused on the sketch. "I woke up with an idea."

Creative people. Christ. Then again, I loved watching him work. Being home in Camassia, in our new loft, was keeping me spoiled rotten where his work was concerned too. Partly because his shop was right across the street and I could visit whenever I wanted. Partly because of what he'd done to our home.

We'd picked out furniture and stuff together, the goal to keep that cool, New York loft feel, but then he'd gone above and beyond with two of the walls. They were the ones that weren't made of brick, and he'd used his artistic skills. The plain wall in the living room had a huge oak tree painted with names hidden in the crown, names of our friends and family. And then there was the wall that our bed rested up against. He'd painted it a dark, dark red, and in a lighter shade was a silhouette of me in hockey gear, captured the second before my stick hit the puck.

Photos filled the other walls, along with sketches of his I'd had framed.

In the guest room, Mad had even painted the hardwood floors to look like a page in a coloring book. Stark white met black-lined patterns that made my sister and Haley go nuts because they could actually color the floor with washable paint.

He'd painted it for me, though. The patterns and figures were mostly hockey-themed, like a bunch of little pucks in a cluster, the detailed net of a goal, hockey sticks, and such. Because he'd researched, and we'd discovered coloring was a good way for me to calm down when I was anxious. It cleared my head.

And let's be honest, Daddy loved watching me when I sat on the floor and colored.

I glanced at the clock again and smiled sleepily. "Six months ago, I would've told you no good ideas are born at four in the morning."

He sent me a wink, then dusted a hand over his sketch. "Without those moments of weakness, maybe we wouldn't be here today."

That was why I wouldn't say no good ideas were born at four a.m. anymore. In fact, the four-a.m. angle was the only one I hadn't played in my quest to get him to agree that we should totally get a pet.

Mental note: set the alarm for four a.m. next time Daddy's extra sweet and cuddly.

"Can you show me what you're drawing?" I asked.

"Not yet." He smiled and worked his eraser on something. "I can give you a hint, though. I was inspired by our little talk about power."

Huh. That was yesterday. Mom and Dad had come over for Chinese food and some rock documentary Dad and Mad had wanted to catch together—partly because they were both in it. And while we ate, I teased Dad about being pussy-whipped. It'd just been a joke and a topic we'd moved past quickly. But afterward, when it was just Mad and me again, we'd talked about how fluid power could be. How it bounced from person to person over the course of a relationship. Then, 'cause Daddy was a *grown* grown-up, he'd droned on about the importance of never abusing said power, to which I'd pretended to snore.

He'd tickled me senseless after that.

"Are you drawing a tickle monster?" I smirked.

He chuckled. "Not quite."

I watched him in silence for a beat. He was too fucking beautiful for words. Moving in together here had changed him in ways I hadn't anticipated. I didn't think he'd seen it coming either, but he was a lot more carefree these days, and this about the guy who'd always been pretty carefree. There was peacefulness in him, and it automatically transferred to me.

To me, it meant the world. It would make future work travels and away games so much easier to get through because we had *this* waiting for us when we came home.

I yawned and looked out the big window, the sky slowly going from black to a dusky blue.

"Wasn't Dad in a weirdly good mood last night?" I asked, thinking back on the dinner.

That made Daddy grin. "Probably because I made him feel important."

"Huh?"

He shook his head, amused.

Great, so he wasn't gonna answer. *Hmph.*

I yawned again and rolled around as I stretched. Our bed was *so* amazing. And fluffy and soft and comfy. We had the biggest duvet in the world, I just knew it. Catching sight of the piggy bank on my nightstand, I remembered I still hadn't taken the change from the pocket in my hoodie. I'd do that after breakfast.

Whenever there was something left over from my allowance, I saved it in my Deadpool piggy bank. Daddy and I were going on vacation before training camp and preseason games, and I was gonna need all the savings to buy souvenirs and stuff.

It was possible he was trying to teach me about saving and "spending money wisely." Boring stuff. All because I'd accidentally bought a four-wheeler when I was away in Canada teaching awesome kids how to play hockey at the beginning of summer. In the woods, four-wheelers were a necessity, okay?

"All right, I think I'm done," Daddy said pensively. He inspected his work critically—two pages of it, it seemed. "I was gonna wait till later—"

"I wanna see them now." I sat up in bed, the duvet pooling around me, and patted down my bed head. "Gimme, gimme."

He left his seat by the window and joined me in bed, and he handed over one of the sketches.

"That's you and me." Positioned slightly behind me, he rested his chin on my shoulder while I smiled widely at the drawing. Two shadowy figures filled the page, one standing tall, and that had to be him. The other silhouette was kneeling and had his head bowed. It was me, submitting to him.

"I love it." I tilted my head and kissed his cheek. "This looks like a tattoo, you know. Can you put it on me?"

Since the first time he'd put his ink on me, I'd added another tattoo. To go with his "Protect him" tattoo, I now had "Serve him" along the side of my own middle finger. It was one of my most meaningful tats, and I couldn't wait to add more of his work on me.

"That's the idea," he murmured, "although, this one goes on me. If you like it, this one's for you." He handed me the other sketch, and I cocked my head curiously.

It was the same shadowy figures, though, this time, with the bigger man kneeling. "Daddy, you never kneel." That wasn't how the power exchange worked.

He smiled into the kiss he pressed to my shoulder. "I do if I'm asking you to marry me."

I whipped my head around, nearly head-butting him in the process, and he swept me off the bed and made my stomach flip-flop. *Oh my God.* Sleep-rumpled and wearing the duvet like a puffy sarong, I gulped as my feet hit the floorboards and he went down on one knee.

The sketch in my hand shook before it fell to the floor.

"I know it's soon." He placed his hands on my hips and pressed his lips to my happy trail. "But you were right, Abel. It was always supposed to be you and me. If I believed in people being destined for one another, no one fits the bill the way we do." He looked up at me, and I swallowed against the emotions. He was blurry to me, so I had to blink hard. "I wasted two years believing my feelings for you were wrong—until you and your bravery knocked sense into me."

I grinned and wiped at my cheek.

Fuck, I couldn't stop trembling.

He grasped my hand in both of his and kissed the top of it, lingering. "Be my little boy forever—fuck." *What!* "I left the rings in the kitchen—"

"Screw them, we'll get them later, I wanna say yes." The words left me in a jumbled rush, my heart hammering furiously.

He laughed thickly and rose to a stand, then palmed my face and kissed me. "Marry me, Abel."

"Yes, yes, yes." I sniffled and threw my arms around his neck and kissed him back super hard. "Tomorrow?"

He grinned and stroked my cheek. "I'm not sure that would make Lincoln feel very important." *Oh...*oh, wow, he asked Dad for permission yesterday. That was what he meant earlier... Holy shit. "Our friends and family should be there," he whispered into the next kiss. "Don't you think so?"

"Yeah, I guess." As long as it happened soon, I was happy. *Unbelievably* happy. I couldn't stop smiling up at him. "I knew I was right."

"You definitely were," he chuckled. "Can I get the rings now? I wanna see it on your finger."

I nodded quickly and bunched up the duvet around my hips, and I wiped at my face again. Silly tears. "Oh, and, Daddy?"

Halfway out of the bedroom, he paused and looked over his shoulder. "Yeah, baby?"

I bit my lip and figured it couldn't hurt to try. "Can we get a pet too? I strongly believe it would complete our little family."

He looked like he was trying not to laugh. "You strongly believe that, huh?"

"Very strongly." I nodded sagely.

He finally broke a smile—or maybe a smirk. "I guess I'll strongly consider it." Then he left the room.

I huffed and slumped down on the edge of the bed, though I couldn't shake an ounce of the excitement. I sat there and smiled like an idiot and palmed my face, too happy for words. I was gonna marry my Mad. I'd told everyone when I was twelve that I was gonna marry him one day, and now he'd proposed.

I was one ecstatic genius.

MORE FROM CARA

In Camassia Cove, everyone has a story to share

Lincoln & Adeline
Jesse & Cass
Gray & Darius
Casey & Ellis
Adam & Alessia
Chloe & Aiden
Jameson

Cara freely admits she's addicted to revisiting the men and women who yammer in her head, and several of her characters cross over in other titles. If you enjoyed this book, **you might like the following where Abel and Madigan appear.**

Their Boy

MMM | The Game Series, #2 | BDSM | Daddykink | Standalone

Left all alone in the world after the loss of his parents, Kit Damien feared his life was over before it had truly begun. Then he met Colt and Lucas, two Daddy Doms who changed everything. The three embark on a journey to learn about true love, growing up, the importance of sprinkles, and the rules of The Game that can make them all winners.

Auctioned
MM | Suspense Romance | Hurt/Comfort | Trauma

At twenty-one, Gray Nolan became a human trafficking statistic. He and seven other young men were taken aboard a luxurious yacht where they would be auctioned off to the highest bidder. Tortured, shattered, and almost defeated, he watched his new owner step out of the shadows in a swirl of his own cigarette smoke.

Path of Destruction
MF | Rock Star Romance | Hurt/Comfort | Family | Standalone

The first time Adeline Ivey danced into my life, high on ecstasy instead of life, was at the party before the kickoff of our seventh tour. We shared an insane summer together on the road, and I knew that she'd ruined me for all others for the rest of my life. But the summer ended in disaster, and the second time she tried to make an appearance in my life was ten years later. The world had forgotten Lincoln Hayes, rock god and guitarist of Path of Destruction, and I was nothing but a number in the system of the Michigan Department of Corrections waiting for my parole.

You might also like...

Out
MM | Comedy Romance | Coming Out Story | Age Difference | Standalone

I had two things on my list when I arrived in Los Angeles. One, track down Henry Bennington, the uncle and guardian of my little brother's best friend Tyler, and tell him to get his ass back to Washington—because his nephew was getting out of control. And two, figure out just how non-straight I was. Nowhere on this list did it say, "Get Tyler's uncle into bed and fall for him." Nowhere.

Check out Cara's entire collection at www.caradeewrites.com, and don't forget to sign up for her newsletter so you don't miss any new releases, updates on book signings, giveaways, and much more.

ABOUT CARA

I'm often awkwardly silent or, if the topic interests me, a chronic rambler. In other words, I can discuss writing forever and ever. Fiction, in particular. The love story—while a huge draw and constantly present—is secondary for me, because there's so much more to writing romance fiction than just making two (or more) people fall in love and have hot sex.

There's a world to build, characters to develop, interests to create, and a topic or two to research thoroughly.

Every book is a challenge for me, an opportunity to learn something new, and a puzzle to piece together. I want my characters to come to life, and the only way I know to do that is to give them substance—passions, history, goals, quirks, and strong opinions—and to let them evolve.

I want my men and women to be relatable. That means allowing room for everyday problems and, for lack of a better word, flaws. My characters will never be perfect.

Wait...this was supposed to be about me, not my writing.

I'm a writey person who loves to write. Always wanderlusting, twitterpating, kinking, cooking, baking, and geeking.

ABOUT CARA

There's time for hockey and family, too. But mostly, I just love to write.

~Cara.

Get social with Cara
www.caradeewrites.com
www.camassiacove.com
Facebook: @caradeewrites
Twitter: @caradeewrites
Instagram: @caradeewrites